HOW SHE CAME TO KNOW

How She Came to Know. 1st Edition

Story concept and text © 2025 by L. Shapley Bassen

Cover design © 2025 by Amedei Arte.

Editing, print preparation, formatting, back cover summary, and final cover design © 2024 Staback Author Services.

Books may be ordered through popular, online retailers, Page Turner Books, Inc.'s online store, or by contacting the publisher at:

Page Turner Books, Inc.*
222 N. Lafayette St., Suite 11
Shelby, NC 28150

Visit our website at www.ptbooksinc.com or contact us via email at contact@ptbooksinc.com.

Page Turner Books, Inc.'s name and logo are copyright of Page Turner Books, Inc.

iBooks ISBN: 978-1-965788-61-5
Hardcover: 978-1-965788-63-9
Kindle ISBN: 978-1-965788-62-2
Paperback: 978-1-965788-64-6

Printed in the United States of America. First Printing: September 2025

Library of Congress Control Number: 2025932653

ATTENTION CORPORATIONS AND ORGANIZATIONS:

Most Page Turner Books, Inc.* books are available at quantity discounts with bulk purchase for educational, business, or sales promotional use. For information, please call or write:

Special Markets Department, Page Turner Books, Inc.

222 N. Lafayette St., Suite 11

Shelby, NC 28150

Telephone: (702) 606-1775

HOW SHE CAME TO KNOW

L. SHAPLEY BASSEN

SHELBY, NC USA

TABLE OF CONTENTS

PART 1

"When an organism grows from a seed, the process of its growth is guided by the genetic materials...If I cut myself, the same genetic process which originally created me now takes charge of the smaller process of healing the cut and guarantees that all the cells around the cut cooperate to form a whole again."

Christopher Alexander
"The Timeless Way of Building"

1

SEPTEMBER 2000

Denim Prix met Marwa on what he considered *his* bench along the esplanade in Battery Park City. He recognized her from their building, that Muslim girl, as he'd once labeled her in passing, but it was not his business to pay attention to other people.

They paid attention to *him*. They paid to notice him.

They paid a *lot*.

His magnified face and sculpted form stared down on mortals in Times Square, the Crossroads of the World, and from similar intersections across the globe.

Prix didn't recall meeting Marwa that particular weekend, just after school started, but he remembered what she said.

"Did you know that if you press a pure, large diamond," she stuck out her pink tongue and pointed at it, "it drains heat from your tongue?"

She slurred the last few words, leaving her tongue out the whole time.

Prix was no stranger to unusual approaches from people of all ages and genders. He considered himself a connoisseur of them.

He laughed.

"How do *you* know that?"

"We did it in Chem," Marwa said.

"You had pure, large diamonds in your classroom?"

"We used quartz as a stand-in," she explained. "But our Chem teacher got another teacher to come in—she'd just gotten engaged—and she let some of us touch her ring to our tongues."

Marwa grinned.

"We tried measuring the heat differential. We couldn't get a clear result, but it's literally a cool theory."

"Where do you go to school?"

"Stuyvesant. That was last year. My sophomore year."

Denim Prix remembered Marwa because of the diamond.

It was from that first meeting with Prix that Marwa began to reckon with the disestablishment of her childhood beliefs, of her "medieval religious fascism."

She remembered being seven years old, proudly spelling that impossibly long word—*disestablishmentarianism*—while her older brother, Sharif, could not.

For the first time in that moment, she considered that being left-handed and a girl might not be such bad things after all. Despite the birth of her younger, much-anticipated and heralded brother, Yusef, whom they called Joey, celebrated as the family's first "real" American simply because he was a boy, Marwa held on to that spelling triumph.

It was her First Sign. Her own *ayah*, the verse of a Qur'an she had written simply by existing.

The day after Marwa met Denim Prix on the bench, she took off the headscarf she had only begun wearing as a freshman at Stuyvesant High.

Her parents had moved the family from Far Rockaway to lower Manhattan just so she and Joey could live as close to the school as possible. They had no doubt Joey would surpass even Marwa's academic success.

"I never had a sophomore year," said Prix. "My mother had me modeling since I was three."

"You're Nautica!" Marwa exclaimed, the realization dawning.

Prix recoiled. He'd been hoping she wouldn't make the connection.

"Yeah...and Hilfiger...and Lauren. *Et ceterah! Et ceterah!*" he added, mimicking the bald, bare-chested king from *The King and I.* Yul Brynner had long been his object of comparison for exposed skin.

"My name's never really been my own," he said, voice flat. "Not even the one on my checks for that matter... 'Robert Doucette.'"

"No one's ever looked less like a 'Ro-bear' than you," Marwa said. "You *sound* Haitian."

Denim Prix told her his mother was Haitian, a former model, which was how she'd met his possible father, a Caucasian entrepreneur from Jamaica. They lived on the Upper East Side, near the mayor's Gracie Mansion, though they also had a house in Jamaica and other residences scattered around the world.

Marwa found herself wondering which genes accounted for Denim's blond curls and green eyes set in an otherwise brown, African face.

His original name, if his mother could be trusted, which he doubted, was Prix Freeman...her maiden name. Her own mother's last name had been De Nîmes, after the French city where denim fabric was first woven.

"Why am I telling you this?" Prix muttered.

"What do you *want* to be called?" Marwa asked.

"My friends call me Prix. My agent and the fashion world call me Grand Prix."

"Why?"

"I make more money for them than any other male model in the world."

He told her he was twenty-two and had bought his apartment in their building because the view reminded him of Alexandria, Egypt; and because he liked that it faced upriver.

"On a map, the Hudson River kind of looks like a vagina, don't you think?" Prix said.

Marwa stood up.

"Sorry," he said quickly. "That was mean. I *felt* mean."

"Why?"

"I don't know. I just wished...," he hesitated, then blurted, "I mean, it would be a relief to wear one of those circus tents you people wear."

"Burkas?" she snapped.

Marwa started to walk away.

Prix caught up to her.

"Come on...two apologies in five minutes. Let's make it a record."

He tried to smile.

"I don't even have a dog to talk to. I travel too much. Only animals and small children actually *listen* to me. I can always tell when a kid stops being a kid. They stop listening and just... stare."

He paused, tone shifting.

"No one takes me seriously as an actor. They say I've got 'no depth,' but it's *them*. They put their hands inside me, pull me out, and throw my insides away."

He gestured broadly, waving his open palm from the top of his curly blond hair down his brown-skinned, handsomely attired length.

"All anyone cares about is *this*. So yeah, sometimes I'm mean."

He looked at her.

"But you were staring."

"Just like everyone else," Marwa said quietly. "I'm sorry, too."

"It's the Fashion Fascists," he said. "People think I'm what they want to look like because the F.F. tell me *how* to look. I don't even know what I'd look like without the costumes they put me in. I'm their...design."

He glanced at her, hesitating.

"Don't run away again; but when I'm alone in my apartment, I stay naked, and I have no mirrors."

They returned to Prix's bench. From that moment on, Marwa thought of him as *Pree.*

Pree...pre-what? she mused privately.

She also thought it would be easier to talk to him online or if he wore a mask.

His hair was a halo of golden curls. His skin, a living mosaic of Hispaniola aborigines, slaves, conquistadors, all blended into one. His eyes, brown-rimmed and green, not the hard green of gemstones, but the tender green of new leaves in spring.

And shaping it all, his face was regal. So was the way he moved, with the lithe, undulant gait of Africa.

"Even naked, you're still Nature's and your parents' design. And all of theirs. We all are," Marwa said. "Nature and nurture."

"You think so?" Prix asked.

"It's a Western obsession, this idea of free will and individuality. The rest of the world thinks it's a joke."

"So, I only feel... what?"

He fumbled for the right words.

"Defined by others?" Marwa offered. "A friend of mine once said, 'Even a hermit belongs to a guild.'"

She gave him a pointed look.

"And you, wishing you could wear a burka!"

"I want to get away," Prix said, his voice low. "Get out. Go away. But where? I've been *everywhere...*"

"Yeah, and you're still *you* when you get there," Marwa said, frustration creeping into her voice as she touched the scarf that, in her opinion, hid her best feature, her long, Nile-wavy black hair.

"Y'know, that, there's no way out of it," she continued. "It's like coloring outside the lines. Changing your name, or *anything*, doesn't really escape the structure. Even if you color outside the lines, you're still inside a coloring book. Someone else drew the pictures, right?"

She paused, then pressed on.

"And even if you draw your *own* pictures to color outside of, you're still limited by the lines *you* drew. That's what lines *do*—they create limits. That's what *definition* means. It's like math, too."

"I've heard about Stuyvesant High, but now I believe it. Do you even understand half of what you say?"

"Sometimes. Not often."

Prix laughed, and Marwa saw the colors in his laughter. This wasn't the time to mention synesthesia, or being left-handed, or any of the rest. It was enough. Her friend Judy would have shouted, *"Dayenu!"*

"My parents are from Alexandria, Egypt," Marwa said.

"Get *out*," Prix said, trying to sound like a teenager.

"I have to go now," Marwa said.

Prix was adept at letting go.

"See you around," he said, turning to look upriver.

The next day, Marwa went to school without her *hijab*. Everyone noticed, but only her closest friend, Judy, said anything.

And, of course, her parents did that night at dinner.

2

OCTOBER 2000

Judy Yamaguchi was Marwa's best friend. She described herself as "Amer-Asian and Jewish because my mother was Jewish." Her father held a prestigious position, sitting on a Chair in neuroscience at NYU. Her mother had passed away when Judy was in eighth grade, leaving her to help care for her younger sister, who was just a year older than Marwa's brother, Joey.

Every day, Judy picked up her sister from the elementary school, the same school where Joey was a second grader.

Marwa's mother had arranged for an elderly woman from Masjid al-Farah, their mosque on West Broadway, to pick Joey up from school and stay with him until either she or Marwa returned home.

Marwa's mother taught part-time at Columbia, offering classes in Arabic and Arabic studies. Her brother, Sharif, commuted to college in Brooklyn. Childcare was never expected of him, and certainly not of their father, a bank executive who had recently moved from a Brooklyn branch to a Wall Street office.

In Marwa's family, there had never been a sentence in which the words *father* and *childcare* coexisted. The idea had simply never occurred to her.

"It's all a matter of translation," Judy argued, leaning over her history notes.

She and Marwa were studying for an upcoming test.

"Translation is like a window into another culture. I speak Japanese, you speak Arabic, and we both speak American English. And even *we* don't always agree on how to say something in English!"

It was late October, just before Halloween, and they were sitting at the white Formica dining table in the living room of Judy's apartment, one of the Washington Square Towers buildings in Greenwich Village. Her younger sister was in her tiny bedroom next to Judy's, a cubicle-sized space of her own. Every so often, Jody, now in third grade, would pop out with a homework question, interrupting the two high school juniors with her questions.

Marwa admired Judy's patience. She also loved the contrast between Judy's daintiness and her fierce arguments. At five feet tall, Judy barely came up to Marwa's shoulder, and her eyeglasses were constantly sliding down her nose. Still, she refused to get contacts. In the classroom, and at home with Marwa, Judy usually won every argument she chose to enter.

Judy was in the middle of a passionate argument about Michael Servetus, a 16th-century scholar burned at the stake for translating the Bible.

"All he did was agree with Erasmus," she fumed.

"The *Nicene Creed*, Judy," Marwa reminded her gently, trying to steer them back to the test material.

"But that's where it *started*," Judy insisted. "It's not important just to know what it *is*, but what it *did*, after. It burned Michael Servetus at the stake for *his* translation. Servetus only agreed with Erasmus."

Marwa examined her notes and compared them to the open textbook by her right hand.

"'The concept of the Trinity arose out of the First Council of Nicaea, convened by Emperor Constantine the Great in 325,'" she read aloud. "That's right after Constantine made Christianity the state religion of the Roman Empire."

"Right," Judy nodded, her glasses slipping down her small nose again.

"...'There was a Libyan bishop named Arius, who was preaching that while God, the Father was timeless, infinite, and divine, Jesus the Son was *created* by God and subordinate to the Father, and therefore not divine. For the Church hierarchy, the problem with this interpretation was...'"

"...'One that plagued Xtianity for more than a millennium...,'" Judy read from her notes.

"*X-tianity?*" Marwa raised an eyebrow.

"That's what Mr. Sullivan says. 'Ex-tee-anity.' I *love* when he does that, like he's calling it *inanity*. He's terrible."

"He just wants us to call him on it," Marwa said.

"'Bee-WARE of political correctness!'" Judy imitated their history teacher, puffing up her voice. "*It is the foolish hobgoblin of modern minds!*'"

"He's so immature sometimes. Two years with him...too much," Marwa groaned, absentmindedly twirling one of her long braids. "What do you think?"

"Braids don't thrill me," Judy said frankly. "They draw more attention to the fact that you're *not* wearing the scarf."

Marwa ignored the comment.

"So, what's the deal with the Nicene Creed? I'm tired, and it's getting late. We can IM the rest later."

"Just this," Judy said, scanning her notes. "If Jesus *isn't* divine, he could've been made divine through faith and acts. And if that's possible couldn't *anyone* do it? And if so, then how could the Church hierarchy say it was the only 'and irreplaceable intermediary between Man and God'? That claim is what gave the Church its enormous political power...even back in the 4th century."

"And from there," Marwa reasoned, "in reaction to the Nicene Creed, and the faulty translations, the Protestant Reformation could begin."

"Yeah, that's the point, I think."

"Y'know, the translation problem kind of reminds me of the seventy virgins promised to Muslim martyrs..."

"*Male* martyrs, of course," Judy cut in. "You're blushing."

Marwa winced. She didn't like discussing her religion with Judy, who had been bat mitzvahed the year before they met as freshmen. But somehow, the virgins had popped out of her mouth.

"No, I am not. And those seventy fair maidens? That's a mistranslation. It's supposed to be 'crystal clear raisins.'"

"*Crystal clear raisins?*" Judy repeated slowly.

"White raisins of crystal clarity," Marwa clarified.

"*White raisins of crystal clarity,*" Judy echoed with a grin. "You're a raisin."

"You're a raisin."

"*Am I* a raisin?" Jody asked, wandering into the living room with a book open to a difficult page, balanced carefully in her hands. "I'm hungry. When's Daddy coming home? Is he bringing supper?"

Marwa and Judy burst out laughing.

Jody's face fell. She thought they were laughing at her, and she was just overwhelmed. Her homework was frustrating, and Judy wasn't helping her like she usually did.

Feeling the mood shift, Marwa quietly collected her backpack and left. She took a cab home but not before undoing her braids and promising Judy she'd eventually explain what had *really* made her blush.

She hadn't told Judy about Prix. He had been her secret for two months.

A month later, after Thanksgiving, Marwa and Judy sat at a crowded lunch table surrounded by classmates. Multiple conversations crisscrossed loudly, echoing off the walls of the lunchroom. Everyone had been forced to stay in because the weather was too miserable for their usual trek to the 23rd Street diner.

"This is *not* sushi," Judy said, eyeing her tray with disdain.

"Oh, you're not interested in religion," someone teased.

"Yes, I am. Just not in any of the religions we *have*," Marcus replied.

"That's a Woody Allen line," someone else chimed in.

"'Amateur poets borrow; professional poets steal,'" another voice added.

"Who said that?"

"T.S. Eliot."

"Religion isn't religion. It's politics," someone argued. "It's all about power."

"No, it's psychology," Judy said. "I swear, I'm beginning to believe everything is just people's personalities. It doesn't matter what they claim to believe or which group they join. It's about who they *are* and how they were raised."

"I don't see that at all. At least, not entirely."

"You can't discount history," another classmate cut in.

"But *which* history?" someone shot back. "Economic? Military? The power elite or the poor slobs on the outs they find in bogs centuries later?"

"In *blogs?*"

"*Bogs*, boob. I'm saying if a meteorite fell in the Middle East hundreds of thousands, maybe *millions*, of years ago, and Stone Agers..."

"Were they stoned, you think?"

"...Excuse *me*, if they were stoned or sober *in* the Stone Age, and the meteorite falls, and they think it's a cooled uterus..."

"I think the uterus is cool," Biren said.

"You *would*."

"Why did they say this is sushi? It's just tuna fish without mayo. *Yuck*."

"He just wants to see your uterus."

"He'll have to wait until he's an ob-gyn. And even *then*..."

"You *wish*."

Then Marcus turned to Marwa.

"So...why *did* you take off your scarf...your *hijab*...if you don't mind me asking?"

"I *do* mind," Marwa said coolly. "And that's personal."

"Which is exactly why it's interesting."

"Drop dead," Judy snapped.

"Oh, *that's* intelligent."

"But we *can* talk about the Kaaba as being some chilled space rock that prehistoric people mistook for Her Divine Box, and *that* doesn't bother you?"

"I *do* have a problem with it," Marwa replied calmly. "I have *many* problems. But they're mine."

"*Her Divine Box*? Oh, that's *awful!* You are a total pig!" Judy fumed.

"There are plenty of countries where they'd be happy to kill you for saying that," someone muttered.

"But they wouldn't eat my flesh, because I'm a pig," Judy shot back.

"You're so funny I forgot to laugh."

"Well, Judaism's not exactly innocent either," Marcus added. "Only the priest class, and those they've initiated, can approach and spread the sacred labia of the ark doors to reveal Her Divine Boxed Law inside."

"I can't *stand* this talk," Judy said, visibly fuming. "I don't *care* if we're practicing political incorrectness. It's disgusting. It's insulting. And it's *stupid*."

"Ah, stabbed through the heart!" someone teased.

"It *is* stupid," Marwa agreed. "It's *reductionist* past belief..."

"That's the point, Stupid, isn't it?" Marcus interrupted. "Getting *past* belief?"

"Oh great, now we're name-calling. That's intelligent. *Very* mature."

"Which perfectly proves my point," Judy said. "It's all personality. Psychology. Everything else is this fake sushi. Which, by the way, I'm *not* eating."

"I will," someone offered.

"You'll eat *anything*," Marcus said.

"I *soy-tanly* will," Biren chimed in.

"Was that supposed to be Groucho Marx?"

"No, he's just being dirty. *Again.*"

"You kiss your mother with that tongue?"

"Anyone *but* my mother...want some?"

"Put that nasty thing away and *shut your labia!*"

"Wait...look...can you curl your tongue like *this*?"

"That's nothing. That's genetic. I'll use you in my Intel."

"I'll go *in-tel* anything you say, *anytime*."

"What else you got? Left-handed, blue-eyed—anything else *interestingly recessive*?"

"Ah, we're back to *recesses...*"

"What kind of meteoric rock?" Marcus asked suddenly.

"What?"

"Inside the cube."

"Cube? What cube?"

"In Mecca. That's what *Kaaba* means... cube."

"Who you calling *Cube*?"

"Stop it," someone said, cutting off the joke. "Marwa wasn't calling *you* a cube. I want to know. What type of meteoric tektite is it? Does anyone know?"

"Oh god, now *textiles*?"

"*Tektites*, not textiles," Marcus corrected. "It could be Libyan Desert Glass. There are at least six recognized geographic distributions of tektites on Earth, and Mecca lies in the path of one."

"How do *you* know that?"

"There are several excellent meteor sites online," Marcus said proudly. "I subscribe to the chief *zine*."

"I read that in pre-Islamic Mecca, the Goddess was worshipped in the form of a black, aniconic stone. It's still kept inside the cube, in the *Haram*, which means sanctuary and is a cognate of *harem*, which originally meant a temple of women.

"Allah is a masculinization of *Al-Lat*, part of a female trinity," the student continued. "The others were Kore... or Q're, the Virgin, and a crone figure. Some think the Koran is like the Word of Kore..."

"*Judy!*" Marwa gasped.

"Aniconic...cool word," Judy said. "*An-iconic?*"

"Please, *stop!*" Biren cut in, dramatically. "I thank my gods every day they're Hindu, free of your Judeo-Christian-Muslim anxiety. This incessant *mind over matter* dialectic! My gods *enjoy* the sex they created. Good *grief!* Relief...frigid uteruses falling out of the sky? The sky is falling!"

"*Uteri,*" someone corrected.

"Say '*frigid uteruses*' like your father," another chimed in. "I love when Biren does his dad's accent."

"Yeah, do the arm dance *and* the accent at the same time!"

"I see we're back to practicing political incorrectness," someone muttered.

"Thank God."

"Which one?"

The bell rang, signaling the end of the lunch period.

"As in... saved by the..."

3

NOVEMBER 2000

That November night, sleet turning into snow promised a snow day. Marwa moved away from her desk and the still-glowing computer, away from IM'd dialogues about math homework and looming Intel project deadline meetings.

She lay down on her bed and closed her eyes. She let herself sink into the shifting sounds outside. First the harsh, metallic hiss of sleet, then the softer, almost inaudible hush of snow gusting against the window.

In her mind, she imagined the differences in sound as beautiful equations for Brownian motion. Crayola Burnt Sienna curves scribbled across a whiteboard, though some of her teachers still stubbornly called them blackboards.

In Joey's elementary school, the boards were made of green slate. His teacher used yellow chalk. The contrast always stuck with her.

The sounds of voices, words written on different-colored surfaces, and numbers and symbols from her physics class. 'An Untestable Idea is Not Even Wrong', declared a poster border in the back of the room. It's message merged with the rhythm created by the sleet, snow and blizzard winds outside.

Marwa didn't feel sleepy.

The phrase 'Her Divine Box' kept repeating in her head, threading through all the other images and sounds. The words aroused her, and she was still furious at Judy.

She wondered, if she put her hijab back on would her heart stop pounding?

Marwa tried to block out the flood of images of Prix on magazine covers, billboards, entire sides of tall buildings, and lately, perfume ads on TV. Those pictures of Prix invaded her from the outside. More often now, he walked out of the dark back of the cave in her mind, carelessly, as if he lived there.

She was convinced it was her visual cortex flashing, connecting directly to her ancient, animal brain, deep in the hippocampus, wired straight to her body's pleasure center…her genitals.

Clitoris.

She knew the word.

The ugly, whispered word for the part which was cut off in African coming-of-age mutilations.

She and Judy had watched that *Seinfeld* episode—the one where Jerry can't remember a girl's name, only that it rhymed with a "female body part."

Dolores.

Clitoris.

At lunch, when the conversation had turned to Mecca and the Kaaba, and when Judy had started poking around the concept of Allah, Marwa hadn't said a word. She hadn't mentioned Prix either.

*Her Div…*the phrase blinded her.

It was terrible to even say the word…*Box*…for the shoebox her mother had given for her secret keepsakes.

Marwa had been seven when she began saving small, sacred things, but she hadn't decorated the box until she was eleven. The first item she had ever placed inside was something she'd dug up while planting bulbs with her mother one fall afternoon in their front yard in Far Rockaway, the place that still filled her dreams with the feeling of home.

At seven, she had eagerly worked the earth with a red-handled trowel, praised again and again for digging perfect holes at just the right depth for daffodils and tulips. Her mother, forever exasperated by non-metric measurements, had nonetheless been impressed by Marwa's precision. The praise had made Marwa feel proud.

Marwa got off the bed and found her Box where she kept it hidden at the back corner of her closet. Upon opening it, she took into her hand that first magic object. She remembered that special find vividly.

That day, her trowel had struck a stone. She'd pulled it out of the dirt and run to her mother to ask what it was. Her mother had examined it, frowning, not in disappointment but in fascination.

"This isn't natural, I think," she'd said, turning it in her hands. "See these marks? Like it was struck by a knife or another stone."

"Maybe it belonged to the Indians!" Marwa had exclaimed. "The Rockaways lived here, right?"

"It's not flint," her mother murmured, still puzzled.

Marwa had taken the small, rectangular wedge of stone to school for Show and Tell. Her classmates passed it around, marveling at its uniqueness. One boy started tossing it between his hands, refusing to give it back. Marwa had shouted and the teacher had intervened.

No one ever identified what the object was, not its composition, its age, or what it might have been used for. She took it home and placed it inside the box her mother had given her.

And though she could barely say the words out loud, she forced herself to now... *Marwa's Divine Box.*

The blizzard kept battering the tall apartment building, wind funneling straight down from Canada through the Hudson's air shaft. But it wasn't the Arctic winds that cooled the heat rising in Marwa's body. It was the small, right-angled edges of the Indian stone in her hand.

It calmed her.

It seemed to whisper, "*I am yours. You are safe.*"

There were many other objects in her...*Divine Box.*

She picked up the carefully folded, lovely cloth that had once been her *hijab* and pressed it to her heart with her other hand, as if apologizing to her younger self.

When she had first been allowed to wear it, the *hijab* had made her feel special, womanly. She believed she was pleasing Allah. She *knew* she was pleasing her father, who had looked at her differently that day.

Then she thought of Juliet in the essay, silently rebelling against her parents. Juliet Capulet, who never spoke again as a child after her very own nurse encouraged her to marry Paris after she had married Romeo and made love with him. She wouldn't even argue with her nurse or mother anymore · or her father who threatened to disown his only child, send her out to the streets where she could only become a whore if she refused to obey him.

'Her chaste treasure,' Marwa thought, knowing that line belonged to Ophelia from *Hamlet.*

They'd read a book about anorexia in Psych class that used Ophelia in the title, so she had read the play on her own. She'd be reading it again soon, in AP English.

Suddenly, she realized she was hungry, and she still hadn't finished her math homework in case the snow day didn't happen after all.

Leaving her room became risky since Marwa stopped wearing her *hijab.* She never knew which of her parents, or her older brother, might scold her or glare in disapproval.

Joey never bothered her about it.

He and Marwa were in some kind of unspoken alliance now, which only angered her parents more as she was such a bad example for her little brother.

Stopped being Mu'hajiba, Marwa thought.

To wear or not to wear.

To be or not to be.

She wasn't thinking of Hamlet, though. She was seeing Prix, leaning patiently in the mental doorway of her thoughts. The poor, small stone in her hand wasn't strong enough to keep him out.

Gently, she placed the stone and the scarf back into her hot, swollen Divine Box and braced herself to face the other side of her bedroom door.

⚱☥

As Marwa had feared, her mother was in the kitchen, preparing the next night's dinner, *wara' enab*. The boiled grape leaves to be filled with spiced rice and the ground meat she was in the process of draining were cooling and drying on paper towels. The kitchen smelled heavenly!

Her mother was giving her the silent treatment

Marwa felt a sharp ache of guilt, followed by an urge to reach out, to take her mother's hands and press her palms to her own face, the gesture her mother had always used to show a love too deep for words.

But then, as had been happening more and more often, the ache twisted into anger so sharp and terrifying it made her suddenly understand all that talk about Achilles during freshman year literature class. *The Iliad*, the rage of the hero.

She thought, *Fine. If she won't talk to me for a minute, I won't talk to her for an hour.*

Unconsciously and instantly, Marwa saw, rather than calculated, how long it would take before she could say a word to her mother. As always, the coolness of numbers and arranging them in equations, cool and predictable, gave her a sense of control. They couldn't replace her mother's love, but they offered a balm for its absence.

Then her mother spoke. First, she recited in Arabic and then, pointedly, translated as if Marwa could no longer understand.

"Every son is a blessing. Every daughter is a curse."

Marwa's resolve to silence shattered as quickly as her mother's had.

"If I ever have a daughter," she said, voice shaking, "I will never say those words to her."

Her mother didn't look at her.

"We will see. We will see," she said softly, turning to scrub the shining stainless steel sink.

Marwa stood her ground.

"When you treat me like this, you're teaching me how to treat *you.*"

Marwa's mother turned to face her, eyes blazing.

"What do you think you are doing? Where do you think this is going? How can you disappoint your father like this? How can you break my heart?"

Marwa fought to hold back her tears.

"*Ummee,* how can you break *mine*?"

"It is one heart between us, and *you* are the one breaking it. Who will pay for you to go to college, then?"

Marwa recoiled, as if slapped.

"You would do that?"

"How can you expect your father to pay for your education when you're no longer his daughter?"

"All my work, all *your* work, and you could turn your backs on that?"

"As *you* have turned your back on us. On *Allah.*"

"This is economic blackmail. This is *politics. Ummee...*"

"You know nothing of the world," her mother cut in. "I love you. Your father loves you. But we cannot let you walk *naked* in this world. *'We have bestowed raiment upon you to cover your shame, as well as to be an adornment to you.'"*

"I am *not* naked," Marwa said, her voice tight. "The hijab is one piece of cloth. *'But the raiment of righteousness, That is the best.'"*

Her mother's mouth twisted.

"Oh, you're too smart for your own good. You're *modern.* You're *American.* You're an *individual.* And when you turn away from us and turn around, there will be an *individual* there, standing alone and naked. And the world will *eat* you alive. This is what happens here…the child rejects the parent. It is *against Allah*."

Marwa struggled to breathe, her voice barely steady.

"That is *paternalism*. That is *politics*, not spirituality. That is *not* Allah."

Her mother's hand flashed like lightning and struck her.

"*Blasphemy!* What follows is chaos, war, rape. You don't know what men are…"

Then her mother began to cry. And Marwa cried too.

Through the tears and running nose, a voice…new, fierce, and steady…spoke from Marwa's mouth.

"So, you think religion is the gang that protects me from gang rape? *If* I can stay wrapped in the folds of *hijab* or *chador* and all the misogynistic laws and hateful sayings, *then* I can exist as a sheep in the fold, protected by the very wolves who keep me penned?"

She pressed forward, breath shaking.

"And *you* left your family behind, didn't you, *Ummee?* Did you think I wouldn't imitate you? That's why you're so angry, because I'm doing exactly what you did, for the same reasons you can't admit. And you feel guilty. You're afraid I'll be hurt because of *you*. But I won't, *Ummee*. Or no more than *you* were, when you left the people, you still love in Egypt."

Her words landed. Marwa could see it. Her mother's dark eyes stayed wide and troubled, but the worst of the storm had passed.

"I came to this godforsaken country because I loved your father, and he loved me," her mother said at last. "There was no work for him in Egypt. His family was poor, and he was the oldest of nine. You know this. I am ashamed to have broken my parents' hearts. But we are one heart, in Allah. They understand that. I do not understand *you*."

Marwa took a breath.

"I think you do. I think you *want* me to argue with you. I think you want me to *win*. I'm just not good enough at it yet."

She paused.

"In seventh grade, when I was voted to play the judge in the class trial, you said I couldn't. That a good Muslim girl couldn't be a judge. What was I supposed to tell my teacher and classmates? That Muslim girls lacked the gene for judicial thinking that other girls had?"

Her voice hardened.

"That's the same hateful, superstitious logic that justified the murder of Hypatia of Alexandria, skinned alive by a Christian bishop because she was a genius mathematician. 'Don't think' doesn't mean '*can't* think.' If you and Baba won't send me to college, I'll go on my own. I'll win a scholarship. I know how to work hard. You made me strong."

Her mother's voice softened.

"All strength comes from Allah."

Marwa nodded.

"Allah is a merciful judge. I got an A+ on that class trial. So, if I have strength, then it must come from Allah."

"This country is poison," her mother said. "It will kill you. It is materialism, individuality, and filthy music."

"Living here isn't just about the money you and Baba make and send to Alexandria," Marwa replied, her voice trembling with urgency. "It's why you left the garden where we planted daffodils and counted worms... so I could go to Stuy. It's Sharif at Brooklyn Poly. It's *everything* for Joey... basketball, baseball, ice hockey, and Internet access to the public library. No, *no*, because in Egypt, yes, there's public school and university, but Baba brought you here for *hope*, Ummee. *Hope*. That's the last, best thing left in Pandora's Divine Box. *People* should make their own laws that *evolve*—not blindly obey the ones that oppress them just because they call *history* God."

"You're so in love with this country," her mother snapped. "A country where *I* can be no more than an *adjunct* at Columbia. I'm not a professor because I'm not a *man*."

"They have women professors at Columbia," Marwa said gently. "But you don't have an M.A. or a Ph.D."

"I *was* a professor at the community college in Brooklyn!"

"No. You were an adjunct there, too. The students called you 'Professor,' but Columbia would treat a man without advanced degrees in Arabic the same way."

"Because he is…"

"No, *Ummee.* Not because he's Muslim."

Marwa's mother covered her ears with her palms, squeezed her eyes shut, and shook her head, lips pressed tight.

Marwa stepped forward and gently placed her own hands on her mother's face, just as she had wished her mother had welcomed her.

Her mother's eyes opened. Marwa released her mother's soft cheeks, returned to her room, and finished her math homework.

They said nothing more that night.

☙ ❧

The next morning, the apartment was strangely quiet. Marwa didn't wake up in time for school since her clock radio had been turned off while she slept.

After the blizzard, it was indeed, a snow day. Only her father had gone to work at the bank. Her mother had kept Joey busy and quiet, letting both Marwa and Sharif sleep in.

When Marwa stepped into the kitchen for something hot to drink, she found that her mother had prepared cocoa from Zabar's. It had been kept warm in the double boiler on the stove.

The container was left out on the counter as a silent peace offering.

4

DECEMBER 2000

It was mid-December, another Saturday night Marwa wasn't going anywhere. She was home babysitting Joey while her parents were out at a holiday party. Of course, Sharif was in Egypt for winter break, visiting their maternal grandmother and aunts.

The phone call between New York and Alexandria, which Marwa had walked in on after school on the last day of classes before the holiday, was entirely in Arabic, fast, clipped phrases that sounded like fingers tapping rapidly on a keyboard...click-click-click. Then, suddenly, the sounds softened, rounded out, melting from ice into water. The words became globules she could almost taste, like the mineral-laced water in Alexandria...unfamiliar, but not unpleasant.

Marwa could have been out. Judy had invited her to a party with a big group of friends, or she could've gone to the movies with Marcus Silbercoff, an attractive classmate who clearly liked her. He lived on the East Side and described his parents as Jewish, as if distancing himself from the label.

They were both strong candidates for the Brookhaven Lab internship on Long Island that summer, but if it came down to one spot, Marwa figured Marcus would get it. She was fairly confident, though, that she had a solid shot at the genetic research position at Stony Brook. Her Intel advisor was friends with the professor running the lab.

Right now, she was torn between experimental physics and genetic research. Both fascinated her. She loved how her physics teacher called the class Stemcell, like it was their shared nickname.

Marcus had an intuitive feel for numbers that Marwa admired and knew she didn't quite share. Her instincts leaned more toward living systems.

She wasn't sure how she felt about Marcus. With Prix, she had known instantly.

That day, when they were alone in the elevator, he had invited her to his apartment.

"Just to see it," he'd said.

Of course she had said no.

He'd noticed she wasn't wearing the hijab.

"Do you miss it?" he asked.

"I didn't *lose* it," she snapped.

"Hey, hey," he said, raising his hands in mock surrender. "It was just a question. You just rejected me."

Later, Judy had apologized for what she'd said about Al-Lat and Allah. That apology opened the floodgates, and Marwa finally told her about Prix.

Judy had dramatically pretended to tear out her own hair as Marwa recounted the elevator scene.

"Prix said it with such a smile, half disbelief, half disinterest, I knew he didn't really have feelings for me," Marwa said. "At least, I *think* I know. I mean... I *know* I don't have enough experience to be sure."

"'Twere to consider too curiously, to consider so,'" Judy quoted.

"I'm not Hamlet," Marwa replied.

They were reading *Hamlet* in AP English and watching the Kenneth Branagh film adaptation.

And I'm not Zohra either, Marwa thought.

She was reading Naguib Mahfouz's *Miramar*, or trying to. Her mother had given her the original Arabic edition, and she was struggling through it, supplementing with an English translation she'd ordered online. She had even copied out a favorite passage, first in Arabic, then in English.

It was the scene where Zohra, the poor servant girl, refuses a marriage proposal as an act of defiance.

"The man said to Zohra, 'You deserve to be killed!'"

Later, Zohra discusses the decision with the wise, narrator-like old man at the small Alexandria hotel.

"Zohra said, 'What do you really think I should do?'"

"'I wish you could go back to your village.'"

"'Go back to misery?'"

"'I said, I wish you *could*, that is, go back and be happy.'"

"Zohra said, 'I love the land and the village, but I hate the misery... Here is where love is. Education. Cleanliness. And hope.'"

Marwa admired Zohra. But she also knew the truth. She wasn't a peasant girl from 1960s Alexandria. She was a Muslim-American teenager in Manhattan. Judy had Beatles posters on her bedroom walls.

And the real irony? Her mother had given her the Mahfouz novel *in Arabic*, hoping it would have the opposite effect.

But it didn't.

GRTψ

Instead of going to a party—or on a maybe-date with Marcus, Marwa was home babysitting Joey. She didn't mind, really. She liked competing with her mother for influence over her little brother.

What she *was* looking forward to was the second half of a movie she'd stumbled upon the night before. She hadn't

27

realized it would end with one of those frustrating cliffhangers, *To Be Continued*, but at least the conclusion was airing tonight.

The story was wild. Passengers on a jumbo jet flying through a sky where the world was literally disappearing behind them in time. They'd landed in Bangor, Maine, only to discover that the airport itself was being devoured by monstrous time-eaters called Langoliers.

Classic Stephen King.

Marwa just needed Joey to be *pretending* to sleep in the bottom bunk so she could watch in peace.

She tried coaxing him into her fourth-level Sims game, but Joey much preferred chaos, blowing up buildings and people in other games. He would frequently hurl himself out of his swivel chair in mock explosions, complete with dramatic sound effects.

At one point, he even launched himself off the top bunk, landing perfectly on a wide cushion she'd set up on the floor.

Tire him out, she thought, *but don't get him wild.*

They switched to building a city, using blocks and wiry magnetic links that allowed for three-dimensional structures and even "vehicular" movement. Joey narrated how everything in his city worked, and Marwa played along, interviewing him like a TV reporter.

"Mayor Joey," she said, holding an imaginary microphone, "can you walk us through your urban design?"

Joey immediately slipped into perfect impersonations of their father and older brother, Sharif.

"And *here,*" he pointed dramatically, "is where Alexander the Great is buried."

Marwa raised an eyebrow, still playing along.

"I thought he was buried somewhere in Alexandria, and no one knows exactly where."

"Oh, *my* archaeologists found him," Joey said proudly. "And as a reward, Alexander the Great lives in *my* city. It's the greatest city in the whole world."

"And what is the name of your city, Mayor Joey?" Marwa asked.

"It is *Joe York*, on *Planet Al-Hal*," Joey declared.

"And how many citizens live in your great city, O Mayor?"

"They're invisible citizens, so it's hard to say. It varies."

"Why do citizens without bodies need buildings?" Marwa asked, genuinely curious.

Joey puffed up his cheeks and let out a loud mouth-fart.

Then he answered seriously, "They honor the past by building buildings they don't need, but they like flying around in them."

He broke character for a moment.

"Wouldn't they crash into each other, flying invisible?"

"Invisibly," Marwa corrected. "Maybe they evolved sensors."

"Invisibly sensors to see invisibly fliers!" Joey cried.

"Invisible fliers fly *invisibly*," Marwa said, but her clever turn of phrase was lost on Mayor Joey, who had already taken flight, arms outstretched, circling the bedroom with dramatic banking turns as he attempted to glide out the door and avoid bedtime.

Marwa stepped in front of the doorway.

"I can see you," she said, catching him mid-flight and lifting him up.

He leaned his head against her chest with a small, tired sigh. Joey managed to bargain for one book before bed, but he was asleep, thumb tucked in his now softly snuffling mouth before Marwa even finished reading it. His nightlight glowed gently from the rotating image on his computer screen, casting moving shadows across the room.

The only TV in the apartment was in the living room's dining L, where the walls were three-quarters window, facing mostly northeast. The view wasn't much, just more buildings, but her parents had traded scenery for space...three bedrooms.

Marwa made herself a cup of cocoa, settled on the couch, and flipped the widescreen to the sci-fi channel. The movie hadn't started yet. With a few minutes to spare, she muted the volume and sipped the hot chocolate, feeling, for a moment, content.

What could we be without bodies? she wondered.

We were, quite literally, *invested* in them—knowing ourselves and the world only through their changes. What utter nakedness invisibility would confer. But then again, would "naked" even *mean* anything in such a state?

Her thoughts drifted to Çatalhöyük, the ancient Stone Age city in Turkey. The sound of the name itself—gargling and gulping—delighted her. She had seen a special on the Discovery Channel and followed up on their website.

Çatalhöyük was the earliest known Paleolithic city on Earth. In one of its dwellings, there was a wall painting of another city, with twin volcanoes in the background. The archaeologist voiceover had explained that, when flying over Çatalhöyük and looking north, you could see another mound site with twin peaks that matched those in the mural—100 kilometers to the south.

So, the archaeologist theorized, the painting might be a memory—a visual echo—of where the people of Çatalhöyük had come from: the older site of Azılhöyük.

Marwa noticed the recap on the TV was wrapping up. She reached for the remote, but her thoughts lingered on Çatal and Azıl.

What would it be like to live in a time before all the religions? she wondered. Before Muslims, Jews, Christians. Before Hindus, Confucians, Buddhists, Shinto. She even knew a few African spiritual words. But nothing from South America. Or the Arctic.

There had once been a time before all the names, before all the laws.

And there would be a time after.

Marwa leaned back and unmuted the television, ready to watch *The Langoliers* devour the past.

5

JANUARY 2001

"*We take life three seconds at a time.*" "*Because light travels at a finite speed, to look out is to look back.*"

The assignment was simple: choose one—or both—of these statements as the basis for a 500–1500 word meditation.

It was the first day back at school, the first week of January 2001. Mr. Haddam handed out the prompt to Marwa's AP English class, and as she read the words, an unexpected image flickered across her mind: Sharif's face.

It startled her.

Then came a voice—an inner voice that wasn't really a voice at all, more like the echo of memory processed through thought:

"*The second-largest city and main port of Egypt, Alexandria was built by the Greek architect Dinocrates on the site of an old village, Rhakotis, at the orders of Alexander the Great.*"

She'd read it recently while browsing online, searching for something—anything—that might prove to her parents she cared about Alexandria, about their roots.

Meanwhile, her classmates were loudly debating the "three seconds at a time" line.

"Who *said* that?" someone asked.

"A brain researcher at the University of Munich, Ernst Pöppel," Mr. Haddam replied. "And Einstein, respectively."

"I'll have to ask my father about this Pöppel guy," Judy said, scribbling in her notebook.

"You might begin your essay with that line, Ms. Yamaguchi," Mr. Haddam suggested.

Judy beamed. She loved when Mr. Haddam called her *Ms. Yamaguchi*—the formality made her feel both important and seen.

"Wait, is it a meditation or an essay?" Marcus asked.

"It's 500 to 1500 words," Biren deadpanned, and the whole class burst out laughing.

But Marwa didn't laugh.

She sat quietly, feeling detached from the warm hum of the classroom—set apart, as if she were floating above it. Not in January. Not even in New York.

Somewhere else.

Some other time.

ᏕᎡᎢᎾ

"Our guide in time is memory," Marwa began to write. *"My older brother, Sharif, returns next weekend to New York City from Alexandria, which my mother still calls 'home.' Before the rise of Christianity and Islam, Hermes was worshipped in Alexandria as the incarnation of Thoth, the Egyptian god of the Moon. I am torn—especially since I removed the hijab. This is the beginning of my meditation on time, which, I believe, is the assigned topic.*

"The quotations we were given do not reflect current scientific understanding, which suggests that at the subatomic level, time—at least as we know it—does not exist."

She paused, then continued with what had been echoing in her mind for days.

"The second-largest city and main port of Egypt, Alexandria was built by the Greek architect Dinocrates (332–331 BCE) on the site of the old Egyptian village of Rhakotis, under the orders of Alexander the Great. That village had developed along the Mediterranean shore, shielded by the island of Pharos to the north.

"Once Dinocrates constructed the Heptastadion causeway to connect Pharos Island to the mainland, the water between the land and island was divided into two harbors: the Great Harbor to the east and the Eunostos Harbor to the west.

"It was the eastern, Great Harbor that mattered most to the ancient and medieval world. The Lighthouse at Pharos— erected on the island's easternmost point—was one of the Seven Wonders of the Ancient World. It guided ships for nearly a thousand years before two massive earthquakes destroyed it in the early 14th century.

"In recent years, underwater discoveries in the Great Harbor are believed to be the lighthouse's remains.

"Cleopatra's palace, built along the northeastern shore, looked directly across the harbor at the lighthouse. This must be where Shakespeare imagined Antony saying, 'I am dying, Egypt, dying.'

"Julius Caesar is often blamed for the catastrophic fire that destroyed the Great Library of Alexandria—a library said to contain the collective knowledge of Western antiquity: the plays of Aeschylus, Sophocles, Euripides; lost mathematical works; and 'Aristotle's own library,' as Stoppard put it in Arcadia, which we read in class."

Marwa's tone shifted, becoming more analytical.

"Alexandria can be seen as a model—or emblem—of Greek reason.

"Later visitors noted that the intersection of its two major thoroughfares resembled a slightly tilted Christian cross, and the eastern promontory's curve evoked the crescent of Islam.

"But to Dinocrates, the layout might have resembled mathematical axes, ready to be graphed.

"The east–west axis, now Al-Horreya (Tariq Abd el-Nasser), was once the Canopic Way, stretching from the Gate of the Sun in the east to the Gate of the Moon in the west. The north–south axis, now Sharia el-Nebi Daniel, was once called the Street of the Soma. It extended south to Lake Harbor on Lake Mareotis."

"It might have looked that way to the Greek architect Dinocrates—like a coordinate grid—if graphing had existed in his time. But mathematics wasn't forced to truly grapple with time until the late 1400s, when Europeans began building wheel-driven clocks, waging artillery-based wars, and circumnavigating the globe.

"Last year in math class, we read a chapter titled What Are Graphs? It said, 'The same social context produced a clock…, revolutionary wars…, exploration which enriched the merchant classes…, and a mathematical invention which could measure the movement of the pendulum, the path of the cannonball, the position of a ship at sea, and the courses of the heavenly bodies.'

"When Mr. Sullivan and Ms. Kelly combined our math and history classes for a joint unit, Ms. Kelly explained how Euclid's geometry deliberately left time out—and how Descartes put it back in. By 1637, Descartes had written Discourse on the Method for Rightly Conducting One's Reason and Searching for Truth in the Sciences, where he effectively founded coordinate geometry: a new way to measure and map the world, inspired by the axes of longitude and latitude.

"E.M. Forster once called Alexandria 'the capital of memory.' Still, most people have forgotten that Alexandria began as the Egyptian settlement of Rhakotis—and no one remembers what it was called before that.

"Who knows? Maybe early humans, proto-Neanderthals, had a name for that sheltered stretch of land, nestled between the great sea and the inland lake. Maybe they fished there, bathed there, while moving west toward the land bridge at Gibraltar, then north and east into the river valleys of Europe.

"For my parents, Alexandria is definitely the capital of memory.

"Each winter break, my brother Sharif visits our mother's family there—our grandparents and three aunts—who live in a spacious apartment in the Maamora district, right on the seacoast. It's crowded in the summer, but peaceful and quiet in the winter.

"My mother is the only one from her family who lives in America. My father, on the other hand, has three brothers and four sisters here. He also has two more brothers: one still in Egypt, the other in Qatar.

"My mother's family doesn't like my father's. They resent that his side left Alexandria—and that he took my mother with him.

"Everyone assumes Muslim society is rigidly patriarchal, but in my mother's family, it seems like the women run everything. Maybe that's just how it is in their homes, or maybe it's how I hear it told—through my mother, my grandmother, and my three aunts.

"My mother is one of four sisters. My grandmother had no sons, but she always says that each of her daughters is a Fatima, even though only her firstborn bears the sainted name. It means they're proud to be women who—like Fatima, the only child of the Prophet Muhammad—raised sons to carry on a legacy.

"Still, no one has ever truly forgiven my mother for leaving Egypt.

"No one believes that more deeply than my mother.

"I think that's why she pushes me so hard to be a 'true' Muslim—to make up for what she and her family see as her betrayal and abandonment.

36

"But I don't think she abandoned them at all. She's in constant contact with them, always apologizing, always carrying the weight of their disappointment. And she directs so much of that pressure at me.

"Meanwhile, Sharif is adored—for being the son, the firstborn, the one who visits twice a year, speaks fluent Arabic, and might very well return to live in Alexandria. My oldest aunt, Auntie Fatima, says that's how it should be: that my mother is lucky to have one "American" son and one real son.

"My mother hasn't said a word to her family about me not wearing the hijab since school started this year. Honestly, it made things easier when I told her I didn't want to go to Alexandria with Sharif this time.

"But summer is coming.

"Unlike my mother, who is tall and slim (like me), Auntie Fatima is very large.

"Lately, I've been thinking about how the Greek worship of Hermes became intertwined with the Egyptian worship of Thoth, the moon god. This fusion happened in Alexandria.

"Greek philosophy and Egyptian mysticism merged there to form Hermeticism, a belief system attributed to Hermes Trismegistus. Those teachings formed a bridge to Gnosticism and became a foundation for many Western mystical traditions. Hermetic thought directly influenced alchemy, the Jewish Kabbalah, Muslim Sufism, Christian mysticism—and even the Tarot cards, which were brought to Europe by 'gypsies' (a word derived from Egypt).

"Basically, the idea is this: Hermes is the guide—not only to death, but through death and into rebirth.

"Hermes, or Mercury—as we know him today in the form of the small, fast-orbiting planet closest to the Sun—was seen in ancient and mythological astronomy as the swift Messenger. Think of the old Western Union logo: a figure in a winged World War I-style helmet, holding a staff wrapped with two snakes—the caduceus.

"The caduceus is still used as a symbol of medicine, representing both death and life.

"That symbol itself is rich with meaning. The intertwining snakes are said to represent Hermes as the serpent of eternal life and Aphrodite (Venus, goddess of love—read: sex) as the serpent of time—birth and death—wrapped around each other at the Tree of Life.

"Our resident classroom guru-Hindu, Biren, claims they're copulating. Of course, Biren would say that. But it's clearly illogical—the sexual act alone doesn't grant eternal life or the knowledge that lies beyond death. I've told Biren this more than once, but it hasn't stopped him. He thinks his teasing counts as enlightened debate.

"Astrology, which people still casually follow in newspapers and online, once served as a kind of spiritual map. The zodiac was imagined as a series of time zones or energetic envelopes around Earth—each one imparting traits as the soul passed through it. But the point wasn't to stay in those zones. The goal was to move beyond them—to escape the limiting layers and reach a higher state of awareness where time itself didn't exist.

"Honestly, a lot of this doesn't make much more sense to me than reading about multi-dimensional branes in Scientific American. Maybe someday one or the other—or both—will click.

"But what really matters about Hermes and Alexandria is that they represent a moment in time and place where human thought shifted.

"Alexandria, Egypt: the city Alexander the Great imagined into being, designed by Dinocrates along rational, geometric lines. A city where myth and logic coexisted. Where Egyptian moon worship of Thoth merged with the Greek reverence for Hermes.

"That merging — called transcultural syncretism — wasn't accidental. Alexander encouraged it. He wanted to create a new world where cultures didn't just clash but combined, layered meaning on meaning. Hermes became the perfect symbol of that: the one who moves between worlds, *between death and life, between cultures—and carries the message forward.*

"I think it was the influence of his teacher, Aristotle, that led Alexander the Great to think so logically and methodically. Aristotle taught him to examine ideas, identify their common characteristics, and connect them in reasonable, purposeful ways.

"In AP European History last year, I learned that the classical Greek ideal of polis—the city-state praised by Pericles—evolved in Alexandria into something broader: the cosmopolis, a world city.

"We can see echoes of that same ideal here in New York City, where so many different nationalities—entire cultures and, in effect, nations—live side by side in a shared civic space. Ideally, the rights of the individual are balanced against the privileges of the powerful.

"At least, that's the 'idea of the ideal', as Mr. Sullivan always said. And it began in Alexandria, Egypt, in the 4th century BCE.

"I don't know if I'm related—Egyptian, Greek, or otherwise—to anyone from that era. But I'd be proud to think so.

"In my mind, related by logical analogy, is Galileo's famous formula for falling bodies: $v = g \times t$ — the velocity of a falling object equals gravity times the time it takes to fall.

"Formulas like this reveal something astonishing: that very different phenomena—a stone dropping to Earth and the Moon orbiting it—are governed by the same physical laws.

"But isn't that essentially the same idea expressed in religion and magic? As above, so below. Don't Christians say, 'Thy will be done on earth as it is in heaven'?

"Looking back at my opening thesis, I realize I need to expand on two more ideas: my decision to stop wearing the hijab, and the implications of quantum mechanics for our understanding of time.

"Current research on subatomic particles suggests that time, at the quantum level, may not exist as we perceive it.

Particles can spin both clockwise and counterclockwise at the same time. Even more bizarre are entangled particles—what Einstein called "spooky action at a distance." If one particle spins clockwise, its twin, even far away, must spin counterclockwise—instantaneously, without any signal passing between them.

"However, in the interest of time, I realize I've written far more than the assignment required. It's late, and I'm tired. I don't have any conclusions or answers—only questions.

"This meditation has made me realize that I don't really know how to think about time right now. Even using time-related words and verb tenses feels overwhelming. Vivian Cheng once told me that Chinese doesn't even have verb tenses, and that always makes me a little nervous—like the floor might drop out from under language itself.

"I've been thinking about people who seem to be born in the wrong time, who never quite fit where or when they find themselves. Maybe I'm one of them.

"Some people are described as being ahead of their time— visionaries. Others are called reactionary, as if they're stuck behind the curve of history.

"But what if, like in a dream, we could travel through time the way we move through space?

"What if one of my great-great-grandmothers, as a teenager, had opened a door in ancient Alexandria and caught a glimpse of me—sitting here at my desk, typing on a keyboard, the words appearing on a 17-inch monitor in a nearly dark bedroom?

"Would she have even known what she was looking at? Could she have recognized me as her granddaughter?

"And if I were given that same freedom—able to see into the future—what could I know of the girl or boy whose great-great-grandmother I will be someday?

"What are they doing now?

"And most of all, I'm curious—what book is this meditation actually supposed to be preparing us for?"

Marwa's AP English teacher, Scott Haddam, read through his students' meditations and returned them with handwritten comments.

She received her paper the following Monday morning—just after Sharif had come back from Alexandria the night before, too jet-lagged to touch the dinner waiting for him.

As she scanned the margins for criticism, Marwa smiled at what Mr. Haddam had written in penciled, slightly exaggerated italics—clearly having erased a few earlier edits.

"Must share for future discussion."

Later in class, he passed around a page of excerpts from her essay. He'd scanned, cut, and pasted sections together, omitting any identifying details.

Still, everyone would know "Alexandria" meant Marwa.

But they were expected to follow the classroom's privacy protocol. No names. No direct comments.

The room fell into a sudden, respectful hush as her classmates quietly read her words.

Then Mr. Haddam moved them forward. He passed out index cards to fill out for their next book:

"The overture volume of the seven novels making up *Remembrance of Things Past—Swann's Way*, by Marcel Proust," he announced.

"What do we write down? All *that?*" Biren Ramanathan asked. "Can we just write *Swann?*"

Mr. Haddam nodded.

"Fine. Just *Swann*."

He then gestured for Biren to begin reading aloud.

"For a long time," Biren began, "I used to go to bed early..."

6

MARCH 2001

O n Sunday, March 4th, Marwa set aside her homework—fine-tuning her prep for the Intel Science Fair in Brooklyn, now just two weeks away—to join Judy and her father on their annual visit to the cemetery on Long Island. It was a ritual: a quiet, solemn trip to place visit stones on Judy's mother's grave.

A massive snowstorm had been forecast to begin that night and continue through Tuesday. TV meteorologists were practically gleeful—storm-tracking this, Doppler-4-ing that. Dr. Yamaguchi, Judy's father, seemed mildly irritated by the media frenzy but not nearly as somber as Marwa had expected. "At least I get to drive my midlife-crisis-red car out of the city," he said with dry amusement.

Marwa had slept over at Judy's on Saturday night so they could leave early Sunday morning. She wasn't entirely sure what the emotional tone of the trip would be, especially since Judy's eight-year-old sister, Jody, was coming along for the first time. But when Judy asked her to join, Marwa had felt quietly honored.

Dr. Yamaguchi was about the same age as Marwa's own father—early fifties—but that was where the similarities ended.

Dr. Y, as he liked to be called (or "Dr. Why," depending on Judy's mood), was medium height and carried a distinct paunch that pushed against the waistline of his unbelted brown corduroy slacks. He usually wore jeans and a neutral-toned sweater over an equally muted shirt, topped off with what Judy referred to as his "tie-up leather shoeboxes."

"If he's gonna wear jeans, why not just sneakers?" Judy would mutter.

"I am not a fashion *plotz*," Dr. Why once said, half-apologizing in front of Marwa.

Judy rolled her eyes at his "faux-Yiddish," which she insisted he used in some misplaced attempt to feel connected to her late mother's Jewish heritage.

"My mom never talked like that a day in her life," she'd groan.

Marwa couldn't imagine her own father ever using slang of any kind, let alone *faux* anything. He was tall, meticulously groomed, and proud of his trim build.

"A banker is not a shopkeeper," he liked to say.

Even at home, he dressed in modest precision. Marwa had never seen him without a bathrobe, or in slippers without socks. She shared his quiet pride in how he presented himself.

But what struck Marwa most about Dr. Yamaguchi was how present he seemed with Judy and Jody—not just as a parent, but as someone genuinely interested in who they were as *people*. It didn't seem to matter to him that they were daughters, not sons.

Judy had told her it was true, and Marwa believed her.

"My father thinks misogyny, or any kind of prejudice, isn't just stupid," Judy said. "He calls it *counterproductive.* 'We need all the help we can get,' he always says."

Dr. Why, as he liked to be called, was a Japanese-American who had married a Jewish woman.

As they drove, Judy explained to Marwa that due to the impending blizzard, they wouldn't be stopping by her Lensky grandparents' assisted-living condo after the cemetery ceremony. But they were still expected to meet "an uncle on that side and his wife" at the gravesite.

Her "Lensky-Yamaguchi mini-genealogy," as she called it, included Dr. Why's late parents—Japanese-Americans who had been placed in internment camps during World War II. He also had a sister and her family who still lived in Northern California, where he had been born and raised.

"Northern California," Dr. Why said from the front seat, "where the mudslides never sleep."

Jody, seated beside him, was busy swapping out a CD.

They had just crossed the Williamsburg Bridge, the car making its way toward the low, rolling hills of one of the massive cemeteries that line Long Island's edge.

Marwa stared out the window, watching the gray-black gravestones rise in rows from the green. The sight stirred a memory.

She recalled driving past this same cemetery as a child, on the way from Far Rockaway into the City. She had once asked aloud, *How do stones grow?*

Sharif had teased her so mercilessly that the moment had lodged in her mind, sharp and complicated. She'd wondered then:

1. Was she truly stupid—and had embarrassed them?
2. Did they expect her to be stupid, because she was a girl?
3. Was there a deep, meaningful difference between stones and living things that she had failed to understand?

Now she tried to recall just how young she had been. She had language, that much was clear. She remembered what she saw: the headstones pushing up from the earth like living things, surrounded by summer green. But she had no memory of sensation—no heat, no seatbelt, no sense of confinement.

Had she still been in a car seat?

Her train of thought was interrupted by Jody.

"A CD has a hole, so it's a donut thing, not a se-vere, right?"

"*Sphere,*" Dr. Why corrected gently.

"And the donut's name is Ferdinand!" Jody giggled.

With the weary authority of an older sibling, Judy said, "Ferdinand the Bull. *Ergo* Taurus. *Ergo* torus."

"*Air-GO, Air-GO,*" Jody chanted, "*Tell YOU where to GO!*"

Dr. Why chuckled and started singing along. Jody joined him as she pushed in the CD and hit *Play.*

"Watch this," Judy said, with a smirk, already anticipating what would come next.

As the CD played a song from Disney's *Beauty and the Beast,* Dr. Why kept right on singing something entirely different:

"*Life is just a bowl of cherries... Don't take it serious, life's too mysterious...*"

Meanwhile, Jody joined in with the actual track, singing along with the motherly teapot's melody.

"My father's very proud of this talent," Judy muttered. "He can keep singing *his* song even when another one is playing."

Dr. Why chimed in mid-note, "Try it—it's not easy!"

He tapped his temple.

"You should see what lights up in your brain. *'You work, you slave, you worry so—'* "

"*—But you can't take your dough when you go, go, go!*" Jody finished gleefully.

"Nice, Dad," Judy sighed.

Marwa patted Judy's hand and grinned.

"Can you imagine the kids of those shark guys last night?"

"What shark guys?" Dr. Why asked, turning down the CD.

"We were watching early sharks on the Discovery Channel," Judy explained. "Some of them were over 100 feet long, with teeth shaped like giant triangles—as big as your hand."

"I don't want to imagine their kids," Dr. Why teased.

"*Not* the shark guys, Daddy," Jody said, exasperated. "*The sharks* had the teeth."

"So, the scientists were toothless?" he asked, feigning confusion.

"Yes, Daddy," Judy deadpanned. "The scientists were utterly toothless."

"They were not!" Jody protested. "They sat inside the shark's open jaw!"

She opened her mouth as wide as she could in demonstration.

"*Two* of them could fit inside it!"

Marwa, drifting in her own thoughts, remembered how the shark teeth had looked—like overlapping artichoke leaves, their symmetry smooth and tight.

Like raspberries mimicking the curve of an igloo. Like snowflakes, all built from hexagons.

Like how arachnids had eight limbs. Octopuses, too.

Oxygen's atomic number? Eight.

She turned to Judy.

"The Chinese consider eight a lucky number. They exchange eight tangerines during Chinese New Year."

"Something to consider," Judy said with a shrug, used to Marwa's tangents.

"Ijtihad," said Dr. Why from the front seat.

"What?" Marwa asked.

"A colleague gave me the word," he said. "*Ijtihad.* It's the ancient Islamic tradition of independent reasoning... questioning, interpreting. I thought you'd appreciate it."

Marwa silently corrected Dr. Why's pronunciation in her head, but she liked the word—and the respectful tone in which he'd said it.

The car had already passed the sweeping ocean views along the Belt Parkway, tracing Brooklyn's sandy Atlantic shore as it curved north toward Far Rockaway. That was where Marwa had been born and lived until three years ago— the same year Judy's mother died. From there, the highway connected to the Southern State Parkway, leading them deeper into eastern Long Island.

Marwa looked out the window at the blur of early spring. The trees hadn't fully leafed out yet; most were still tinged with a reddish haze, except for the willows, already haloed in pale yellow, and the forsythia, blazing neon gold. The scrub pines, deep green and unmoved by seasons, dotted the roadside like anchors in the shifting landscape.

They were going too fast to spot the crocuses pushing up through patches of leftover dirty snow, but Marwa was sure they were there—purple, yellow, and white—just beginning to open. In her mind, she was suddenly back in her mother's garden, in front of their old house in Far Rockaway.

As the car sped east under a soft gray-white sky, Marwa's thoughts shifted to the photographs Judy had shown her the night before, after Jody had gone to bed.

Judy's mother had been a photographer for *The New York Times*. When Judy was twelve and Jody just four, their mother had taken a series of carefully timed portraits— enough to fill a volume. From that collection, she selected a few key images and collaborated with a forensic-computer photography specialist, a friend of hers, to create future projections—composite images of herself with her daughters as they would age.

What had given Marwa chills was the image dated for the *present*—Judy at sixteen, Jody at eight. It looked *exactly* like them. It was eerie, beautiful, and oddly comforting.

Marwa had read about this method before. It was used in child abduction cases—projecting what a kidnapped six-year-old might look like twenty-two years later. There had been a *Times* article about it not long ago, when one such child's remains were discovered and her killer identified.

Marwa had gently steered Judy away from the morbid topic of projected photographs and future faces, turning their attention to other objects in the room. One was a sculpture on the windowsill beside a large, blooming geranium: a *star tetrahedron* made of bronze wire. It resembled Judy's tiny two-dimensional Jewish star— "Solomon's Seal," as Judy insisted—now reimagined in three dimensions, its nine-inch wire outlines mounted on a wooden base.

They placed the sculpture on the coffee table between them and sat cross-legged on the floor, facing each other like they were about to summon spirits over a Ouija board.

Judy began solemnly, "Mer—"

"Light," Marwa echoed.

"Ka—"

"Spirit," Marwa translated again.

"Ba," Judy finished with dramatic flair, pronouncing it "*bah!*"

"Body," Marwa said, completing the incantation.

"You really think it's worth waiting around for Thoth to align our chakras?" Judy teased.

"Nah," Marwa said. "But I did like solving for the volume of two intersecting triangles and figuring out what percentage of a cube is occupied by a star tetrahedron."

"I liked cutting, pasting, and folding the paper models we printed out. That part was fun."

"Marcus liked that part better too. But enough about Platonic solids and Pythagorean mysticism."

Marwa stood and stretched her long legs, wandering over to the white Formica dining table.

"Hey, this is new."

"It's a glass *Klein bottle*," Judy said. "Hand-blown. Though I think that means *mouth*-blown," she added, giggling with exaggerated innuendo.

The transparent object stood shorter than a Barbie doll. It looked like a one-legged stork bent low, its beak curled under like an elephant's trunk, snuffling around its own foot. Judy picked it up and stuck her tongue through the glass, making a face at Marwa.

Marwa returned the gesture with a mock grimace.

"You're such a prude!" Judy laughed. "Wanna see if it whistles like a regular bottle if you blow into it?"

Marwa carefully took the delicate piece from Judy's hands and placed it back on the table.

"We do *not*," she said firmly.

"You and Queen Victoria?"

Marwa wandered over to the wall above the sleek black Scandinavian couch, where two large, framed prints hung. She recognized the *Magritte* immediately. The *Escher*, though…that was new.

"You know which Magritte I like?" Marwa said. "The one with all the men in black bowler hats falling straight down like raindrops, all in the same direction."

"Which isn't how rain actually falls," Judy replied. "Wind blows it in all directions at once. That's why no two snowflakes are exactly alike—each one falls through its own turbulence."

"But they're always hexagons," Marwa said. "Like people. Or schools of fish. Or birds flying in formation. Like the scales on a fish—all moving in one direction. Like worshippers in white, bowing toward the Kaaba. It's beautiful."

"You think *conformity* is beautiful?" Judy raised an eyebrow. "You think that's what's happening to the iron in our hemoglobin when a hot guy walks by and all the blood rushes to engorge your—"

"—*Engorge?*" Marwa interrupted, half-laughing. "You are so Saturday night."

Judy gave her the look she got right before delivering checkmate—but this time, she backed off with a grin.

"Ever wonder if there's really anything new under the sun?" she said instead. "Like, if reincarnation is real, where did the first souls even *come* from when humans evolved? Also… are you hungry?"

"I dreamed last night that I was eating my way out of a bathtub filled with spaghetti."

"I'm hungry, too," Judy said. "As hungry as a shark."

She opened her mouth wide, baring her teeth like a playful monster, and chased Marwa into the tiny kitchen.

"Let's see if we can make something entirely new out of old ingredients."

They made grilled cheese sandwiches, adding sliced tomatoes and sour pickles Dr. Why had picked up from the Lower East Side.

As they cooked, Marwa said how strange it was that in dreams, you sometimes saw people you *knew* but had never actually seen before.

"...how the mind naturally creates novelty," she said.

Even though they were visiting Judy's mother's grave the next day, Marwa couldn't bring herself to talk about the dreams she'd been having. About Descartes. About the number three. About the fiery sparks that seemed to fly out of men's eyes.

GRTV

Marwa hadn't told Judy about seeing Prix two weeks earlier, during February break, while the Yamaguchi sisters were away in Florida visiting their maternal grandparents— the ones Marwa was about to meet.

That week, as always, Marwa's parents had gone to work, and Joey had been looked after by Mrs. al-Banna. He called her "Banana" when their mother wasn't around—she'd scolded him for it once, reminding him that "al-Banna is a name honored in Egypt for the Muslim Brotherhood."

Mrs. al-Banna was an elderly Egyptian widow from their mosque on West Broadway, about a dozen blocks north of Battery Park City. She had no children of her own, but she faithfully picked Joey up from school and stayed with him until their mother or Marwa came home. Her favorite afternoon TV program featured a psychic who claimed to communicate with the Other Side.

During the school break, Marwa's mother dropped Joey off each morning at Mrs. al-Banna's apartment over on East Broadway. As they walked, Joey sang his invented jingle— always outside their mother's hearing:

"Goin' to Banana's, goin' to the fair, See the sen-*YOUR*-ee-tas with flowers in their hair..."

50

Marwa had been left to herself that week to focus on preparing for the Intel Science Fair. And she had—diligently—until the weather changed, abruptly and unexpectedly, like a brief dream of spring.

On Thursday, the sun rose into a cloudless blue sky, and by noon the temperature had climbed to 50 degrees. Marwa might not have noticed this rare shift, so absorbed was she in her spreadsheets and graphs, if not for the pigeon that landed on her windowsill, pecking at the glass and startling her.

She hadn't seen a pigeon fly that high all winter. Only seagulls and terns had appeared, distant silhouettes over the Hudson.

She stared at the bird—white with a shimmering blue neck—just before it flapped away. Then she glanced down to the street and noticed people walking without coats. A breeze blew along the pavement with a light, festive energy.

She hadn't eaten breakfast, only downed cups of coffee as she worked, and decided it was a fair trade to step out for a quick lunch.

Though remnants of last week's storm still lay in dirty mounds of snow, the air had shifted—soft and wet with melt. Puddles reflected the pale light everywhere. Marwa threw on a thick sweater over a turtleneck and pulled on a long denim skirt but left her parka behind.

She walked the esplanade, sunlight glittering off the river, trying to decide where to get lunch.

Prix wasn't on *his* bench—it was still wet from snowmelt—but he was there, leaning casually against the black railing. He wore a dark wool cap pulled low over his blond curls.

When he turned and saw her, the hat framed his face like a soft outline, making his green eyes—ringed in brown—stand out even more vividly.

In the noon light, the tone of his skin made Marwa, for the first time, understand why coffee was called *brown gold.* Her mind filled with the scent of it.

Then her *nose* caught the scent, too.

They ended up having lunch together at a small nearby café, decorated for Valentine's Day—red hearts, bow-and-arrow Cupids draped across the windows, the doorway, even the cashier's counter.

"February is named after one of the aspects of the Roman goddess Juno," Marwa said. "The month was sacred to Juno *Februata*, the patroness of fever—*febris*—especially the fever of love. The original Valentine's Day came from the Roman festival *Lupercalia*. Guys handed out proto-valentines with girls' names on them—for, um, erotic games. I take Latin."

Prix raised his hand to signal the waitress, who nearly tripped when she saw him. She spilled a bit of the water as she set it down at their table.

"It's a good thing she's not carrying knives and oranges," Marwa said.

"What? Why?" Prix asked.

"Oh, there's a story in the Qur'an—about Yusuf, Joseph. He's called 'the noble angel.' When a group of rich women see him for the first time, they're so overwhelmed by his beauty that they accidentally cut their hands with the knives they were using to peel oranges."

"Seriously? On purpose?"

"No. Their hands just... slipped."

The waitress returned, still a little shaky, with iced tea for Marwa and hot coffee for Prix. They placed their lunch orders.

"She looks at me like it's acid," he said.

"The coffee?"

"No, her look. The way she stares at me—it's like acid."

Marwa looked down at the table, suddenly unable to swallow.

"I don't want you to think I *like* it," Prix added.

Marwa stared at a red cardboard heart taped to the window.

"The Catholic Church replaced Juno Februata with Saint Valentine. According to legend, he was a Roman teenager who was executed right as his girlfriend received his message—supposedly the first valentine."

Prix didn't respond right away.

Then he said, "People look at me like I'm food. Like they're starving."

Marwa had no appetite. She forced herself to sip the cold tea.

"There are people worse off."

It was something her mother would have said.

Prix laughed softly and pulled off his dark wool cap.

The sight of his golden curls made Marwa dizzy. Her thoughts snapped to her hijab. Without thinking, she blurted, "There wasn't any observable differential."

At that moment, the waitress returned with their food.

"What?" Prix asked, confused.

The flustered waitress set the plates down.

"Isn't this what you ordered?" she asked.

Prix gave her a glance that made her blush even deeper—then turned his full attention back to Marwa.

"*Deferential?*" he asked.

"*Differential,*" Marwa corrected. "The diamond I told you about—the first time we talked. You were right. It was too small to measure any kind of heat transfer. I don't know why I exaggerated. Why I lied to you."

"To impress me," Prix said easily, taking a bite of his sandwich. "It worked. But I didn't believe you."

He nodded at her plate.

"Don't you like your salad?"

Marwa looked down and registered the food, but it felt abstract, like a diagram or a photo of something to be consumed. She remembered how to eat, took a forkful, and swallowed it with help from the iced tea. She tasted nothing.

"Why didn't you believe me?" she asked quietly.

Prix shrugged.

"I never believe anyone."

On the walk back to their building, he invited her up to his apartment—then laughed.

"I only asked so I could see you narrow your eyes like that. Like a cat. Who'd guess eyes that big could get so...," he made a motion with his left hand, fingers pinched together in a small, sharp gesture.

Marwa noticed the gold ring he wore on his middle finger. He was left-handed.

Prix kept walking beside her.

"I mean it—I'd really like you to see my view. You said yours is lousy. But—wait, don't freak out."

He placed his left hand gently on her sweatered arm. His expression changed; he was serious now, even unhappy.

"Listen," he said. "You may never talk to me again after this, but I want you to know something."

He hesitated. Then, "The way I look—ever since I was half your age—people, all kinds of people, have tried to buy and sell me. And they did. And I thought I liked it. I *did* like it, for a while. But then it got... old. And it got... ugly."

He exhaled, eyes not quite meeting hers.

"And now—if anything—I'd rather out-virgin you."

Marwa's face went hot. Her vision swam. His hand was still resting on her arm.

"Oh," Prix winced. "That came out wrong."

He pulled his hand away.

"I don't mean—I don't *want*—I just...," he shook his head. "I don't know how to talk to anyone."

Then he turned and strode off, leaving her frozen on the sidewalk.

Why hadn't she said anything? Why hadn't she called after him, caught up?

Because he didn't want her. She hadn't misunderstood.

It was just the heat of the moment. The *Ides of February*. Everyone else's fever for him—and her own.

⚔ ℜ ♄ ⚑

Marwa's body temperature dropped quickly in the bitter wind at the cemetery.

54

Dr. Why walked a few steps ahead, gently taking Jody's small hand from her coat pocket and tucking it inside his large brown leather glove. Jody had grown quiet the moment they left the highway for the wide avenue that passed several sprawling cemeteries.

They had stopped earlier at a strip mall of gravestone shops and a florist, where Dr. Why bought green metal cones and three bouquets of daffodils. The air had a sharp, metallic edge—you could taste the storm coming.

At the gravesite, Judy's grandparents, uncle, and aunt were already there, shivering. There were subdued greetings, brief embraces, and murmured small talk. Then Dr. Why, Judy, and Jody carefully inserted the daffodils into the cones and pressed them into the frozen ground.

Judy's Uncle Robert opened a prayer book and began reading.

"*Yis'ga'dal v'yis'kadash sh'may ra'bbo...v'imru. Omein.*"

The others responded, "*Omein.*"

Judy and Jody echoed the word a beat behind, following their father's lead. The prayer continued only a short while, but Marwa could tell it was finished when the final "*Omein*" came—firmer, echoed.

Judy's grandfather wept quietly, but her grandmother only pressed her lips together and held his hand, her face still and resolute.

Uncle Robert's wife unfolded a piece of paper and read a short poem aloud.

> *"Once out of nature I shall never take*
> *My bodily form from any natural thing,*
> *But such a form as Grecian goldsmiths make*
> *Of hammered gold and gold enameling*
>
> *To keep a drowsy emperor awake;*
> *Or set upon a golden bough to sing*
> *To lords and ladies of Byzantium*
> *Of what is past, or passing, or to come."*

Afterward, each family member bent to pick up a pebble from the ground and placed it gently on top of the headstone. Marwa watched, wondering: where did all the pebbles come from? Did cemetery workers scatter them deliberately so mourners would always have one to place?

Once out of nature, would the questions nature compels us to ask still matter if we were no longer made of matter?

But those questions, Marwa thought, were the most important ones we ask while we're still here.

Just then, a huge black crow flew to a tall yew hedge, landing with a heavy flap before folding its wings. It waited, cawed loudly, waited again, then flew off.

Jody huddled between her father and her sister. She didn't cry until Judy did. And when Judy did, Marwa felt the sorrow surge up and spill over inside her too.

Uncle Robert's wife passed tissues around. There were more embraces, tearful goodbyes, and finally, the group dispersed.

Back in the car, Jody sat silently and made no move to put in a CD.

Judy turned to Marwa and asked, "Do Muslims observe annual mourning?"

"In the twelfth lunar month—Dhul-Hijjah—at the end of the hajj, the pilgrimage to Mecca, we visit the graves of our relatives for *Id al-Adha*," Marwa said. "It usually falls in late January or February. The Feast of the Sacrifice. But all my family's graves are in Egypt."

No one had asked, but the silence invited explanation, and Marwa continued, ever gently, "The *Id* marks Abraham's willingness to sacrifice his son at Allah's command, according to the Qur'an."

"Did he kill him?" Jody asked, wide-eyed.

"No," Judy answered quickly. "Same as in Judaism. It's Abraham's son Isaac—there's an angel, or a scapegoat. A goat appears instead. Abraham kills the goat. That's actually where we get the word *scapegoat.*"

"That makes no sense," Jody frowned. "An *escape* goat? It didn't escape. It should be an *instead-goat*. A *stead goat*."

She paused, thoughtful.

"Why'd God want him to kill his son—or even a goat?"

"Abraham wanted to show that nothing was more important to him than Allah," Marwa explained. "For Muslims, it's a sheep, not a goat."

"But Marwa said Allah *commanded* it," Jody said, still trying to make sense of it.

"Who knows?" Judy said, her tone lighter but edged with something else. "Which came first—the chicken or the egg?"

Marwa recognized that voice. Judy was trying to be playful, but there were tears hidden in it.

"I don't think he should've killed a goat or a sheep," Jody declared. "I'm going to be a *vegetablarian.*"

"A *vegetarian,*" Judy corrected gently. "Or a vegan. Tell Marwa your theory about where babies come from."

"Doesn't Marwa know?" Jody asked, suspicious.

"She'll admire your reasoning," Judy said, encouraging her.

"Well," Jody began, "I don't believe it anymore, of course—but when I was little, when I saw fat pregnant women, I couldn't figure out how the baby got out. Then I thought about belly buttons. I figured during pregnancy, baby buttons grew around the belly. When it was time for the baby to come out, a special baby-button doctor would unbutton them. Like those trapdoor pajamas kids wear."

"Did you have any trapdoor pajamas?" Marwa asked, smiling.

"I had feet-ins," Jody said. "They made my feet sweat."

It was then that Marwa realized Dr. Why had been silent ever since they left the cemetery. He hadn't said a word on the drive back to Manhattan. Not until they were nearly at the Williamsburg Bridge did he finally speak—asking Marwa about her Intel Fair project.

When she explained it and mentioned that his research had inspired her, he expressed quiet surprise. But there was a flat, gray tone to his voice, and Marwa could tell—he wasn't really there.

7

SHREDS & PATCHES

W as the universe cut from whole cloth, or was it stitched together from shreds and patches?

Everything in the universe was spinning—from the interior of an electron to the spiraling arms of the widest galaxy. When a black hole spun, it dragged spacetime itself along with it. Understand how an object moved, and you could infer its size, structure, even its life story.

People once believed the moon was the only object in the sky that spun. The one thing that *didn't* appear to move was the universe itself.

"*Yoni-verse*," Biren called it—much to Marwa's endless irritation, which, of course, was exactly why he kept saying it.

Biren's Intel Science Fair team—which included Judy— was investigating cosmic rotation by measuring distortions in the faint microwave glow left over from the Big Bang.

By the end of the 20th century, the most sensitive measurements showed no evidence of universal rotation. It appeared the universe had completed no more than one-millionth of a full turn since its birth 13.7 billion years ago.

But wasn't one-millionth of a revolution still *something*? A sizable movement, even?

Biren had winced when Marwa asked that. He'd been trying to impress her with the point he *really* wanted to make...that roughly five billion years ago, the expansion of the universe had suddenly accelerated.

He called it a "cosmic jerk" and threw up his palms in mock surrender before Marwa could say what she was thinking—who the *real* cosmic jerk was.

She wished Biren would stop flirting with her. She wished Marcus would stop circling her like a mantis. And she wished the erratic spring weather—sunshine one minute, hail the next—would settle down by the Intel Fair weekend in Brooklyn, where the crocuses were already in bloom and daffodils stood at least six inches tall.

The Ides of March had just passed. The Latin Club, of which Marwa was Vice President, had celebrated by parading around Stuyvesant High in white-sheet togas, carrying a symbolic coffin for Julius Caesar and chanting funeral dirges in Latin.

As a freshman, when she'd first read Shakespeare's *Julius Caesar* in English class, it was the Latin Club's theatrical performance that drew her in.

Her mother had always said it was a shame Stuyvesant didn't offer Arabic—Judy had chosen Japanese—but now, in Marwa's junior year, Arabic was finally in the works.

Marwa was one-third of her Intel Fair team, along with Marcus and Vivian Cheng.

Marwa didn't like Vivian, but she respected her. They had a lot in common, something Marwa begrudgingly admitted, including the fact that neither of them was particularly fond of the other.

Vivian was the first American-born child of her Taiwanese parents and had two brothers, one older and one younger. Her family also lived in Battery Park City, though her father worked in investments, not at a bank like Marwa's, but in a firm uptown.

Vivian was shorter than Marwa, though not as petite as Judy. She looked more typically East Asian than Judy did, but her skin tone was nearly as dark as Marwa's. Like Marcus, she was left-handed.

Marcus was tall and skinny, with curly dark hair and bright blue eyes. He lived on the Upper East Side and had attended an elite all-boys private school since kindergarten. He had taken the Stuyvesant entrance exam in secret, impressing his father and shocking his mother.

According to the version of events his mother told her colleagues, Marcus bore a refined Roman name, carefully chosen to reflect cultural elegance. In reality, she had simply given him her own maiden name—and a bris. He'd been bar mitzvahed the year before starting Stuyvesant, though both parents emphasized it was a cultural milestone, not a religious one. They were corporate lawyers, each working at different firms. Marcus took Spanish, not Hebrew.

Vivian Cheng was, without question, the smartest person Marwa had ever met her own age—which, frankly, was part of what irritated her. Vivian never *tried* to compete; she simply *won*. Always.

She had scored a perfect SAT Verbal in eighth grade. She was studying both Latin and Chinese. In class, she was consistently the only one who knew obscure vocabulary— words like *lucubration* (late-night studying or writing, originally by candlelight), *ukases* (Russian edicts issued by czars, carrying the weight of law), and the most recent: *jejune* (something intellectually unsatisfying or superficial).

That last word led Vivian straight to *Juno.*

"Juno was the feminine counterpart to *genius,*" she explained one day as the three of them arranged their Intel Fair display in the university exhibition hall. "Both mean soul—*genius* for the masculine, *Juno* for the feminine."

Then, with academic flair and a touch of mischief, she continued.

"So, I propose that *geno* means a homosexual soul, *junius* a lesbian soul, and..." she paused dramatically, eyes twinkling, *"gee-june* is the all-purpose soul of the transsexual."

Marcus laughed in that awkward way boys often did when a girl said anything even vaguely sexual.

Vivian, like Marwa, had synesthesia—more intensely than Marcus, who only experienced it mildly. That shared trait had brought the three of them together as a team to study the neurological and genetic dimensions of the phenomenon.

Through Judy's father, Dr. Why, Marwa had been connected with a former colleague of his at Rockefeller University—a neurogeneticist working on the genetic roots of synesthesia. The scientist, a Greek woman, had quickly gravitated toward Vivian's confident plan to center her senior-year Intel project on gene mapping. This junior-year team effort was, for Vivian, just a warm-up.

Marwa, on the other hand, had no idea what her own senior project would be.

And that uncertainty, combined with the pressure of the fair, Vivian's precision, Marcus's erratic energy, Biren's provocations, her unsettling dreams, and her cowardice—the one time she'd seen Prix since Valentine's Day—all left her on edge.

Marcus, sensing her mood, tried to lighten it by singing a parody from the Herskowitz Lab, *"I've Been Workin' on the Genome."*

It didn't help.

When Marwa didn't respond, he snapped, "Lighten the freak up, will you?"

Marwa snapped back. She aimed her thumb and forefinger at him like a mock pistol—a callback to a private online conversation where Marcus had once shyly admitted that, for guys, every morning was a question of "when the gun would go off."

"How can you *stand* it?" she fired.

"You bleed every month," he shot back. "How do *you* stand *that?*"

Marwa glared, turned on her heel, and stalked away.

Two weeks earlier, she'd seen Prix across the street, heading toward their building lobby—and had panicked. Instead of approaching him, she had ducked into the stairwell behind the elevators and hid.

He had looked like a golden idol, impossibly luminous. And just the *sight* of him had triggered something: her heart hammering with an extra beat, pulsing in rhythm to the memory of his voice—*Outvirgin. Outvirgin.* Sharp. Red. Metallic.

It made her chest ache.

Vivian, meanwhile, was also a nationally ranked saber fencer. She starred on the Fencing Club team and was, in every way, blade-sharp.

In the cavernous university hall, Marwa stormed past the other schools' displays, her pulse still pounding. As she swept by, she noted the familiar banners of her main competitors: Bronx Science— "Sigh!"—and Brooklyn Tech— "Eck!" Just as surely, she knew they clocked her from Stuyvesant— "Sty!"

That sharp, comradely ill will between rival schools had its usual effect: it grounded her. It slowed her down. Her heart stopped thudding.

What a thing of shreds and patches I am, she thought.

As she crossed the wide floor of the Polytechnic exhibition hall, Marwa passed a booth manned by sophomores from a Staten Island high school. Their project banner read: *Pangaea Earth, Past and Future.* It arched brightly over a tidy display of geological timelines, graph work, and old globes demonstrating ancient and projected continental drift. Their poster boards were clean and colorful, their ideas neatly glued into place.

They were only sophomores. They had no chance of winning. *But maybe next year,* Marwa thought.

And what about this year? This moment?

Was it possible, as Hamlet's classmates might have put it, that she lived in the very middle of Time's favor? That humanity was poised in scale between quark and quasar, gluon and galaxy?

Pangaea had once been—and "Pangaea Ultima" would return, 250 million years from now, raising new Himalayas, sinking new Death Valleys.

How completely insignificant it seemed to try and restore, to any continent of history, this one small island of time: 2001.

There were no words for her stupidity.

Outvirgin. What a ridiculous word.

Marwa wasn't used to feeling stupid. As a child, she had realized that adults often spoke to her without the condescending tone they used with other kids. She'd noticed Sharif was sometimes resentful—because she and Joey were the ones in whom their parents placed their biggest hopes.

She stepped outside, into the March sun warming the Commons area. A sharp gust lifted scraps of paper into tiny tornadoes, biting through her light sweater.

So, this is where Sharif always said he "took classes," never "went to school."

Marwa had been in the Gifted Program by second grade. Sharif never qualified. She looked around at her older brother's world—and realized something. He never talked about what he did here, or where, and maybe that was because no one ever asked him.

Why shouldn't he prefer Alexandria?

There, he was treated like royalty. At home, he didn't even have his own room. He shared a bunk bed with Joey, who was seven.

It struck Marwa that this was the *second* time in as many weeks she'd run away and hidden—and felt stupid.

Why had she walked out on Marcus? Why had she fled from Prix?

She was annoyed by the shame of it. But she knew what it really was: fear. That's what she'd felt in the stairwell.

Ralph Waldo Emerson had been right, she thought. It wasn't just Hamlet mocking Claudius— *"the king's a thing of shreds and patches."*

Man was a thing of shreds and patches.

A misfit from the start.

So was woman.

So was Marwa.

Pigeons and seagulls pecked around the chained garbage baskets nearby. There were fewer seagulls, but they were much bigger than the pigeons—and far more aggressive.

Marwa didn't notice the footsteps behind her until the familiar voice spoke.

It was Mr. "Spin" Spinelli, the Stuyvesant Intel advisor, holding out her parka.

"Coming or going?" he asked.

Marwa tried to laugh.

"I wish I knew."

"Don't we all."

She turned and gestured broadly, taking in the concrete expanse of the Polytechnic Commons, and the world beyond it.

"Does it even make sense that all the land above sea level—*all* of it—would clump together once, and then reclump in an entirely new configuration, 250 million years from now?"

"To clump or not to clump isn't my department," Mr. Spin said with a shrug.

Then he paused, "What about Gondwanaland?"

"*Godwannaland?*" Marwa raised an eyebrow.

"*Gon-dwana-land,*" he enunciated. "Pre-Pangaea clumping."

He made slow, sweeping gestures with his hands, mimicking the drift of continents.

"They come together, they drift apart, they come back together again. Like daisies...loves me, loves me not, loves me."

"You think it lands on *loves me*?"

"The house never bets against itself."

Then, after another brief silence, he added, "As they say in zero gravity—what's up?"

"Do they *actually* say that in zero gravity?"

"How would I know?" he smirked. "But I do know it's five days a week, all of us getting up before sunrise, working in that classroom an hour and a half before school starts— staring up the dark, unknowable *anus of Nature*, hoping for a little light at the end of the tunnel. The westward route to the Orient. Or whatever the hell it is you're all searching for."

Marwa looked at Mr. Spin's tired face. For a moment, he looked older than her grandfather in Alexandria.

His young assistant Intel advisor—an elegant Black woman who, like Marwa, stood taller than Mr. Spin—walked over and joined them.

"How we doin' out here?" she asked.

"I just needed some air," Marwa said.

"We got air inside," Mr. Spin replied. "Come and breathe."

꧁ꗍ꧂

Marwa sat cross-legged on the thick carpet in Joey's room, her gaze drifting up to the window cubbies that stretched to the ceiling soffit. One of them now displayed a toy she recognized—a clear plastic top filled with colorful beads that bounced and clattered when spun. Joey's long-abandoned toy reminded her of a whirling dervish or King David dancing in ecstatic joy.

Downstairs, the buzzer rang. Judy had arrived. Joey darted out to the living room to open the door for her.

The Intel Fair had gone well for Stuyvesant, and the AP exams were still weeks away. It was Saturday night—a rare lull in the whirlwind of school and stress.

Joey no longer let Marwa sing him lullabies when she babysat, but he still enjoyed her company—especially when Judy was around.

Judy appeared in Joey's doorway, pulling off her hooded jacket. From one of its oversized pockets, she produced the video she'd brought for the evening. With a flourish, she dropped the case for *LILI* into Marwa's lap, then turned her attention to a new poster on the wall, which Joey eagerly ran over to explain.

"What's this you've got here?" Judy asked, crouching beside him.

"It's rocks. It's *geology.* Did you know there are *three* kinds of rocks?

"I may have known that, once upon a time," Judy said, playing along.

"Ig-nee-us, metta-MORE-fo-sis—"

"*Metamorphic,*" Marwa corrected gently.

Joey, undeterred and delighted to have stumbled onto a word that *sounded* slightly naughty, repeated it with exaggerated glee, "Metta-more-FICK! And *sedentary!*"

"Sedentary?" Judy raised an eyebrow.

Joey turned to Marwa for confirmation, his dark curls bouncing above his wide, expectant eyes.

"*Sedimentary,*" Marwa said.

"Right! Sedimentary. Like, sediment—what drops down in the water. Like fish bones and stuff. Et-cet-er-RAH."

Marwa stood up, taking Judy's jacket from her.

"Joey's new favorite word is *etcetera,*" she explained with a smile.

"So, what's your favorite kind of rock, Joseph?" Judy asked.

Before he could answer, Marwa dropped the jacket over his head like a blanket. He collapsed theatrically beneath it, groaning under the imaginary weight.

"*MetamorFICK!*" he shouted. "Because it crushes limestone into marble!"

The teenagers were already leaving his room, headed to the kitchen, but Joey followed close behind, still reveling in the performance.

⚨⚨⚨⚨

"A song of love is a sad song—Hi Lili, Hi Lili, Hi lo," Judy sang softly later as she and Marwa pulled out the trundle bed. "A song of love is a song of woe—don't ask me how I know..."

"Joey only understood the puppets," Marwa said, opening her closet door.

She undressed behind it, pulling her nightgown over her head before slipping out of her clothes beneath it.

Judy, already in her bright pajamas from her backpack, waited for Marwa to get into bed. Then she turned out the light and slid quickly into the trundle, pulling the sheet and blanket over her shoulder and turning her back to Marwa.

"Good dreams," she mumbled sleepily.

Marwa rarely fell asleep easily. Sleep felt like a traitor to the realm of consciousness—the Land of Marwa. In sleep, she ceased to be Marwa, vanished into somewhere undefined.

Where does Marwa go, she wondered, *when her usurping sister—Dream—takes her place?*

Dream mocked her in waking hours, whispering in flashes of red and black. *The Country of the Two Lands is our name.* Even in daylight, Marwa couldn't escape the symbols Dream sent—images of things in twos, strange twins of meaning, like encrypted messages.

If Dream could reach her without resistance during the day, why didn't *she* have equal power in Dream's domain?

In dreams, Marwa felt like Joey watching *Lili*—completely absorbed, unconfused by its unreality. By the end of the movie, Lili had outgrown her crush on the married puppeteer and realized he lived inside all of his puppets. The final dance was like a waking dream, her passage from adolescent fantasy to adult awareness.

"Oh, don't ruin the movie," Judy had said afterward, irritated—not even bothering to say, "for Joey," because Marwa's interpretation had clearly annoyed her, too. Joey hadn't even heard Marwa's comment. He'd been too engrossed in the film.

Marwa knew she would lose the wrestling match with Dream eventually. Dream would overpower her. Dream always did.

Judy lay beside her now. Marwa listened to her breathing, recognizing the moment when it changed—the soft shift from waking to sleep, that crossing of the boundary between dreamless quiet and Dream's dominion.

It was a sound Marwa had studied since childhood: beside her mother, who always fell asleep before Marwa did while trying to comfort her; beside Joey, who tumbled into sleep as easily as he threw himself into everything else; beside snoring cousins in Alexandria, sleepover friends in Far Rockaway.

And now, beside Judy, in the heart of New York.

8

MAY 2001

Was it really 60,000 years ago—600 centuries—when the Nile began its modern flow, swelling from June through September? Marwa couldn't remember where she'd read that. In truth, she couldn't remember much of anything now. The AP exams were finally over, and her brain felt completely drained.

It was mid-May, midweek.

Her predictions had come true: both she and Marcus had won summer internships on Long Island, just as she'd expected. She would be on the north shore, at Stony Brook, working in genetics; Marcus would be farther south, near the Atlantic, at Brookhaven, studying physics. That arrangement suited her just fine.

There was a gene associated with synesthesia. A genetic mutation that emerged around 60 centuries ago had allowed certain humans to digest milk into adulthood. The *Lactose Tolerants*, as they were called, had spread across the globe—

speaking the early languages that would become the Semitic, Indo-European, and Uralic families.

Her head still swirled with these factoids, sediment of knowledge settling slowly on the riverbed of her memory.

And then there was the unexpected: Prix had mailed her a birthday invitation—*snail* mailed it, in fact.

Her father, self-appointed lock and key of all household correspondence, opened it first. He interrogated her, then forbade her not only from attending the party at the club, but even from replying.

Still, Marwa felt more lifted by the invitation than crushed by the command. Prix had thought of her. That mattered.

Mr. Haddam had given their English class a wonderful assignment: to write—or retell—a fairy tale from any ethnic tradition, preferably one passed down aurally from their own pre-literate childhood. In Art, they were working on a project using and reflecting on Crayola crayons and color.

Marwa felt something unusual.

She felt happy.

Descartes made her happy. So did Denim Prix. And the month of May.

What were the colors of Descartes' dreams? she wondered.

What if mathematics wasn't the natural language of the universe after all?

"Don't go throwing the baby out with the bathwater," Mrs. K., her math teacher, had told her recently.

Marwa wasn't sure if that was meant to be ironic—a metaphor about metaphor itself—or just a warning not to abandon math entirely for metaphor.

With Mrs. K., teasing and teaching often blurred together.

But in Marwa's current mood, it didn't matter. She leapt from one thought to the next, happily—even the sharp, metallic ones.

It had been such a relief to discover she wasn't crazy. There was a word for it—*synesthesia*—and this summer she'd be working with someone studying the actual genetics behind it. Now she understood why new ideas and sensations came to her eyes filtered through orange gauze, why colors had shapes and moods, why days of the week each carried their own hue: gray Monday, yellow Tuesday, and brown Wednesday.

Brown. A color with no true opposite, which was probably why everything went so well with it. A stable, nonargumentative hue—reliable, grounded, and impossible to hew. *Whew!*

There was a whole private party going on in Marwa's brain—and it was one her father couldn't keep her from attending.

On the night of November 10, 1619, the night Descartes—just twenty-four—believed he had found "the foundations of a wonderful science," he had three dreams. He was certain they had come straight from the Divine Box.

The first was strange, almost Holden Caulfield-like: wandering, chased by phantoms, afraid he'd fall with every step.

In that dream, Descartes's right side was weak; he walked bent to the left. When he tried to straighten up, a whirlwind caught him, spinning him around three or four times on his left foot. He tried to reach a chapel to pray, but someone stopped him—someone Descartes thought might be carrying a melon from a foreign land.

Strangest of all, the people around them, who stopped to chat, were untouched by the wind that had nearly knocked him over—but which now seemed to be dying down.

Descartes woke in pain, turned onto his right side, and prayed for protection from the evil effects of the dream.

To Marwa, that first dream *looked* brown.

But which brown?

She thought of the original 1909 Crayola box—eight colors: black, green, violet, blue, orange, yellow, red, and, of course, brown. Her favorite, *burnt sienna*, hadn't appeared until forty years later. Crayola added *mahogany* and *tan*, then *raw sienna, sepia,* and, more recently, *beaver* and *fuzzy wuzzy brown.*

Descartes's dream, she decided, was *cocoa-before-you-add-milk brown,* with a faint wash of violet at the edges.

In the dream, the man—possibly melon-bearing—had said Descartes might like to seek out someone named Monsieur N., who "had something to give him."

Marwa thought, in dreams, *speech* sounds like speech, not like thought. You can tell when someone's talking versus when you're just thinking. You can hear with your ears, or only in your mind.

But when you're awake, thoughts don't sound like anything at all—unless, of course, you're a mystic. Or a schizophrenic.

And/or was such a lovely expression, Marwa thought. Bright yellow. Filled with possibility.

Marwa's art teacher had introduced the day's lesson as an exercise drawn from modern architecture. He presented two images: a pair of buildings, two drawings, and two ordinary household objects—a salt shaker and a ketchup bottle. For each pair, he asked the students to choose which had "the most life" or was "a better picture of the self."

"*And/or?*" Marwa had blurted out during class.

"Yes," her teacher replied with a smile, which made everyone laugh.

He continued, "Eighty percent of people tend to choose the same one. The architect behind this exercise believes that order is inherent in space and systems, and that some things are more—or less— 'alive' depending on the quality of order they express."

Marwa suspected he was steering them toward a discussion about which colors held "the most life." But she thought that was the wrong question.

The bell rang. Marwa left art class frowning in thought.

How does the brain process visual information? And/or, what color dress—if she wore a dress—should she choose for Prix's forbidden party? And/or... should she go at all?

Which of those questions had "the most life"? And which answer would be a better picture of herself?

Descartes's second dream was stranger than the first. It was all sound, sight, and fear: a loud thunderclap woke him, startling him into consciousness. When he opened his eyes, he saw bright sparks—so vivid he could make out the objects around him.

Descartes claimed this had happened before—not the thunderclap, but the sparks.

Before Marwa had known anything about synesthesia, those "eye sparks" had comforted her. If Descartes had experienced them, then they weren't madness. Awake, seeking a rational explanation for his vision, Descartes had reached "satisfactory conclusions." That alone helped soothe his fear—and by extension, Marwa's.

His third dream wasn't her favorite, but she had referenced it once in Latin class. In the dream, Descartes opened a book and read a line of poetry: *Quod vitae sectabor iter?—What path shall I take in life?*

Marwa had used that same question as the topic sentence for a five-minute Latin dialogue. It was a good question. Timeless.

What path was she going to take? To Prix's birthday party—or not?

"*Est et Non*," Marwa murmured aloud. "Yes and No."

Walking beside her in the current of students between classes, Vivian tilted her head.

"Yes and no, *what?*"

"What fairytale are you telling in Mr. Haddam's class?" Marwa asked, trying to redirect.

"I'm hoping he doesn't call on me today. I haven't decided yet."

"How was art?" Vivian asked, pulling out a small bouquet of crayons and offering it with a grin.

Marwa looked down and realized her backpack was unzipped and she'd been leaving a trail behind her. When she and Vivian stopped, passing students dropped crayons into their open palms, giggling.

"Sunny's doing *Zulaikha and Yusuf*," Vivian said as they walked toward their English classroom.

"As a fairytale?"

"Not from the Qur'an," Vivian clarified. "From..."

She paused, thinking.

"The author's name is Jami. Sunny said he died the same year Columbus discovered America. She double-checked that. But she's telling it the way her grandmother used to—before she could read. Or, as Sunny put it, 'before I even knew stories had authors.'"

Mr. Haddam was seated at his desk, which sat angled in the front corner of the room, tucked between the window sill and a tall metal cabinet, forming a triangular nook. A few students milled around, handing in late assignments and chatting quietly while he took attendance.

Sunny was already in her seat, nervously flipping through a stack of note cards. She was a Muslim, and her family had come from Pakistan.

Biren had once remarked—trying to be clever—that when she and Marwa stood next to each other, they looked like the number 10. Then, trying to dig himself out of the hole, he'd added that Sunny looked more like a Buddha than a Muslim.

Sunny had raised an eyebrow and summed it up.

"So I'm fat and short. Thank you very much, Biren."

But Sunny was neither. She was just shorter and rounder than Marwa, and she quietly looked to Marwa for guidance as a fellow Muslim girl. When Marwa had stopped wearing her hijab, Sunny hadn't asked why—she'd simply taken hers off too. But she still put it on each day before returning home.

Her full name was *Sunniya*, but in her second year at Stuyvesant, she'd asked everyone to call her *Sunny*.

Mr. Haddam called the class to gather in a circle for a discussion, then turned to Sunny.

"You're up."

She glanced once more at her note cards, tapped them against the desk arm of her chair, then looked at Marwa, who gave her a small, encouraging nod.

"This is how my grandmother used to tell me the story when I was very little," Sunny began. "She would lie down next to me, and while she told it, she'd do this—"

Sunny raised her hand and gently mimed the motion.

"—with her first finger, she'd move my hair back and forth over my ear, over and over again."

She paused, her voice catching.

"I miss my grandmother."

Around her, the room fell still.

Her classmates leaned in, quiet and attentive.

Sunny cleared her throat and began:

"Once upon a time, there was a beautiful princess, the daughter of the King of the Maghrib. When she was young, she had three dreams.

"In the first, she saw a young man—noble and impossibly handsome.

"In the third dream, it took all her courage to ask the young man his name. And he told her: he was the Wazir of Egypt."

She paused, likely just as her grandmother had when telling the tale. The room was silent. Even Mr. Haddam was fully attentive.

Marwa's long face had flushed with color; her dark eyes were wide, almost comically so—like the saucer-eyed dogs from yesterday's fairytale. She pressed her fingertips to her lips, her chin supported by her thumbs, elbows braced against the desk. Sunny was thrilled—but also nervous. Marwa had never listened to her like this before.

"When it came time for the princess to marry," Sunny continued, "she refused every offer—from kings and princes across the world. In her heart, she held only the image of the man she had seen in her dreams.

"When her father, the king, learned that she would accept only the Wazir of Egypt, he sent a wise man to Egypt to arrange the marriage.

"The wise man discovered that the Wazir—his name was Aziz—was both ambitious and reluctant. He was a eunuch. Yet the wise man also knew that if he returned to the Maghrib without securing the marriage, the princess would die from longing.

"When Zulaikha—yes, that was the princess's name—heard the news, her joy knew no bounds. She journeyed to Egypt in a litter made from fragrant wood, adorned with gold and jewels, veiled behind curtains of golden brocade.

"At last, she arrived.

"Peeking through the curtains, she looked out eagerly, ready to see the face of the man from her dreams.

"But when she saw the Wazir of Egypt—Aziz—it was not the young man she had dreamed of.

"Her heart broke.

"'I planted a palm tree,' she cried, 'but all I see are thorns! What shall I do?'"

Sunny shifted her tone, her voice softening into something ethereal.

"And then a voice came to her from the unseen world: 'True, he is not thy love. But thy desire for thy true love will be fulfilled through him. Fear him not. Thy jewel is safe with him.

"If a great sleeve is shown, but there is no hand within— what is there to wield a dagger?'"

"The princess knew she must marry the eunuch Wazir of Egypt, Aziz—and so she began to sing a song of grief," Sunny said softly.

Then she paused and added, "My grandma used to sing this part, but I can't.

"'*I know I will win thee,*'—she meant Yusuf—'*at last, and when that happy day comes, I shall not be I, but thou. May I see thee soon. I shall roll up the carpet of life when I see thy dear face again, and I shall cease to be—for self will be lost in that happiness, and all the threads of my thought shall fall from my hand. More precious than heaven, more dear than the earth, myself were forgotten, if thou were near."'*

"Then a slave was brought to the marketplace, and Zulaikha's husband, the Wazir, went to present him before the King. But when Zulaikha saw the slave, she was overcome—for she recognized the face of the man from her dreams. It was Yusuf.

"She had to have him.

"She ordered her husband to double the bid of anyone else at the auction—even that of Princess Baziga, a noblewoman descended from the ancient 'Ad race.

"When Baziga later met Yusuf, he told her something profound. He said that the visible world is only a mask—a veil—covering an invisible beauty beyond imagining. What we see is just a reflection, he said, of the true and eternal Beauty, Goodness, and Truth.

"Baziga was so moved by Yusuf's words that she began to sing joyfully.

'From a fond, strange love thou hast turned my feet,
The Lord of all creatures to know and meet.
If I had a tongue in each single hair,
Each and all should thy praises declare!'

"And after that, Princess Baziga gave up her wealth and her crown. She spent the rest of her life serving the poor and praying along the banks of the Nile.

"As for Yusuf, he became a slave in Zulaikha's household. But one day, she could no longer restrain her desire. She reached out to take hold of him—he ran, and in the struggle, his shirt was torn clean from his back.

"Zulaikha, furious at his rejection, accused him of wrongdoing. But when her husband saw that Yusuf's shirt had been torn from behind, he understood the truth—Yusuf had been fleeing, not pursuing.

"Still, Zulaikha burned with shame. She was humiliated, especially in front of the women of Egypt, who had already begun whispering behind her back.

"So, she invited them all to a grand banquet.

"And when dessert was served, and all the ladies were slicing oranges with their sharp, shiny knives, Zulaikha called for Yusuf to appear.

"The moment they saw him, the women gasped—they said he looked like an angel.

"And so shaken were they by his beauty that they cut their fingertips without even noticing."

Sunny paused and noticed that Mr. Haddam had placed a small paper cup of water beside her. She smiled at him gratefully and took a sip.

Marwa slowly lowered her hands from her mouth and folded them in her lap beneath her desk.

Sunny continued, "All the women were overwhelmed by Yusuf and understood why Zulaikha desired him. Each of them wanted him for herself. So, they advised her to weaken his resistance—by having him thrown into prison.

"But while Yusuf was imprisoned, he became a source of hope to the other inmates. He taught them Truth. He interpreted their dreams so they would no longer be troubled by them.

"While Yusuf healed the men in prison, Zulaikha's husband died. She fell into sickness, lost her beauty, and went blind.

"Later, when the King needed help interpreting a troubling dream, Yusuf was summoned from prison. His interpretation saved Egypt from the famine foretold in the dream. Afterward, Yusuf became the most powerful man in the land—second only to the King.

"Zulaikha, meanwhile, had lost everything. At her lowest, she cried out to Yusuf. He pitied her and prayed for her.

"Her health, beauty, and eyesight were restored.

"And Yusuf married Zulaikha—with true love."

Sunny looked up, set down her last note card, and finished the water in the cup.

"That's how it ends," she said simply.

"She even goes blind," someone in the circle murmured.

"You stayed awake through all that?" another joked lightly.

"I just wrote down all the parts I remembered," Sunny said.

"Did you even know half the words you just used back when you first heard it? Like *famine*, *humiliating*—all that?" a boy asked.

"I guess not," Sunny admitted, glancing toward Marwa for support.

"Didn't Yusuf lie in the dream?" someone asked. "I mean, what was that about?"

Marcus, who had waited quietly, finally jumped in.

"That's just the Joseph and Potiphar's Wife story from the Bible, right?"

Marwa snapped, "They share elements, yes, but they make *very* different points."

Marcus noted her irritation but remained focused on understanding.

"Okay, but...don't both stories show that Joseph—Yusuf— ends up on top because he's God's favorite?"

"On top of *what?*" a girl muttered, to scattered laughter.

"I mean," she continued, "does she *really* have to go blind? Am I the only one who thinks this whole story is kind of... misogynist?"

Marwa had calmed herself.

"She doesn't just go blind—I mean, yes, she does—but the point is, she's blind *until* she can see beyond superficial things."

"Superficialities like lust?" Biren asked.

"Here's what I think," Judy cut in. "It sounds to me like the old Adam and Eve story all over again—only this time, Yusuf is the apple. And every woman wants a big bite of him.

But he's not just the apple—he's also the snake *and* the tree of wisdom, all wrapped into one."

"And Zulaikha," Judy went on, "she's humanity. She's Job. She has to suffer in every way possible before she learns what she needs to and finds her way back to Paradise. It's always the same story—journey for knowledge, suffering to get it, happy ending."

"So what fairytale are *you* telling us, Judy?" a classmate asked.

"I was hoping to go last," Judy said, smiling at Mr. Haddam just as the bell rang.

It was lunch period, and Marwa was determined to get out of the building as fast as possible. But Sunny caught up with her first—Biren wasn't far behind.

"I told it wrong, didn't I?" Sunny said, breathlessly.

"I'm up tomorrow," Biren added. "You'll like mine."

At the foot of the stairs, Marwa paused, stepping aside to let the tide of students pass. She tried to think of how to tell them she wanted to be alone without hurting their feelings.

"You told it fine—great, actually," she said to Sunny.

Then to Biren, "Why does everyone think they have to apologize to me?"

Biren blinked his wide, dark eyes—tilted slightly inward, as if made for sympathy. When he blinked, it felt like something *happened.*

"I wasn't apologizing. I just wanted to tell you the story."

"I'll hear it tomorrow," Marwa said curtly.

But as Sunny walked away, guilt tugged at her. She turned back to Biren.

"Okay, tell me. But outside."

"Where you grabbing lunch?" he asked as they exited the building. "We're heading up to 23rd."

"I'm not hungry."

Biren, sensing the window closing, spoke quickly—like he'd rehearsed this moment. Once outside, beneath the bright May sun, he slipped on a pair of new sunglasses. The effect noticeably boosted his confidence.

"I figured I wouldn't use note cards. You know... it feels more like *real* storytelling without them. My uncle never used them."

He hesitated, then added, "My dad's younger brother. He lived with us when I was little—he's the one who told me all the stories I still remember. He lives in Phoenix now."

Marwa turned to look at him. "Biren?"

"Okay, okay," Biren began, animated. "So, there's this old stonecutter working in the sun, and a young woman walks by. She says, 'That's very hard work you're doing,' and gives him a drink from the river.

"'Yes,' says the old stonecutter, 'sometimes one is fated to do hard work. Fate is strange. See that young man resting over there?' he adds, 'He's doomed—and only a loving sister can save his life.'

"Since it *was* her brother, the young woman asked how she could save him.

"'By pretending to be crazy,' the old man says. 'Do everything the opposite of what's expected. Curse him.'"

"You must've loved the cursing part," Marwa said, half-smiling.

Even with the sun heating the crown of her head—*hijab* or not—she was curious to hear the rest.

Three classmates, including Sunny, had joined them. Marwa offered her a warm smile.

Biren beamed with momentum.

"So, the sister has to act this way until her brother's fate changes—which, according to the old man, would happen only *after* his bride has been in his house for a full day. So, she and her brother head home for his wedding, and the whole trip she's yelling at him, cursing like a lunatic."

He grinned.

"On the wedding day, she ups the crazy—puts on this ragged old sari, screaming and spitting out curses nobody's ever heard before. When they put the wedding crown on her brother's head, she starts jabbing at it with a long needle. People think she's completely nuts.

"But then"—Biren made a sinuous gesture with his right hand— "a *very* thin viper slithers out of the crown."

"Viper," one of the boys echoed, impressed.

"Yeah, *viper,*" Biren nodded. "Next, the groom gets up on the wedding horse, but the sister starts yelling that *she* wants to ride it. Everyone just wants to shut her up, so they let her get on. Just as she's leaving the house, a giant gateway falls right where he would've been. Crushes the spot. She's fine."

There were a few murmurs from the group. Marwa raised an eyebrow.

"So now the family's like, 'Okay, maybe she's crazy, but... maybe not?'" Biren continued. "Later that night, when the groom and bride go to their flower-strewn wedding bed, the sister *again* throws a fit, insisting she has to sleep there instead."

"With them?" Sunny asked, horrified.

"No—*instead* of them," Marwa replied, catching on.

"Exactly!" Biren said. "Turns out, *bam,* giant *scorpion* in the bed."

Gasps and laughter rippled through the group.

"A week later," Biren said, "the groom's mother tells him they have two choices: send his crazy sister back to her husband or lock her in a back room. Either way, she's *not* getting the golden sari she's owed for attending the wedding."

He switched to a falsetto, imitating his uncle's storytelling voice.

"'Now I will leave with my golden sari,' the sister says calmly, 'because I followed the advice of the wise man. I cursed my brother. I acted crazy. I did the opposite of everything expected of me. And I took all your insults. But with my love, I saved a mother's son, a sister's brother, and a bride's groom. And I am *not* crazy.' Then she grabs the sari and says goodbye to them all."

"Not bad, not bad," one of Biren's friends said, stretching. "So, where we grabbing food?"

"You all go," Marwa said, stepping back from the group.

"She's not hungry," Biren explained to the others.

Then, quietly to Marwa before following them, he added, "Thought you'd like that one. Girl hero."

He turned away quickly before she could answer.

⁂

Marwa went to walk along the river. It wasn't quiet—not with the sounds of city traffic, the occasional siren, and the steady flow of people from the nearby high-rises, all with the same idea on a beautiful May lunch hour. She strolled the esplanade, passing babies and toddlers chattering alongside their nannies, the occasional mother, and the even rarer sight: a stay-at-home father.

Above, the sky was a flawless blue. On the Hudson, sailboats dotted the water, dwarfed by larger ships gliding farther out. In the distance, the George Washington Bridge glittered like something imagined.

Under a vendor's umbrella, she bought a pretzel and a bottle of water. Checking her watch, she saw it was almost time to head back to Stuyvesant for her afternoon classes.

She didn't notice Prix behind her until he slipped into step beside her. He didn't even say hello.

"Hey," he said. "You didn't even RSVP. Where've you been hiding?"

Marwa took a grateful sip from her bottled water. He wore a short-sleeved, collared shirt in a shade she immediately recognized as Crayola *Purple Mountain's Majesty*, paired with chino shorts. The logo on his shirt was designer—one she didn't know. He looked like he had just woken up, but that was always part of his look. No lines on his face, and his green-rimmed eyes stayed wide open, even in the sunlight.

"I have to get back to school," Marwa said.

"That's your hello?" he teased. "You could've at least RSVP'd."

"My father only showed me the invitation yesterday. When did you send it?"

84

"Two weeks ago. My agent's secretary swore she sent yours. Seriously, where've you been?"

"I haven't been hiding," she replied sharply.

"Don't be mad. I really want you to come. It's at a comedy club. Bring as many friends as you want."

"I'll be late for class," she said. "And my father says I can't go. All my friends are underage. We're not allowed in clubs."

Prix stopped himself from laughing.

"You wouldn't be the only sixteen-year-olds in the clubs, y'know. But I guess at Stuyvesant, you're all too smart to get fake IDs."

"And I guess you're amoral."

That made him laugh, really laugh. It took him a moment to recover.

"You're a dream," he said. "He only told you yesterday? I can't believe it."

"Well, believe it," Marwa snapped. "I have to run now. Literally."

As she turned to go, Prix reached out and took her bottle of water, drank from it, and handed it back. That stopped her.

"You either want to come or you don't. Yes or no. If it's yes, we'll figure it out."

Then he turned and walked away without another word.

Marwa walked fast back toward Stuyvesant, water sloshing from the bottle. She couldn't decide whether to put her lips where Prix's had just been or to screw the cap back on.

Yes, or no? Not even that. *Yes and no. Est et Non.* Descartes's three dreams.

Zooley, Judy had called her. And yes, Yusuf had lied—but not in Zulaikha's *first* dream. It was the *third,* wasn't it? He'd said he was the Wazir of Egypt. That was the lie.

Yusuf, in a Purple Mountain's Majesty designer shirt, torn from his back.

Running now along the crowded sidewalk, Marwa had to watch her step very carefully because she thought she might be going blind.

9

KNOWING SOMETHING

ꜥ ꞉ ꜣ

Marwa remembered her mother beginning, "Why were Hands and Feet angry with Head?"

And she would answer dutifully, "Because they had to do all the work, and Head just sat still on the neck."

Then Ummee, slipping into a deep, regal tone, would continue in Head's voice.

"I keep all in order. I see, I hear, I speak. You, Hands, are strong and proud—but I am your Queen, and I shall punish you..."

That was the shortest Egyptian fairytale Marwa knew. A fragment, really—lifted from a schoolboy's copybook over 5,000 years old. It had no ending. Her classmates wouldn't let her get away with telling just that. Not in Mr. Haddam's class.

The color of her mother's bedtime stories was always Crayola Apricot. On warm nights, if the window was open in her bedroom in Far Rockaway, the scent of the ocean would drift in. Her mother tasted of peaches. Marwa remembered the Egyptian word: *khukh*. She used to call her

Ummee *Khukh*, and her mother would respond by calling her Plum—*Berkuk*.

Ummee never read to her from books. All the books were in her head.

No one had told the Egyptian version of Cinderella yet, so Marwa knew she could claim that one. In this version, Rosy-Cheeks's sandal is stolen by an eagle and dropped at the Pharaoh's feet.

"As sure as I am Pharaoh," he declares, "I will wed the maiden who fits this little sandal."

When Rosy-Cheeks's stepmother drags her along—after the sandal fails to fit any other girl—Rosy-Cheeks recognizes it at once. The court ladies don't believe her. But then she reaches into her pocket and pulls out the matching sandal.

The Pharaoh silences the doubters.

"The word of Pharaoh cannot be broken," he says, taking Rosy-Cheeks by the hand. "I will wed this pure maiden."

But Marwa preferred another story... *The Road to Damascus.*

"What are you looking for?" asked an Arab man, seeing another racing across the desert.

"I'm looking for my friend," the man panted. "We were traveling together, but I overslept. He started on without me this morning. Now I see him nowhere. I've almost given up."

"Was your friend," said the Arab, "a lame and heavy man?"

"Yes! Have you seen him?" the stranger exclaimed.

"Since sunset last night," said the Arab, "I have seen no man—until you came along. But tell me—was your friend lame in his right leg? And did he carry a stick in his left hand?"

"You *must* have seen him!" the stranger exclaimed. "He limped badly—he injured his foot. Please, which way did he go? Tell me! Without him, I'll surely die."

"I've not seen your friend," the Arab replied calmly. "But three hours ago, a man matching your description passed this way. He wore a blue *galabiyya* and led a pale camel, blind in one eye and burdened with a load of dates. He was headed toward Damascus. If you hurry, you will surely catch up."

The stranger stared at him in disbelief.

"Are you a wizard? You've described my friend exactly, even his old camel—and yet you say you've never seen him. How do you know all of this?"

"Stranger," said the Arab, "Allah has given all men eyes, but only a few the wisdom to truly *see*. Everything I've told you—you could have seen for yourself, if only you had used your eyes."

"Say not so," replied the stranger. "I *have* looked. I have searched everywhere—and I've seen nothing."

The Arab said nothing in return, but with a small gesture, he motioned for the stranger to follow.

They walked a short distance across the sand until they reached a fresh trail of camel prints, and the footsteps of a man beside them.

"Look," said the Arab, pointing. "There are your friend's tracks."

"I see the tracks of a man and a camel, yes," said the stranger. "But how do I know the man was my friend?"

The Arab walked beside the footprints and gestured again.

"Do you notice any difference between his steps and mine?"

The stranger bent down to compare.

"Your feet press equally into the sand. His do not."

"Exactly," said the Arab. "A lame man walks lightly on the injured side. A heavy man leans more into his good leg. That's what you're seeing here."

"But the color of his robe? The pale camel? The dates?" the stranger insisted. "How could you know *those*?"

The Arab pointed to a thorn bush nearby.

"Is it so hard to see the scrap of blue cloth caught there, or the pale hairs scattered on the ground where the camel rested?"

"And the dates? The blindness?"

The Arab only smiled.

"Can you not see," said the Arab, "the flies feasting on the drops of date juice spilled beside the camel's tracks? And notice—wherever the camel grazed, it fed only on one side—the side on which it could see."

"Truly, you are a man of remarkable perception," the stranger said. "But tell me—how did you know it was *three hours* ago that my friend passed this spot?"

"Have you eyes and still do not see?" the Arab replied with a touch of scorn. "Look there—where they rested in the shade of this palm tree. The shadow is the hand of a sundial. You can tell from its position that no shade has fallen there for three hours."

He turned to go.

"Farewell. Follow the road to Damascus. You will find your friend."

And that is exactly what the stranger did.

That's when Marwa's mother would kiss her on the forehead and whisper, *"Now follow him—follow the stranger on the road to Damascus, the path to Dreamland."*

But of course, Marwa was too busy searching for more clues to fall asleep.

Maybe she could end the story like that in class.

But how could she lie to her father about going to Prix's party? How could she ask her friends to lie with her? In social studies, they'd studied something called the *technological imperative*—the idea that once you *know* how something can be done, it becomes tempting to do it.

This was the first time Marwa truly felt how dangerous that could be. She wasn't even asking *if* she should do it. She'd already skipped ahead to *how*. And *how*—she realized—was already halfway to hell.

Just then, a familiar tangle of curls appeared at the threshold of her bedroom door. Joey was crawling in on his stomach, inching his head forward so just his forehead and eyes peeked over the edge of the bed.

Marwa exhaled. She was relieved by the interruption.

"Homework question?" she asked.

"I already did my homework," Joey replied. "Banana's got the sidekick on."

"You mean *psychic*. Mrs. Al-Banna," Marwa corrected gently.

Joey knew their mom didn't like him watching Banana's favorite TV show when he was around. But he said nothing.

"You can hang out with me," Marwa offered. "But I've still got loads of homework."

"You *always* have loads," Joey grumbled. "I don't want to go to high school."

"You'll be the king of high school."

"I don't want to be the king," Joey said. "I want to be a *vice president*."

"Just like Daddy," Marwa said.

"Well, I don't want to be Ummee," Joey replied.

"You couldn't be an Ummee."

"I don't want to be one."

"Then you're lucky. You don't have to do something you don't want to. A lot of people in the world can't say that."

"It's a free country. I'm the boss of me," Joey declared, bouncing on Marwa's bed to punctuate his point.

"If you fall off and break your neck, you'll be the boss of a broken neck—and *I'll* be in so much trouble."

Joey froze mid-jump.

"You're supposed to know better," he said with mock severity.

"That's the law according to Ummee."

Joey didn't jump again, but flopped dramatically into a full-body sprawl, swiping his arms and legs across the bedspread like he was making a snow angel.

"Joey. Mr. Entropy. I've got work to do," Marwa said.

"But I can't go in there. She's listening to dead people again."

"So go play in your room."

But Joey's face turned red.

"I saw the movie with the boy who sees dead people."

"What? Joey—when did you see that? Where?"

"At Ositadimma's. He had the tape. Don't tell Ummee."

"Oh, Joey... you know you weren't supposed to watch that."

"Why not?"

"Ummee explained—it could bother you."

"It didn't bother me. It was just weird. Osit's big brother mutes the scary music and says stuff. If I saw a dead person, I'd ask what it's like—unless he was too yoo-glee. If he was yoo-glee, I'd stop, drop, and roll!"

Their recent school trip to the Fire Department Museum had clearly made an impression. Joey demonstrated the drill on the floor, then popped up triumphantly. Ghosts forgotten.

"I want to be a fireman. They're big." He paused. "I'm gonna tell her to turn it off."

"Find a nice way. Be diplomatic," Marwa said.

"I'll say I'm hungry."

Marwa gave him a thumbs-up. Joey saluted and marched out like he had a mission.

Great, she thought. *My seven-year-old brother can come up with a plan—and I can't.*

She opened her laptop and sent Judy a message.

Mars429: Houston, we have a problem

YAMsky: copy that. which is?

Mars429: prix invited me—us—to a party. my dad says no

YAMsky: *us?*

Mars429: "bring as many friends as you want"

YAMsky: what do *you* want to do?

Mars429: that's the prob

YAMsky: copy

Mars429: which priority? disobedience or desire?

YAMsky: if your dad said yes, would you go?

Mars429: dangerous territory

YAMsky: Marcus + Biren, you + sunny, me + jimmy

Mars429: you'd ask *burro*?

YAMsky: hypothetical. he did ask me to his prom

Mars429: also, Vivian + Lem? you're sharing the limo

YAMsky: *HAR*lem, if you please

Mars429: since when?

YAMsky: since Vivian

Mars429: I can't

YAMsky: call him Lem when V's not around. she goes orbital
Mars429: i live for that
YAMsky: you can't what?
Mars429: you are *quick*
YAMsky: your dad knows the time + date?
Mars429: bingo
YAMsky: sleepover cover story?
Mars429: obvious. no qualms?
YAMsky: *having* qualms. count   my   qualms. devil's advocate here
Mars429: appreciate
YAMsky: what friends are for
Mars429: get back 2 u
YAMsky: copy. Chill

Closing the IM window, Marwa leaned back in her desk chair and stared blankly at the screen. An image of a page from a medieval Arabian medical text glowed in front of her— ornate, intricate, unread. She had no energy left to keep researching. Instead, she printed one copy in color and another in black-and-white, satisfying just enough of her art homework to feel justified.

The coloring portion still loomed. Ignoring the original manuscript's palette, she reached for her crayons and began filling in the spaces. But the impulse to color outside the lines—strong, mischievous, almost thrilling—swept through her. It felt laughably close to the tug she felt every time she thought about disobeying her father. About Prix. About doing things she couldn't even speak aloud. The moment she picked up Crayola's *Hot Magenta*, her left hand trembled with intent. She dropped the crayon and pressed that hand against her forehead, trying to steady herself.

She stood abruptly and crossed to the closet. Kneeling, she reached beneath the shoe rack and pulled out the Divine Box. Sitting cross-legged on the floor, she rested it in her lap and slowly lifted the lid. From within, she took out the blue bottle cap—the one from the water bottle Prix had drunk from. The one she couldn't throw away.

This is madness, Marwa thought as she pressed the cap against her lips. But she closed her eyes anyway and began to sway, pretending. Oh, the colors—like a kaleidoscope exploding behind her eyelids.

"Whatcha doin'?" Joey asked, appearing in the doorway, a piece of milk-soaked raisin cake dripping from his fingers.

"Banana gave me *umm ali* cold. I like it better hot," he added, chewing.

"Ummee's going to be furious. You're going to spoil your appetite."

"You said be a mechanic."

"Diplomatic," she corrected.

"Want some?" He extended his palm like a makeshift plate.

Marwa had already tucked the bottle cap back into the box and slid it out of sight. She watched him as he ate, content, observing her.

"You don't have to hide it," Joey said after a moment. "I know what's in it."

There was a long pause.

"You don't know anything!" Marwa snapped, her voice rising sharply. "Get out of my room!"

Joey's eyes filled with tears.

"I *do* know," he said, stepping back, voice gaining strength as he left. "I *do* too know something!"

Marwa stared coldly at the empty doorway.

Then, with quiet precision, she shut the door—no slam, just finality. She crossed to her bed, lay down, and closed her eyes. Her nostrils flared slightly as she exhaled.

And then, she smiled.

10

JUNE 2001

Did she feel guilty? Marwa had all of Sunday—and several days afterward—to ask herself that question. She didn't have a fever, but she lay in bed, sick. Her parents suspected food poisoning from something she'd eaten or drunk, maybe at the movie theater or from a street vendor. They couldn't believe she'd be reckless—or disobedient—enough to buy anything like that.

They were more worried about the final exams she was missing, and what the consequences might be for her summer internship. Her father came into her room, placed a hand gently on her forehead, smiled reassuringly, and left without a word. In that moment, Marwa sensed that he felt somehow responsible for her illness—as if his strict ban on going to Prix's party was, in some way, to blame.

Her mother, meanwhile, was on the phone with other parents, quietly gathering intel. None of the other girls were sick. She didn't ask where they'd been. Vivian's mother, however, let something slip—something about the girls being with boys. She said she intended to call their families. Once more negative food poisoning reports came in, Marwa's mother decided to hold off on any interrogations until her daughter felt better.

Unbeknownst to either parent, Marwa had made a similar decision: she'd postpone the question of guilt until she no longer felt physically miserable. And if it *was* food poisoning, she was sure the movie theater had nothing to do with it.

The previous Saturday night, around nine, Marwa had gone uptown to Judy's apartment in Greenwich Village with Vivian and Harlem ("Lem") Jordan, a senior who was taking Vivian to the prom after exams. There, the trio joined Biren, Sunny, and Judy's prom date, Jimmy ("Burro") Wagstaff. That made seven of them.

On the Upper East Side—where Prix's birthday party was being held at a comedy club—Marcus waited to take charge. He knew the neighborhood. Marwa had been anxious, her heart pounding so hard she wondered if it might cause an electrolyte imbalance. But it was a warm June night, the stars just starting to appear, and the waxing crescent moon hung sharp and bright in the sky.

No one else seemed nervous. Just excited. Not even Sunny—who had long since conceded to Marwa the moral and Muslim high ground.

When Sunny was very young and thrilled by her elementary school discovery that words could rhyme, her mother banned *Dr. Seuss* books from the house. As she got older and began borrowing books from the public library, her mother told her to stop asking what unfamiliar words meant.

By the time she reached Stuyvesant, Sunny turned to Marwa with her questions. But any attempt Marwa made to untangle Sunny's circular reasoning—especially when it came to the "immorality" of adopting someone else's choices as your own—had always proven futile.

Now, though, Sunny's presence felt oddly reassuring to Marwa, and she couldn't help but feel a bit betrayed by her own logic. She was hoisted on her own petard. Walking into the club thinking about everything she *should* say no to was pointless. If she had intended to refuse anything, that intention had long since sailed—and sunk.

It didn't help that the club's awning screamed the name TSUNAMI in bold letters.

"Terrible name for a comedy club," Marcus said. "Everyone thinks it's a Japanese restaurant."

Had any of them even laughed at that point in the night? Time had started misbehaving on Saturday evening, slipping and looping strangely.

Later, in the throes of relentless nausea—retching painfully into the toilet—Marwa realized how dreamlike the night had felt.

Had that bizarre comedienne on the tricycle appeared before or after Prix first came over to welcome them?

They had been shown to a booth. Prix wore something white that caught the light with a glint, while the club's velvet-covered walls shimmered in a deep, Crayola Outer Space blue, scattered with pinpoint lights like stars. Mirrors were everywhere: floor-to-ceiling on the walls, glittering disco-ball centerpieces on the tables, and rotating pendant lamps overhead.

Had there been music at that moment? Or was it just the chatter and clamor of guests and partygoers? Many were young celebrities—faces Marcus recognized.

Prix's skin gleamed a tea-colored brown, the kind that defied easy description. (The Japanese language, Marwa once read, had no general word for "brown.") His eyes were ringed with brown, then shaded into gold-flecked green, like the veins of a leaf.

Judy leaned over, pulled Marwa's shoulder down, and whispered into her ear, "Wow."

Then the comedienne made her entrance, tricycling onto the stage. She was dressed like a clown, her face hidden behind the mesh eyes of a long blue burka hiked up just enough to keep from catching in the wheels.

On her head perched a parody of Egypt's ancient Double Crown—tall and teetering, more like a pope's mitre than anything regal. She steered skillfully with elbows and forearms, holding in her crossed hands a glittering crook and flail—the Pharaoh's dual symbols of power.

Her entrance music was Steve Martin's song about King Tut, and the crowd roared with laughter and applause.

As she dismounted—with help from two waiters—the room quieted, the music fading. Marwa's table was right near the stage.

Was Prix beside her then, handing her a goblet of apricot nectar? She remembered the flavor—rich, thick, velvety. It had tasted wonderful at the time. Now, just thinking about it made her gag.

On stage, the comedienne began to explain her costume through the mechanics of a striptease. She reached up to steady, then remove, the elaborate headpiece in two parts.

"The *pschent*," she announced, "the crown of Upper and Lower Egypt—the red and white crowns combined to represent unification."

She set it aside and next mimed placing down *"the copt,"* the hooked staff of pharaonic authority. The gesture exaggerated its shape—a large, crooked royal phallus—and was followed by a flourish of the whip. More laughter erupted.

Returning to the dismantled crown, she playfully examined the tall white portion.

"This is the *hedjet*—symbol of Upper Egypt. Its icon was the lotus flower," she said, pronouncing *"lo-tus"* with a rhythmic sway of her blue burka that hinted—suggestively— at feminine allure.

She reached for the narrower red crown.

"Symbol of Lower Egypt, where the Nile flows into the Mediterranean. This *deshret* represented the papyrus plant. Its patron goddess was the cobra, Wadjet of Buto. The unification of the two lands—Upper and Lower Egypt—was embodied in the merged crown," she continued, holding them up together.

"Called *nebty*, meaning 'two ladies'—lesbians, feel free to cognate—cobra and vulture goddess, clasped in union!"

She held the pieces aloft dramatically.

"I swear on an onion, as they did in ancient times," she intoned, then added mockingly, "Head Jet and Dish Rag, makin' a crown!"

The crowd around Marwa howled with laughter.

The comedienne segued into politics.

"Since they had no books to burn, the Taliban in Afghanistan had to blow up the Bamyan Buddhas—those massive statues carved into the cliffs, like erasing Mount Rushmore from the South Dakota hills."

Then, with a slap, she flung down her striped headcloth.

"The Pharaoh's *nemes!*"

Finally, in a theatrical climax, she bent forward, grabbed the hem of her burka with both hands, and in one sweeping motion tossed it aside—revealing a jarring red bikini, long black hair cascading like Marwa's, and comically oversized gold-rimmed eyeglasses.

The room exploded with cheers and laughter.

At that moment, Prix was standing close beside her. She knew it by the scent of his cologne—a sharp mix of sweat and lime.

The comedienne adjusted her glasses and zeroed in on their booth.

"There's our birthday boy!"

Voices rose in unison, crashing into a jubilant chorus.

"Hap-py Birth-day, Den-nem PREE-EE! Happy Birthday to YOU!"

The comedienne turned her attention to their table.

"How'd you puppies get in? What are you even drinking?"

Prix replied coolly, "They're relatives."

She raised an eyebrow.

"Relatives? Of whom? Oh—what's that guy's name, the one on the thousand-dollar bill? Prix, you'd know."

Then, suddenly, her eyes locked onto Marwa.

"Honeybee, what are *you* doing there among the infidels? You better not be drinking anything *bloody*."

She turned to address the crowd.

"We don't have a Virgin Mary, and Allah knows we wouldn't name a drink after a woman... But maybe she's sipping a—what is it..."

She leaned in closer, peering into Marwa's glass.

"Oh, I see. Let's call it an *Apricot Aisha*."

Raising her voice for the room, she explained, "Aisha was the Prophet Mohammed's favorite of his eleven wives. And hey, after Mohammed—P.B.U.H.—died, Aisha led men into battle!"

The moment blurred after that.

Somehow, Marwa had moved to the dance floor, spinning beneath star-like lights in the dark. Music pulsed through the room.

Marcus and the others were there. Vivian was dancing nearby, jabbing the air with imaginary sabers near Lem, who was darker-skinned than Prix. Jimmy Wagstaff loomed like a giraffe over petite Judy, bobbing clumsily.

Sunny spun like a whirling dervish, wild and uncoordinated, so much so that Marwa half expected her to topple over like Joey's toy top. None of the eight of them could really dance.

What kind of errant particles were they, drifting like scattered electrons through the night? Where was the music even coming from?

At one point, Marcus held her close, the beat slowing. Then Prix cut in. His shirt—white, shimmering—was soft beneath her hand, but underneath it she felt solid muscle. That familiar, dizzying scent: sweat and lime.

But after that—nothing.

Marwa couldn't remember leaving the club. Or how they got home. Or even saying goodbye.

Why did she have an image—vivid, persistent—of Prix and Marcus standing together off to the side, reflected in a fractured mosaic of mirrors, like the multifaceted eye of an insect?

Now she was home. In bed.

The phone rang. She was falling.

It was June.

She fell asleep.

☥☥☥

Rising, buoyant, through water, Marwa could see bright light above. She broke the surface—and then the light dimmed. She was no longer underwater. She was looking into her mother's dark eyes.

"Ummee," Marwa murmured.

Her mother sat beside her, palm resting gently on Marwa's forehead.

"How do you feel?"

"Hungry. Thirsty. What day is it? It's raining."

"Thursday."

"I'm starving."

"Juice. Just some apple juice."

Marwa tried to sit up.

"I'm dizzy."

"Don't move. I'll get it for you."

What surprised Marwa most was the way her mother looked—still in her bathrobe, her hair uncovered and uncombed. The dream still clung to Marwa. She had been a fish, the sunlight overhead blinding. Now, the gray rainy morning felt thick and warm. The open window let in the humid scent of rain and river.

In the dream, she'd seen like a fish—flat, in outline—like a hieroglyph, or that Christian fish decal, the intersecting ellipse people stuck on their cars. That symbol reminded her of the *Eye of Horus* elements on a dollar bill.

She reached for the juice.

"Slowly," her mother warned. "Your stomach's empty. Is it good?"

100

"Delicious." She paused. "It's Thursday?"

Her mother nodded.

"Your guidance counselor called every day. So did Judy. The Chinese fencing girl dropped off your makeup Latin test. That boy from your Intel group wants to call—you father said yes. Marcus Silbercoff."

"It's Thursday," Marwa repeated, finishing the juice. "Physics Regents. What time is it?"

"It's still morning. I should call your father."

"I dreamed about Alexandria. Where's the Latin test?"

Her mother handed it to her with a look that said, *Don't overdo it.*

Marwa sat up—and felt fine. She recognized her Latin teacher's handwriting, but her mind was on food: *ful* with eggs, falafel fried the way only her mother could make it, and kufta—spiced lamb grilled into frankfurter shapes. She craved pizza. Buttered corn. *Why would anyone do anything but eat and drink?* Water, ginger ale, apple juice... apricot. *Denim Prix.*

Had he put something in her drink?

Put it out of your mind, she scolded herself.

The practice test was a Pliny letter—79 A.D., to Tacitus, about his uncle's death during the eruption of Vesuvius. She reread her translation.

"He was at Misenum in his capacity as commander of the fleet on the 24th of August, when between 2 and 3 in the afternoon my mother drew his attention to a cloud of unusual size and appearance... He called for his shoes and climbed to a place where he could better see the phenomenon (correction: 'get the best view'). The cloud was rising from a mountain. At such a distance, we couldn't tell which, but later learned it was Vesuvius.

"I can best describe its shape as a pine tree. It rose on a long trunk with branches spreading at the top. I imagine it was caused by a sudden blast (correction in red), which then weakened, allowing the weight of the cloud to cause it to spread sideways. Some of it was white. Other parts were dark with dirt and ash. The sight awakened the scientist in my uncle—he wanted to see it more closely."

The makeup exam was another Pliny letter—this time *to* him, not from him. *"Traianus Plinio."* Marwa read the opening line.

"Actum quem debuisti, mi Secunde..."

"Trajan was laying out a kind of first-century "Don't Ask, Don't Tell" policy regarding Christians. A world before Islam. Before the New Testament was even finished. Before the arguments over what would be included in Christian scripture. While sculptors were still carving the Bamiyan Buddhas—one of which had just been blown up by the Taliban in March."

Marwa's stomach growled. *Latin could wait.*

She was sitting at the dining table when Marcus called. Her mother brought the phone, but Marwa took it to her room and shut the door.

"How was physics?" she asked.

"How was the test? *How are you?* We thought you were dying or something."

"I'm fine. I just ate five days' worth of food. How was the Regents?"

"Ridiculous. He said if anyone gets less than a 90, we should wear bags over our heads."

"When will you know?"

"He's grading them this afternoon. You're signed up to retake it in August. No big deal."

"Did he put anything in my drink?"

"What?"

"Prix. Did he?"

"Jesus, no. He's been calling me every day. What happened? We all ate the same stuff."

"We ate?"

"We never stopped eating. Monster shrimp. We smoked, drank, and did the hootchie-coo—*not*. We were *so* underage it was comical. Lem and Burro were furious—both eighteen— but no one would check their IDs. Prix wouldn't let them."

"Why's Prix calling you every day?"

"He asked me at the party. He wanted a way to contact you. He doesn't want you in trouble. I felt like your big brother. Marwa, I don't get it. You asked me about the club—he invited you. He keeps saying he wants to *go backward*."

"I don't know why I got so sick."

"F.U.O. Fever of Unknown Origin."

"I never had a fever."

"The important thing is, you're better now. You can skip the math final and write a paper. I can help—something on power law and the number of webpages with exactly k links. Probabilities. She'll love it."

"Immoral. I'm more interested in translation symmetry. Like fish scales."

"And honeycombs. That's new," Marcus said.

"You're the network guy. Anyone would know it was your work."

"Prix is a hub, you know."

"In what network?"

"*Quien sabe?* But that party was definitely scale-free. Burro and I agreed. Prix was the hub—linked to a crazy number of disparate nodes: juniors, seniors, Stuy High, who knows what else."

"Did you calculate it?"

"Were *you* there?"

"Apparently not."

"Don't you remember Jordan ranting about those doctor jokes from the short, fat comedian? Does everyone need to know he got a Duke med school ride for free? Good thing Vivian's saber shut him up—or raised his voice a few octaves."

"Harlem said Islam created the first secular hospitals."

"So, you *do* remember."

"I remember *he* said it. I don't remember when. Or the comedian."

"Relax. It doesn't matter."

Something about reassuring Marcus made Marwa feel better. By the time Judy called—after her Japanese final—

Marwa had showered and dressed. The rain had stopped, and the sun was heating the long June afternoon.

Judy had only one thing on her mind…Burro Wagstaff.

"He's actually a better kisser than dancer," she said.

"He doesn't like being called Burro, you know."

"Really? Wasn't it his idea?"

"He acts like it now. But when he was a freshman, someone teased him about being from an outer borough. He turned it into a joke in Spanish class. It stuck. He's from Bayside, Queens."

"*Burro, the Bayside Émigré.*"

"*Jimmy,*" Judy corrected.

She liked saying his name.

"Did Jimmy explain choosing that Christian school in Hartford over Dartmouth?"

"Trinity's not really a Christian school. They gave him a full scholarship. When he met the Math Chair, she called him Shakespeare. Wagstaff—Shakespeare? Get it? So now I call him Shakespeare."

"In the same way you say 'Jimmy'?"

After the call, Marwa felt normal. Hungry again. Her mother was delighted to feed her. Her father came home early. That evening, Marwa finished the Latin translation, ready to return to school the next morning.

"Trajan to Pliny: The method you have pursued, my dear Pliny, in handling the cases of those denounced as Christians is appropriate. It is not possible to set a universal standard for all such cases. No search should be made for them. If denounced and proven guilty, they must be punished—but if they deny being Christian, and offer evidence by worshipping our gods, they should be pardoned, even if previously under suspicion.

"Anonymous accusations must not be admitted—they set a dangerous precedent and are contrary to the spirit of the age."

11

JULY 2001

Grover Cleveland was on the $1,000 bill. Marwa was in her dorm room at the State University at Stony Brook, Long Island. She was reading an email from Mr. Haddam, who wrote from Tunisia. He was visiting his old Peace Corps family before heading to Santorini (Atlantis) and Hisarlik (Troy).

"Teachers can only travel to archaeological hotspots when they're literally hot," he wrote. "I'm consuming cases of bottled H_2O!"

Marwa took a sip from her own bottle of water and glanced at her laptop screen. A standing floor fan swiveled warm air around the room, while a smaller table fan beside the couch blew over her bare shoulders and neck, trying to keep the heat at bay. She wore a clingy tube top and shorts—immodest by her usual standards. Her hair was piled up and pinned with what one of the other summer interns (who said, "It's okay, I'm Jewish") called a "JAP clip."

The clip, the top, and the shorts were all borrowed from Desiree Lipshitz— "Is that a name or a punch line?"—a Long Island native. Marwa was taking a break from lab research, the kind of repetitive work better suited to machines. The Intel-winning project they were helping to develop had simulated interactions among genes, proteins, enzymes, and growth mediums—a six-figure idea with no actual machine yet built. Just grad students and interns like Marwa. The lab was air-conditioned. Her dorm room was not.

At least she didn't have to share it. Mr. Haddam had written that she now had "Virginia Woolf's room of [her] own." There was a small study area with a desk and couch, cantilevered below a lofted sleeping space with two twin beds and a nightstand. A large window above let in the suffocating heat, despite the third fan churning air with little result. But Marwa didn't mind. She was not in Alexandria. She was not at home with her parents or with Joey.

Sharif pinged her just as someone knocked lightly at the open door. Desiree's blond curls poked in.

"Come in," Marwa said. "My brother just IM'd me—from the new library in Alexandria."

"In Virginia?"

"In Egypt."

Desiree kicked off her flip-flops and stretched out on the couch, tucking a cushion under her head.

"What time is it there?"

"Seven hours ahead of us."

"So...nine o'clock. Library's open late."

"Day and night shift differently in hot climates."

"What's up with the Sharif-ster?"

"He's meeting a friend. I'm amazed he messaged me at all." She glanced at the screen.

"Oh. There he goes. Offline."

Marwa shut the laptop and swiveled in her chair.

"You left lab early."

"Later than you," Desiree said. "But I couldn't handle the co-opting of any more innocent RNAi today."

She grinned, "I'm going swimming at the gym. That rhymes. You wanna come? Need to borrow a suit? I don't think it matters if I wear a cap or not."

She sat up and pressed her halo of tight curls flat against her head with both hands.

"The genetic code has no Constitution. This heat and humidity are cruel and unusual punishment for my skull protein. Your hair doesn't puff up like a dandelion."

"It *does* look like a dandelion seed."

"Thank you."

"But don't you find it fascinating how different systems reflect one another?"

"Like what?"

"Like how we talk—saying 'um,' 'like,' 'y'know.' It's like our verbal junk code."

"My father always says, 'No, I *don't* know,' every time I say that. When I was a kid, he'd never tell me what a word meant—just yelled, 'Look it up!' He *always* yelled. Which explains why they're divorced."

"Let's gym-and-swim," Marwa said.

"Gorgeous."

Desiree stood and reached into her pocket.

"Oh—here."

She handed Marwa a folded piece of paper, pretending to have just remembered it.

"Read it if you get a chance."

It was another of Desiree's poems.

Much later that night—after the swim, their guilt-driven return to the lab for extra grunt work, dinner, and a campus movie that flickered during a lightning storm—Marwa was finally alone again in her now much cooler room. She stretched out on her couch, content in the quiet.

Earlier, as she and Desiree had walked from the gym to the lab, Marwa's cell phone jingled. Judy's voice, bright and familiar, had burst through like sunshine. Her father had just been dragged back to the City for jury duty, ruining his retreat to his lab at Woods Hole.

"Shit does so happen," Judy declared.

Now, alone again, Marwa noticed Desiree's poem on her desk and thought of the word *disfluencies*. It fit not only gaps between genes, but also the quirky, awkward hesitations in people—Desiree's personality, her own. Maybe the most important data wasn't in text or code, but in what people didn't say. Maybe meaning lived in the in-between.

Even rice had more protein-coding genes than humans, but the proportion of non-coding DNA—so-called *junk*—scaled with complexity. Like glial cells in the brain...once thought to be janitors, now known to outnumber neurons 9 to 1. Einstein had more glia than the average brain. And the angular gyrus—the neural crossroads of temporal, parietal, and occipital lobes—was disproportionately large in humans.

I mean, Marwa thought, catching herself. *What do I mean when I say, 'I mean'?*

She clicked on the table lamp and lay back to read Desiree's poem. The fan swept cool air across her skin.

A Poet's Directive

Resist the tyrant,
even God.
Nurse the unwholesome and help
to safety those desperate for asylum.
Speak simply, quickly, and in whispers
as though overheard by an informant.
Avoid cameras.
Copy down artlessly the dying words of saints
and carry their messages at personal risk to able translators.
Remember the names of ten thousand ghosts
and feel their hands move through yours to open doors for
each of them.
Sleep only to dream.
Praise explorers and those who seek cures.
Encourage commerce,
for it created the great metaphor, Money.

Finally:
cast in silence,
the setting of your stone.

What a *disfluency* this was. Desiree, so brash and loud (like her father), had written something delicate. The quiet, poetic offering was more intimate than anything Marwa had expected.

She stood up. She needed to rest before making up for lost lab time tomorrow. And she still hadn't answered Marcus's email, which had been interrupted hours ago.

The granularity of matter is old news. Here, they're trying to count the grains of sand that make up space and time. It's testable. I can drive you. We'll go to the beach. There's a math guy here who says phylogenetic analysis can apply to language dispersal—like your gene/language stuff. Get back to me, okay?

Marwa left the fan running but turned out the light. She locked the door, climbed the ladder to the loft, and plugged in the baseboard nightlight. The room above was softly lit by campus lights outside. On the nightstand sat the book of Arab poetry Desiree had bought her. Mr. Haddam would have approved.

She turned off the fan, pulled out a sheet, and velcroed it to the window frame for privacy. Then she knelt on the mat, naked—free in a way she never could be at home. She bowed toward the east-facing window.

There was just enough light for her to look under the curve of her body, between her breasts, past the hollow of her torso to her heels. If she were male, she thought, her genitals would obscure the view. But instead, her inner complexity folded inward—hidden, dark matter.

She felt suddenly silly. *Blasphemous.* Her mind overflowed with thoughts.

She got into bed.

Mr. Haddam, with his plastic bottles of H_2O, was somewhere between Tunisia and Troy. His delight in oddities reminded her that strangeness could be normal. That students like her—still figuring themselves out—were safe with him.

When you're thirsty and drink water, it feels like one perfect action. But water is H_2O—two atoms of hydrogen, one of oxygen. And even those atoms are made of smaller parts. This was known. Matter was granular. Marcus had said it was *testable.* He wanted to take her to the beach.

Prix had sent her a postcard from East Hampton. An aerial view of the ocean. Endless waves. All that water.

And inside it…hydrogen. Oxygen. Attracting. Coupling.

12

MARCUS & DESIREE

"You can never solve a problem on the level on which it was created."

~Einstein (1879–1955)

"The limits of my language mean the limits of my world."
~Wittgenstein (1889–1951)

At some point in the future, what now seems incomprehensible or impossible will appear as simple as child's play. We'll look back on ourselves as curious children—ignorant, and at times, dangerously so.

Marwa had handwritten those quotes in her notebook, copying them from a recent email exchange with Marcus. As she wrote with a plastic ballpoint pen, she found comfort in the sensation of her left hand gliding the pen along the paper's soft resistance. The image reminded her of the Escher drawing—two hands sketching each other.

"Children," she thought, and instantly missed Joey.

She paused, memories flooding in—Joey at three years old, sitting at the kitchen table in their Far Rockaway home before they'd moved to Manhattan.

It was a Monday in late April, just before her birthday.

She had asked him, "What day of the week is today?"

"February," he replied.

Now, sitting at her university dorm desk on a brilliant July day, Marwa marveled at both of them. Joey would turn eight on November 2nd; she had just turned seventeen on April 29th. Four years ago, she hadn't even considered the workings of his angular gyrus, tucked up at TPO, learning to distinguish days and months. At three, he'd already mastered his loud, clear-plastic top filled with colorful wooden shapes. She remembered him on the floor, plunging the spiral shaft over and over, storing up the energy that would send the top spinning wildly.

I feel like that toddler now, she thought. *I'm just waiting for Marcus to arrive.* She stopped writing and changed "come" to "arrive."

Then her phone rang.

"I'm here," Marcus said. "Come and get me."

"I'm here I me get come and. Here am I get me and come."

As she descended the dorm stairs, her mind spiraled through the layers of syntax and meaning. Latin encoded meaning in word endings, English in word order, and the universe in the one-way flow of time—History.

At the bottom of the staircase, she thought, *This is a portrait titled Marwa Descending.*

She was stunned by the car his parents had rented.

"The biggest sedan Mercedes makes, and blacker than an Amazon beetle's back," Marcus said.

"Which Amazon beetle?"

"Scarabaeidae, subfamily Scarabaeinae," he replied, patting the hood. "Tribe Coprini. The name says it all—this dung beetle lives its life consuming filth and wears the color to prove it."

"Remember when we read *The Insect Play* freshman year? Did you tell your mom what genus the car belongs to?"

"Are you kidding? She'd be heartbroken. Since they didn't have to pay for the summer program, she went big on something else."

"We look like German ambassadors."

"Or Colombian drug lords."

He popped in a music disc. The volume was loud as they drove back to Brookhaven Labs.

Marwa leaned into the leather seat, glancing over at Marcus in his new sunglasses. He touched the frame with one hand.

"You like?"

"Another gift from Mom?"

"Nope. My own fashion statement."

"You don't look like a physicist-in-training. When did you even learn to drive?"

"I'm a year older than you. I was sick when I was three—basically out of commission for a year. So I started school late. Or at least, that's how my mom remembers it."

"But she's a successful lawyer."

"Her brain's like a primitive library—some areas are meticulously catalogued, others are just ancient scrolls scattered in urns and caves."

Marwa laughed. Marcus blushed, ejected the disc, and replaced it with another without checking the label.

As they pulled into Brookhaven, he slowed and showed his ID card at the gate.

"You've got three ID cards now," Marwa noted. "Stuy, driver's license, and this."

"Tree rings," Marcus said. "Count them, and you get someone's age."

He navigated through the campus, stopping at a sign for Cavendish House.

"It's a men's dorm," he explained. "We're not going to my room—just grabbing bikes. I've got one for the summer and borrowed one for you."

"Can I ride a boy's bike?" she asked.

"We'll see," he said, suddenly uncertain.

"I didn't think to ask a girl."

"Don't worry. I picked up ice skating right away. Sharif, on the other hand, once biked straight into a neighbor's house."

They picked up two 10-speed, 28" bikes—his was black, hers silver.

"You should ride this one—Silbercoff," Marwa teased.

"But I raised the seat on mine," he replied.

Though Marcus was 6'1" and six inches taller, she didn't think the crossbar would be much of a problem. She wore red shorts, sneakers, a white tank, and a red-checkered blouse tied at her waist. Her long, wavy hair was braided and clipped up (thanks to Desiree). Marcus wore cut-off jeans and a dark T-shirt that fit him well.

"I haven't ridden since Far Rockaway," Marwa said.

Feeling awkward under Marcus's gaze, she swung her leg over and mirrored his stance.

"It's getting off that worries me," she admitted. "On a girl's bike, you swing through the frame and hop off with both feet."

They circled the mostly empty lot while Marcus coached her on dismounting: slow down, plant your left foot, and swing your right leg back. Soon, they were riding side by side in the July sun, wind carrying ocean scents.

"I bet being left-handed made that harder," Marwa said.

"I'm left-handed too."

"Yeah, but you learned from a righty—you're totally right-oriented."

"So are you. You said you dismounted with your right leg."

"We're adaptive misfits," she smiled. "In my gut, it still feels right to dismount through."

"Probably a design thing—for long dresses. But that bar does give better stability. Watch out for turkeys—flocks come out of those woods."

They crossed Brookhaven Avenue. No turkeys yet. Marcus pointed out buildings.

"Cafeteria...Accelerator Development...the synchrotron's that way."

"Where do you work?" she asked, noticing something moving in the trees.

"Physics. You can see the Van de Graaff cyclotron from our window."

"Turkeys!" Marwa shouted.

Two massive toms strutted with a dozen hens and chicks.

"They were extinct on Long Island by the mid-1900s," Marcus said. "Couldn't cross NYC or the Sound. Environmentalists reintroduced them from upstate. Now they rival the geese. One even landed on our team leader's car and stared at him through the windshield."

Marwa, pedaling past, thought of *The Bell Jar* and turkey necks described like male genitals.

She tapped the stabilizing bar and said, "You'd think this would be more dangerous for boys."

"We learn quickly not to make that mistake."

They turned around and stopped in the shade.

"You're good at dismounting," Marcus praised.

Under the trees, they drank water Marcus had brought. Marwa leaned back against a pine, inhaling its scent.

"Avicenna called physics the 'inferior science.' Math was the middle, and theology the highest," she said.

"Lots of free time in Chromosome Country?" he teased.

"Desiree found him. 'Your Ibn Sina,' she says. She even bought a book."

"I hated *Ibn Battuta*. That guy never went home."

"Avicenna was the backbone of medieval medicine. He was Persian. Wrote in Arabic. *Intellectus in formis agit universalitatem.*"

"Which means?"

"Our ideas are universal because of how the mind works— but not because reality isn't objective. Desiree checked."

"You talk to Judy?"

"She's busy at Hopkins. Doesn't want to go. She's aiming for Columbia."

"She's close to her dad and sister."

"Avicenna died at 57. My father's 57."

"Five million high-energy solar neutrinos pass through every square centimeter of your beautiful body every second."

"Desiree calls farting 'spider barking.'"

Marcus choked laughing.

When he recovered, he said, "You're too close to that girl. She's into you."

He offered his hand to help Marwa up and leaned in to kiss her, but she turned the wrong way. He apologized. It was awkward. They rode back in silence—even past the turkeys.

Marwa scraped her thigh dismounting. Marcus ran to get first aid and gently cleaned the cut.

"Avicenna to the rescue," he said, and the awkwardness dissolved.

They drove to Smith Point Park, the highway packed with people leaving the beach. It was a long walk from the lot, past Mister Softee, football-playing teens, and a curved granite memorial wall—names of victims from a France-bound jet crash five years earlier. A ring of tall poles with colorful flags flapped loudly in the ocean breeze.

As sunset neared, Marwa overheard a tiny woman say to a friend with Atomic Tangerine hair, "He's there again."

A bald man was sculpting in the sand. The old woman noticed them.

"He's a sand sculptor. What's he making today?"

The four walked over and Marcus took the women's bags. The sculptor had created a likeness of himself, bald head and shoulders, gripped by a massive octopus dragging him under. The tide was rising. Soon, both would vanish.

Marwa bowed her head in praise. The sculptor smiled.

Later, at the barbecue, Marcus grilled as Marwa set the picnic. He told her about Mr. Haddam getting lost en route to Fez.

"He doesn't speak Arabic."

"But he speaks French. He asked a shepherd for directions and pointed to Fez on a map. The boy didn't want to disappoint him, so he pointed to a dead-end road and a crumbling village."

They ate. The air was thick with sea salt, grilled mushrooms, and evening light.

"Arab culture," Marwa said, reclining, "centers on feeling, not reason."

"You mean like logic, the Enlightenment?"

"No, like strong emotion being its own truth."

They kissed.

"You taste like mushrooms and relish," Marcus said.

"Marcus, stop. You have more—"

"Experience? Nothing compared to your heartthrob Denim Prix."

"He's not my anything."

"I'd just like to know where I stand—behind Prix? Desiree?"

"Why are you angry?"

"Let's walk. I bet the ocean's taken the octopus by now."

GRTW

It was after eleven when Marwa opened the door to her dorm. She didn't see the envelope until she stepped on it. Dropping her bag and keys on the couch, she climbed the ladder to the loft and collapsed onto her bed. Too tired to pull down the window cover, she closed her eyes. The envelope now lay on her stomach. She was already drifting off when the door opened.

At the sound, she bolted upright.

"Well?" Desiree said, climbing up the ladder. "Did you let him into your pants or not?" She switched on the nightstand lamp. "Did you read my letter?"

"I just got in."

"I know. I was lurking in the hall."

"Desiree, that's creepy. I'm exhausted."

"Fine, I'll read it to you."

She pulled a handwritten page from the envelope.

117

"It's not mine. It's a poem by Adonis—he's considered the greatest influence in Arabic poetry today. I bought it earlier and kept rereading it because you weren't around."

"Are you okay?"

"Do I sound manic? It happens. Which is why I don't think I'm cut out for this science crap. I'll still have to go to med school, though—otherwise, my mother will kill herself. So, listen.

"New York,
you are a woman standing in the wind's archways,
a figure remote as an atom,
a mere dot in the numbered sky,
one thigh in the clouds, the other in water.
Tell me the name of your star.
A battle between grass and computers is coming.
The whole century is hemorrhaging.
Its head adds disaster to disaster.
Its waist is Asia.
Its legs belong to nothing...
I know you, O body, swimming in the musk of poppies.
You bare one nipple and its twin to me.
I look at you and dream of snow.
I look at you and wait for autumn."

Marwa had already fallen asleep.

Desiree watched her silently, then continued reading in a whisper to herself.

"...Faster than the air I ran
beneath the jailing sky until I disappeared in darkness.
The wind kept calling me by name.
I heard the echo of an old man's voice:
'You will discover a mountain filled with your necessities."

"Marwa," Desiree added quietly, "whose name means *mountain.*

It will protect you and grant you victory.'
Then I heard a voice from within the mountain:
'Pull aside the curtain and enter.'
I entered the mountain as through a window...
A hand beckoned me toward an ageless place
that glowed in the light.
A bed awaited me there, and on it lay an image
with breasts and thighs and all the rest."

She turned off the light and lay down beside Marwa. In the dark, she finished the poem from memory.

"I awoke beside a woman
who became my other nature,
and that nature flowered suddenly like poppies or plants.
My body started to prepare itself for something
like the fall of planets."

ꓢꓣꓔꙮ

Marwa jolted awake and, without meaning to, shoved Desiree off the bed. Desiree landed on the floor, giggling.

"What are you doing?" Marwa mumbled.

"You fell asleep while I was reading to you."

"I'm sorry."

"You got a little sunburn, right here." Desiree pointed.

"I don't sunburn."

"Right—*copper glow*, whatever."

"And the answer is no."

"To what?"

"My inviolate underwear."

"So, what *did* happen?"

"Walking, swimming, a lot of arguing."

"And making up? Or out?"

"More or less."

"Marwa..."

"More than I wanted, less than he did."

"You *know* you want to tell me."

"We smoked. Well, *I* smoked because he had to drive. I choked. It made me sleepy. I passed out in the car. It was pot."

Desiree switched on the light.

"That was your first spliff?"

"It was my first *cigarette* ever."

"Nasty boy corrupting my sweet girl. And it made you sleepy?"

"Are you not supposed to get sleepy?"

"What else? You look like you're about to break."

"Spliff?" Marwa looked at her. "Desiree, are you gay?"

"Knowing the word *spliff* doesn't make me gay. I was competing with Drug Boy. Alexander the Great was gay. So was Grover Cleveland's sister, Rose Elizabeth. I did start my school's Gay and Lesbian Club."

"I woke up when the car stopped. My face was in his lap."

"How'd it get there?"

"Last thing I remember, I was leaning on his shoulder, falling asleep."

"Gravity, then. Or he will be murdered."

"He didn't do anything."

"You're telling me he just sat there in a parked car with your face in his crotch? I bet he *loved* it. Titillated amygdala. Males are beyond pigs. Giant, hard-on pigosities."

"He did. Have," Marwa admitted quietly, her stomach twisting in confusion. "Desiree, do me a favor, please—"

"Anything."

"Leave me alone, okay?"

Desiree stood up, folded the poem, and placed the envelope gently on Marwa's night table. Marwa leaned back, eyes closed. Desiree turned off the lamp and climbed down the ladder. Marwa heard the firm click of the door behind her.

Still dressed in her sandy clothes and flushed from the heat of a growing sunburn, Marwa reached over and pulled the spread from the other bed to cover herself.

"Rose Elizabeth Cleveland," she muttered. "Fuck."

13

AUGUST 2001

"Ummee, do you know Adonis? His poetry?" Marwa asked her mother the next time they spoke on the phone.

"There's a *fatwa* against him."

"Have you ever read his work?"

"A student once brought in a poem. We translated it together in class, then compared our version to Said's original Arabic. His real name is Ali Ahmad Said—son of Syrian peasants. Is he helping you forget Allah?"

"A friend of mine just likes his poetry, that's all."

"He renamed himself after a Western god of lust—Adonis. Have you forgotten?"

"I haven't forgotten *you*. But what I'm trying to understand—it's hard, Ummee. Don't you think it would take more than a human lifetime to truly know Allah?"

"So, we follow the Prophet, peace be upon him, who heard the words of Allah."

"Do you think those were Allah's *last* words—the ones spoken to the Prophet?"

"Peace be upon him."

"Allah is brilliant in math and science. But He didn't talk about them with Muhammad."

"I don't *think*," her mother said. "I *believe*."

"I can believe while standing and thinking. Do we have to kneel to do it? Isn't there a difference between humility and humiliation, Ummee?"

Her mother hung up.

When Marwa called back, she got only Joey's little-boy voice on the answering machine.

Strike two, she thought, staring at her phone. It was a sweltering August afternoon. She sat on a bench outside the lab, under a peeling sycamore tree that gave off a thick, ancient musk.

She had been avoiding Desiree. But before the call, they'd crossed paths.

Marcus *Sibercoff* ($Ag_{47}coff$, as in silver) had been emailing and IM'ing her regularly. Since their beach date, Marwa had felt a sticky guilt, like peanut butter on the roof of her mouth, whenever she saw Desiree, who seemed to embody the mood of August: heavy, sullen, and unrelenting.

That morning in the lab, they had been paired to analyze part of an experimental run. They worked in silence—until Marwa broke it.

"How do you know you're gay?" she asked.

Desiree's eyes welled.

"How do you know you're not?"

"That's what I'm asking."

"What's your favorite candy?"

"Halvah."

"What food do you hate?"

"Okra."

"But you didn't know you loved halvah or hated okra until you tasted them, right?"

"There's a lot I haven't tasted yet—foods I'd love or hate."

"Exactly my point."

"I don't think it's like food," Marwa said softly.

Two tears slipped down Desiree's face before she could stop them.

"I get it. I get it. You don't like me."

She walked out.

Strike one.

Marwa stayed, finished the analysis on her own, and turned in the results. Then she headed outside, sank onto the sycamore bench, and called home.

Three strikes and you're out, she thought, staring into the distance. She still didn't want to go back to her room.

Desiree's words came back to her—*amygdala*. Why had she used that term when talking about Marcus?

Marwa went to the library and began digging. On BrainInfo, she read that deep inside the brain, dopamine—DA—was the "drug of choice," the principal neurotransmitter for three major midbrain systems. DA cells projected into the neostriatum, the anterior, and the amygdaloid areas. More clicks led to more research: primate sexual arousal increased dopamine and norepinephrine, while serotonin levels dropped. No one yet knew which genes were active in these responses.

. In her mind now: a vivid Crayola image of her own brain—yellow like *Dandelion*, orange like *Macaroni and Cheese*—lighting up during that moment in the car, her face in Marcus's lap. Desiree's brain would glow the same colors when looking at Marwa. And Prix—his face, body, groin—flooded her neuroanatomy with DA and norepinephrine.

Strike three.

She finally returned to her dorm room. Coincidence collided with omen…a voicemail.

Prix's voice.

"Marwa, my hostess just flew off to Iceland. Let me send one of the cars for you."

TSUNAMI.

Only two weeks remained in the summer program. Since she was still a minor, Marwa couldn't sign herself out overnight—or even for a weekend—without parental permission. Deception was an option, but after her act of rebellion in June (also spurred by Prix) had left her physically ill, she no longer trusted her body to be a willing accomplice.

She'd made it through a long, official day-and-night outing with Marcus without any adverse effects, so she figured a similar plan would be safe. She scheduled a day with Prix for her final Saturday on Long Island. Conveniently, her parents would be taking Joey up to Niagara Falls that weekend—Joey himself called to deliver the news, his voice bright with excitement.

There would be time after summer to mend fences—with her parents, and even with Desiree.

That Friday night, Marwa was in a good mood. Prix had promised to pick her up at eleven the next morning. She was IMing with Marcus while half-heartedly surfing for information on Grover Cleveland, his sister Rose Elizabeth, and the mythological—not poetic—Adonis.

Marcus, meanwhile, was nerding out over oscillating neutrinos and his mentors' excitement about them. He asked how her Physics Regents makeup exam had gone.

Mars429: what a trip. no more work talk. *i like "agog,"* tho

Ag47coff: let's play Metaphor: *he was as tall as a 6'3" tree*

Mars429: *her vocabulary was as bad as, like, whatever*

Ag47coff: *long separated by cruel fate...*

Ag47coff: *the star-crossed lovers raced...*

Ag47coff: *across the grassy field toward...*

Ag47coff: *each other like two freight trains...*

Ag47coff: *one having left Cleveland at 6:36 PM traveling at 55 mph...*

Ag47coff: *the other from Topeka at 4:19 PM at 35 mph!*

Mars429: Biren tried to solve it! new topic: ADELPHOPOIESIS, gay men's marriage, legit in early Christian Church till 14th c.

Ag47coff: back to Stuy research already?

Mars429: Grover Cleveland = $1000 bill / his gay sister… gender sites, Greco-Roman, Latin…

Ag47coff: sounds like Desiree—pants on fire.

Mars429: whose?

Ag47coff: what?

Mars429: mine's on first. who's on second?

Ag47coff: touché. please (da dum *DUM*)

Mars429: touché yourself. NO sabers! NO Vivian Cheng! NO Stuy!

Ag47coff: it looms…

Mars429: like a tidal wave…

Ag47coff: tsunami — gotta run — naked girl at door.

GRTΨ

The next morning, Marwa was fully dressed when Prix opened the car door for her. Though it was mid-August, the day felt like a clear, cool September morning. She wore chinos with socks and loafers, a long-sleeved cotton sweater tied around her shoulders, and a ribbon headband holding back her long hair. She had even put in her Sweet Sixteen pearl earrings. The dark green Bentley smelled faintly of tobacco, and its uniformed chauffeur—Dennis, a humorless, middle-aged European—sat behind the wheel.

"We have to return Cinderella by midnight, Dennis," Prix said. "Or who knows what we'll turn into."

"Sir," Dennis replied stiffly.

As they drove to the Hamptons, Prix explained that the oceanfront home they were visiting belonged to a film star currently in Iceland shooting a mystery thriller.

"Did she do it?" Marwa asked.

"Do what?"

"Commit the crime."

"I forgot how many questions you ask. Have you cloned anything deadly this summer?"

"I don't clone," Marwa said and burst into laughter.

For some reason, it struck her as hilarious. She had to sip designer water to calm down.

"It's like hiccups," Prix said, watching her.

She looked at the bottle.

"You mean the water?"

"No, the giggles."

"Must be Stupid Water," she said, still apologetic.

"Probably. It's all I drink," he said with a grin.

Marwa looked so sincerely sorry that Prix took the bottle from her hand and pressed her palm to his cheek. His skin was warm, slightly rough with post-shave stubble.

"When you blush, your face is almost as dark as mine," he said. "I love it."

After that, she could barely hear anything. Prix returned her hand gently to her lap and continued talking about the actress, how they'd met when he was five or six during a mink coat photo shoot his mother attended. She received a fur coat. Then he fell silent, turning to look out the window.

East Hampton was packed with cars and people like Rockefeller Center at Christmastime.

"It's much nicer here in winter," he said.

"There's too much 'there' here now," Marwa replied, hoping he'd catch the Gertrude Stein reference.

He gave her a polite smile to acknowledge she'd said *something*, though not necessarily what.

"You come here a lot, then?" she asked, trying again.

"She gave me a key," Prix said. "I only come out when I have it to myself. When I'm tired of being looked at."

Marwa turned toward tourists crowding around a weathered windmill. Prix gently tilted her chin back toward him.

"Not you," he said. "You can look."

Then he laughed softly, "Just don't look so sad."

"I'm not sad. I'm anxious."

"My face is like a police mirror," Prix said. "People can't see me watching them behind it."

"I'm no different."

"You are. You look at things and wonder how they work, whether they're mirrors."

He paused.

"Also, you're..."

"What?"

"Clumsy doesn't sound like a compliment."

"It isn't."

"I think it is."

"Then I'll have to fall down a lot," Marwa said.

"You won't even have to try," he replied with a smile.

She wondered if his teasing was meant to make her feel more comfortable. She rolled down the car window, inhaling the sea air.

Dennis turned onto a narrow, rose-hedge-lined road that led to a circular driveway fronting a large, gabled, shingled house. Striped awnings fluttered in the strong wind above the many windows. In the distance, the ocean boomed against the shore, its rhythm pulsing beneath their feet.

Dennis opened the car door.

Marwa stepped out, holding her hair back with both hands.

"When we go outside again, I'll get you one of her scarves," Prix said.

Inside, the entry hall faced directly onto the ocean, giving the illusion—at high tide—that the sea was charging straight toward the house. To the right, three steps led to a dining room: to the left, a living room. The décor was blue, white, and yellow, full of windows, mirrors, and French doors. Marwa felt off-balance on the fringed rugs.

Prix led her to the dining room, where a long table was set for two—goblets, glasses, battalions of silverware, and a thick white napkin folded into a rose in the middle of her plate. Portraits on the wall featured the actress in her radiant youth.

"You never really imagine a movie queen actually *living* somewhere," Marwa said.

"There's a screening room," Prix said. "A real mini-movie palace."

"Mini-movie or mini-palace?" she asked.

"You'd rather eat in the kitchen," he said. "I was trying to impress you."

"You don't have to try."

"I want you to like me. But this isn't me—or mine."

A young maid brought lunch on a tray table and served them. After she left, Prix made himself a lobster and endive roll.

"Let's get out of here," he said. "But make one first, from your plate."

"We can't take the iced tea."

"Too bad. It's got cloves—like in ham—and mint."

"We don't eat ham. Muslims, I mean."

"I'll get you a scarf," he said.

While she waited in a pantry near a massive refrigerator, the cook and maid were kind to Marwa but nearly reverent toward Prix—as if he were the sun. He returned with two bottles of water and a bright silk scarf.

"How ironic," Marwa said.

Prix raised an eyebrow.

"This is the first time I've been *Mu'hajiba* since I met you."

He didn't understand, but he smiled anyway, alchemizing awkwardness into charm.

"Let's go," he said. "We've got everything we need."

They passed a putting green to a grove of pines and Adirondack chairs, where they ate lunch. A peacock strutted toward them, magnificent and self-important. Behind him waddled his smaller, duller mate.

Prix and me, Marwa thought.

"She's got bees too," Prix said.

"A real apiary?"

"I know a guy in the Village who keeps one on his roof garden. A New Jersey guy picks up the honey and sells it in

Union Square. There are greyhounds too. Not in New Jersey. Here. Lady rescues them from racetracks. They're sweet. Not like that peacock—he thinks he owns the place. I know people like that."

On their way to find the dogs, they passed gardeners working in flower beds—red roses, blue anemones, and tall white flowers with a licorice scent.

Marwa asked the name of the unfamiliar flower. The gardeners only spoke Spanish but understood her gesture.

"*Anís,*" one answered.

"Oh," Marwa told Prix, "The Romans loved anise. They used it in cakes to end feasts. It's also a lure for mice. Its oil can poison pigeons. It produces a toxic alkaloid—anemomine."

Prix grinned, "So... pigeon poison caused the fall of the Roman Empire?"

Marwa turned to the glittering ocean.

"'It depends only on the dose whether a thing is poison or not,'" she said. "'A lot kills, a little cures.' Paracelsus. I lost points for omitting the word 'only' when I translated him."

"Not always true," Prix replied. "Some things, *any* amount kills. Let's find the greyhounds."

Two lanky greyhounds yelped and sprinted in an enclosure. Prix entered alone to leash them, but when released, they nearly tackled Marwa. Prix held them back as they licked her hands. Their thin, eager bodies seemed too long, their fur oddly patchy.

The dogs dragged them toward the beach. People recognized the dogs—and the house they came from—and gave them space. The greyhounds raced the crashing surf, leaping with wild syncopation. By the time they slowed and trotted back, Marwa and Prix were drenched and freezing.

"Shower, bath, and sauna," Prix announced.

Marwa took off the scarf as they went upstairs. He led her into a palatial bedroom—another portrait of the Lady gazed down from above the bed.

Inside the bathroom—clad in gold-veined marble, stone, wood, and mirrors—Prix pulled robes, slippers, and a black bathing suit from a vast closet.

"This'll be too big," he said. "But better than nothing for the tub. I'll wear one too. Meet you in the jacuzzi."

The spa tub was massive.

Marwa slowly undressed, stepping into the steaming shower, her body relaxing under the many jets. When she finished, Prix was already in the jacuzzi.

"Don't worry," he said as she hesitated in her robe. "I'll shut my eyes."

He submerged, resurfacing with water cascading from his blond curls.

Marwa put on the oversized swimsuit and slipped into the hot, swirling water.

"Talk more Latin," Prix said.

She did. She quoted phrases about healing and the goddess Sulis. Later, in the cedar-scented sauna, whale songs drifted through hidden speakers.

"I sound like you," he murmured, half-asleep.

Afterward, they watched a movie in the private screening room. Marwa fell asleep. When she woke up, the screen was gone—replaced by a blown-up photograph of a $1 bill.

"Lady says that was her first paycheck," Prix explained.

Marwa translated the Latin. *Annuit coeptis* — "He has favored our undertakings." *Novus ordo seclorum* — "A new order of the ages." *E pluribus unum*— "Out of many, one."

"She thinks that means her," Prix said.

That evening, they walked the beach without the dogs. It was cold. Prix took Marwa's hand—his warm, hers icy.

They sat on a low dune.

"This," Prix said softly, "this is what I want. Things to go slow. I never thought I'd be happy here."

"Then why come?" Marwa asked.

"Old habits," he said. "Especially the bad ones. What do *you* think? You think more than anyone I've ever met."

"What happened here?"

"You don't want to know. I don't want you to."

"But she gave you a key."

"Marwa, what do you want?"

She hesitated.

"You don't know?" he asked.

"I want too much. No, I want the wrong things."

"Says who? Your father?"

"And my mother. And... everything."

He kissed her gently, cradling her cheek. Then he stood.

"We should get you back."

They were quiet on the drive. Just once, Prix said, "I'll miss you. I have to go down to DC, then LA."

The goodbye kiss was brief, different.

"Don't look so sad," Marwa said. "Are you?"

Outside the car, with his voice low so Dennis wouldn't hear, he said, "I'm waiting for the moment you realize it's hopeless—and I hope you never do."

⸎⸎⸎

Back in her dorm room, Marwa refused sleep.

I want to make as objective a record of my subjective experience as possible. All right, I want to relive it. I want it never to end.

To make it immortal, it has to be repeated and repeatable. It is sacred. I am ridiculous, but I feel compelled. This is religion.

Adonis, she wrote. Important in Greek and Roman myth, but his name comes from the Semitic Adonai—Lord. Born of incest between Princess Myrrha and her father, King of Assyria. Myrrha became a tree. Adonis was born from it. Red roses or anemones sprang from his blood when he died.

I keep seeing the bees by the blue anemones and white anise flowers. "Anemone" means windflower—petals lost to a breeze. Adonis suits anemone more than rose. A-NEM-oh-knee. It sounds like a sneeze—or a prayer:

Anemone, we pray to Thee. How I envy bees...

14

JOURNAL, PHONE, EMAIL

*I*s it envy or jealousy I feel toward bees? Marwa continued writing.

Mr. Haddam had always suffered over the misuse of those two words. Also fortuitous, *which doesn't mean* fortunate, *it means* accidental. "Poor Grendel's had an accident, so may you all," *is the last line of* Grendel, *which we read after* Beowulf.

But is accident even possible? Or is everything determined? And if there are too many variables for us to determine causation, does that define accident?

Grendel, before Beowulf arrived, believed things were fixed—his world governed by irony and repetition. But Beowulf is the agent of Romantic possibility, a figure whose presence changes reality. He is Accident Incarnate. Beowulf liberates Grendel from his endless cycle of violence and meaninglessness. His death is a kind of release.

"Poor Grendel's had an accident, so may you all."

Bees can go to any flower they choose and walk boldly into its most private places. They are not shy or embarrassed, even if clumsy. They never think they're stupid, or ugly, or guilty, or ridiculous. They don't even realize they're pollinating. They just feel compelled to collect pollen—to make food for the hive. Their intestines turn pollen into honey.

Straw into gold. Rumpelstiltskin. Their intestines. Bees shit honey.

Marcus's dung beetles live off excrement. Bees eliminate the middleman.

I would like to be a bee. Not a queen. Not a drone. A worker bee. Up in the morning, observe the dance, fly to the source, dive in. Rub and scrub, gather until I'm too heavy to fly—but I do—and return to make my deposit in the honey bank.

Envy is for things. Jealousy is for feelings. Do I want Prix, or do I want Prix's feelings?

But he doesn't want me. I don't think he even wants my feelings. I don't know what he wants. He says he wants things to go slowly. Ly. Maybe it's not about me at all—it's about Time.

I don't even feel tired. What is hopeless?

Desiree. She left a package at my door. It's still unopened. It's heavy. Someone could've stolen it. No one did.

Oh, Great Goddess Sulis of Bath, I worshipped in your hot springs today. "Healing springs help cities grow," said Uncle Pliny. Sulis, also known as Minerva or Athena. Aquae Sulis. Her thermae maximae—the best baths!

Jonathan Swift mocked people who traveled to Bath, England, to sit in and eventually drink their own filth in the name of health. But Roman baths were as normal then as restaurants are now. In the 4th century, Rome had 856 baths. 600 years later, Córdoba had even more.

Every place is given its character by patterns of events that keep happening there. We read this in The Timeless Way of Building by Christopher Alexander. These event-patterns are intertwined with geometric space patterns. Interior information becomes external formation.

I'm thinking genes. I'm thinking brain gyrations. I am consciously thinking, calling on my invisible Brain Rumpelstiltskin to spin the right word for Lady's bathroom.

Spin, angular gyrus, spin straw into gold. Give me the Word.

A noise down the hall—someone using the bathroom. Morning was coming. Marwa twisted her head and then bent back to her writing.

"The specific patterns out of which a town is made may be alive or dead. If they are alive, they free us. If they are dead, they trap us in conflict. The more living patterns a place has, the more it holds the fire—the quality without a name. And when a place has that fire, it becomes a part of nature. Like waves or grass, it exists in a play of repetition and variation, held in the truth that all things pass.

"In nature, everything begins and develops as a whole. A mountain is born whole. Earth's crust heaves and the mountain forms. Even each grain of sand is whole. Nothing is unfinished—even after thousands of years.

"Bathing is not just cleaning. It's sensual, therapeutic. Societies that restrict bodily pleasure—especially in childhood—are the ones that glorify warfare and sadism."

"I don't know.

"The top of the pyramid on the $1 bill hovers, unfinished, above its base. I looked it up after discovering Grover Cleveland is on the $1,000 bill.

"The apex is surrounded by a halo—a glory. It's not attached. It's intentionally incomplete. But the more living patterns we place in this country—the more fire we add—the more we become part of nature.

"And I feel unfinished. I suppose all the physical implications were encoded from the moment egg met sperm. But I wasn't there yet. I'm not fully here now. I'm my own Cheshire Cat, watching parts of myself appear.

"The Eye of Horus was staring at me when I woke up with Prix.

"And Prix was staring too.

"The Eye of Horus—Wedjat, the Whole One. His left eye, restored by Thoth (god of wisdom and the moon) after Horus avenged Osiris, his father, killed by Set, god of night.

"Set tore out Horus's eye, but Horus killed him, and Osiris was reborn in the underworld. If you can call that living.

"Left eye. Right eye. Do the hokey pokey and turn yourself around.

"Horus's eye, the restored one, stared at me from the blown-up dollar bill on the wall of a movie star's mansion.

"Odin also lost an eye. How Norse is that? And doesn't Norse sound like mucus? Like snort, a little snot?

"Norcus — new word. A neologism for mucus. Norse = Crayola Timber Wolf gray.

"I had an Egyptian children's book once. The Eye of Horus represented fractions. Each part of the eye symbolized a different sense.

"But the parts never added up to 1. The message: knowledge can never be total. One part is always missing. One part can't be known.

"There are six parts of the eye. Six senses. Not five.

"320 ro = 1 heqat.

"The ro is the smallest unit of perceptible input— the minimum energy to register sense data.

"Its symbol is the mouth.

"One ro = one mouthful.

"But Ummee – my mother – always said it meant one kiss.

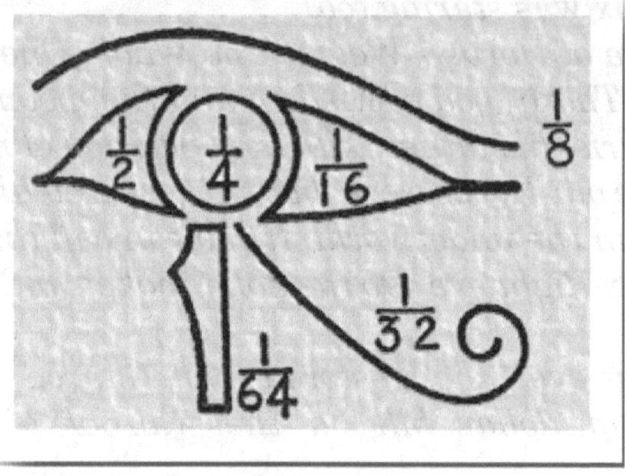

"*Each of the sacred unit fractions the ancient Egyptians assigned to the six parts of the Eye of Horus were: 1/2, 1/4, 1/8, 1/16, 1/32, and 1/64. Each has a denominator that's a power of two, and together they were used to represent parts of the heqat, a unit of grain measurement. According to legend, the pieces of the eye were lost in battle and restored by the god Thoth.*

1. *"Touch = 1/64 heqat = 5 ro*
2. *"Taste = 1/32 heqat = 10 ro*
3. *"Hearing = 1/16 heqat = 20 ro*
4. *"Thought = 1/8 heqat = 40 ro*
5. *"Sight = 1/4 heqat = 80 ro*
6. *"Smell = 1/2 heqat = 160 ro*

"We never got as far as Thought with the kisses—Hearing's 20 ro led to too much laughing, and then I had to calm down.

"When I read this book with Joey, we never made it past Touch's 5.

"With Prix, I barely made it to Touch."

When Marwa finally closed her journal at dawn, her left hand throbbed from writing. Her eyes burned. She climbed into bed.

Five hours later, her phone rang. It was Joey, calling from Niagara Falls. But when he spoke, she couldn't hear him—the roar of the falls drowned him out.

"We're going to brunch!" he yelled. "That's br-ek-fist and luh-unch. We did a tour yesterday. Did I wake you up? You sound funny."

"I *am* funny," she replied. "How are Ummee and Daddy?"

"They're fine. You know what Niagara Falls is? It's runoff from the Great Lakes! They spill where the ground's lower. Like when you said stars curve space like bowling balls. But the guide didn't know about graffiti. Or is it graffeety? Daddy bought me a pop-up book. I had cheese curly fries for dinner. Ummee said I'd get sick—but I didn't!"

"You know erosion?"

"Personally."

"Niagara Falls was born 12,500 years ago and in 15,000 years it'll be flat! You'll be able to walk right off it and not drown because it won't be there! They know that from carbon-dating. What's carbon-dating?"

"It's how they tell how old something is by how much radioactive carbon is left."

"Niagara Falls moves seven miles a year. It erodes the shale under the top rock. Makes a backwards road! I asked if the guide knew shale was sedimentary and he said, 'Yes, my dear Watson.'"

Everyone laughed.

"Who's Watson?"

"Sherlock Holmes's doctor friend. He always says, 'Elementary, my dear Watson.' Is Ummee there? Want to put her on?"

"You know what else? The water crash makes spray, and when you breathe it in, the ions get in your body and make you drunk. What's ions? Who's Sherlock?"

"I'm losing you," Marwa lied gently. "Call me when you get home. I'll email you about the ions."

CRITY

She lay back on her pillow, smiling. Joey was still a bee—light, curious, unselfconscious. The air outside was wet and warm again. September would hold off a little longer. And even though Ummee was still angry, Marwa felt better.

Graffiti. Graffeety. Gravity. Graffiti. And those ions—what *about* them?

She slid out of bed and climbed down to her laptop. There was an email from Judy, which she saved for later. First, she searched *ions* and *waterfalls*.

"On the seashore, where water constantly falls, there are about 2,000 negative to 1,000 positive ions. This is believed to be the ideal ratio for human well-being. At Yosemite and Niagara Falls, sprays of negative ions are thought to lower serotonin levels in the blood. Even home showers act as natural ionizers, splitting neutral air particles and releasing electrons to produce that serotonin-lowering effect. In contrast, positive-ion-rich winds—like the Chinook, Santa Ana, Sharav, Simoon, Hamsin, or Harmattan—have been linked to irritability and mood disorders..."

It sounded more like a New Age health site than hard science, but still—*a likely story.*

She clicked back and read, "Where in the H is the H in H2O? Water may not be H_2O at all. On molecular timescales—about 100 quintillionths of a second—quantum effects make the hydrogen nucleus act more like a wave than a particle. Then strange things happen. The wave-like proton and wave-like electron interact with other nearby atoms, pulling themselves out of their original atoms...

The number of hydrogen bonds a protein encounters along a DNA helix may determine where it binds. Quantum blurriness could be embedded in the very chemistry of life."

Marwa copied and pasted the article and sent it to her lab mentor.

Then she opened Judy's long email about upcoming lab and social events.

In reply, she wrote, *The neuro-biological basis of my synesthesia suggests metaphor could be key to how human language emerged. The brain has cross-wiring rules for converting visual and auditory signals into motor control—especially in the hands and mouth. It's called synkinesia. Like I told you, when my mother cut my bangs, she would tilt her mouth the same way her scissors went.*

My angular gyrus elves are spinning, trying to name the bathroom I was in with Prix. Luxurium? Your dad would love mapping the network I'm visualizing—like chalkboard brainstorming in "Elementary-my-dear-Watson" school. Maximum Bathnasium? Bath plus gymnasium?

See you in a week or so. Love, M.

When Judy read it, all she saw was, *"...the bathroom I was in with Prix."*

Marwa rolled her chair back and noticed the package Desiree had left.

A card, tucked under rubber bands on a manila envelope, read in careful block letters, "Don't freak. Don't open till you get home. —D.L."

She replaced the card and added the envelope to her "to take home" pile.

Then she headed to the showers.

The moment she stepped into the communal bathroom and saw the red-doored toilet stalls and blue-doored showers, a new phrase popped into her head...Aquae Excess.

Thank you, Angular Gyrus—and all your poetic elves.

15

RETURN TO NYC

Returning to her parents' house felt like being Cinderella's uglier stepsister, trying to jam her foot into the glass slipper. She'd been home for a week, with just one more left in August. Then Labor Day would come, and school would start that Thursday.

Marwa was meeting up with Judy in an hour. She opened her notebook—and froze. There, written beneath her last journal entry, was a message in Joey's handwriting:

"Your wrong about bees. Honey isnt bee doody. Bees have 2 stomicks. 2 kinds of worker bees—1 gets nectar and pollen, the other kind chews the nectar for a 1/2 hour and adds ENZYMES. Bees also eat pollen. Bees do 2 dances—a Waggle Dance and a Round Dance. About how far away the flowers are. Waggle Dance looks like 8 for more far away food. Bees can see where the Sun is even when its clowdy. It isnt doody. A man in 1973 had to share the Noble prize for discovering The Rose Stone of the bees dance. It is pyook. The collector bees vomet to the chewy bees. They throw it up and put it in

*the hive chambers wich have 6 sides like snowflakes.
Sorry, Your Brother, Joey"*

Marwa was furious. He'd *read* her journal. He'd written in it.

She stormed into Joey's room, looking for something to take…something personal enough to make a point. His Niagara Falls pop-up book was lying beside his pillow, so she snatched it and stashed it in her room, where she knew he'd find it. That wasn't the point, though. The point was, from now on, she'd have to take her notebook *everywhere.*

She was outraged.

But grudgingly, she was also relieved—glad, even.

Because honey, it turned out, wasn't doody.

ᏕᎡᎢᎳ

Marwa met up with Judy halfway between Greenwich Village and Battery Park City, at *Adonis Piercing & Tattoo* on Canal Street, where Judy had scheduled an appointment to get a boat tattooed on the back of her right shoulder. Afterward, she suggested they play tourist and visit the South Street Seaport.

It was a steamy August day in New York City. Both girls wore tube tops. Judy paired hers with shorts and sandals. Marwa wore two-thirds of an outfit her mother had laid out as a welcome-home gift…a royal blue tube top and a reversible yellow-and-blue maxi skirt. The final third—a long-sleeved blouse—was, as Marwa put it, "too hot even to *talk* about."

"Your mom's trying," Judy offered.

"I thought I'd be the black sheep," Marwa said, "but thanks to Sharif not coming back from Alexandria, my parents are so upset—and my dad's so mad at my mom like it's *her* fault. I'm, at best, third on the family doody list."

Judy entered *Adonis Piercing & Tattoo* first. A brief electronic chime sounded at the door.

"What's going on with Sharif anyway?" she asked.

"(A), the bank's computer department doesn't want him to leave—they're paying for him to finish school in Alexandria. And (B), he just got engaged to a distant cousin who works at the bank. My mom's family engineered the whole thing. My dad's furious."

A muscled Black man with a shaved head stepped through a curtain of beaded strings.

"I'll be right with you. Ms...?"

"Yamaguchi," Judy said.

He checked the appointment book, then looked at Marwa.

"I'm not sure yet," Marwa said.

"Never let anyone talk you into something you don't want to do," the man said. "That's how you know whether a shop's legit. People call me Adonis. You're welcome to choose something from the wall or just have a seat."

He disappeared again behind the beaded curtain.

Judy and Marwa browsed the framed samples: flowers, animals, names, vehicles—rockets, motorcycles, jet planes, boats.

Judy pointed to a small, high-prowed yacht.

"Shakespeare and I rode one just like that around Baltimore Harbor," she said. "It's exactly what he got tattooed on his right shoulder."

"So why are *you* getting a boat?" Marwa asked.

Judy's expression darkened.

"To make a blood memory. My mom took me to get my ears pierced when I was thirteen. I thought it was for my birthday. I didn't know she was dying. Shakespeare got his tattoo right after."

"After the boat ride?" Marwa asked.

"No," Judy said.

"You didn't."

"We did."

Marwa felt faint.

"Stop calling him *Shakespeare*. He's giraffe-Jimmy-Wagstaff."

"Keep your voice down! He's not on a billboard, but his eyes are pale as vodka."

"Vodka? *Amantes sunt amentes*," Marwa muttered.

"Who're you calling a *sunt?*" Judy grinned.

"'Lovers are lunatics.' You're crazy about him."

"I am. He leaves for college in three days. It hurts so much."

"Did it?"

"What?"

"*Hurt* so much?"

Judy lowered her voice.

"You know how your mouth waters when you see or smell something amazing?"

Marwa nodded.

"It's like that. Women have two mouths. The better to eat you with!" Judy growled and leaned forward.

Marwa swatted her.

"You're insane."

"What about Marcus and the Brookhaven turkeys? Prix and the Hampton *bathnasium*? Desiree Lipshitz?"

Before Marwa could answer, Adonis reappeared, guiding a tall, androgynous client with a freshly bandaged forearm.

The person smiled and said, "He knows what he's doing."

Adonis led Judy and Marwa to the back, where the room resembled a salon. Two other artists were already working. Judy showed Adonis her sketch, and he set her up in a barber chair, prepping the area like a surgeon.

The needle buzzed—sharp, dental, mechanical—and when it first touched her skin, a drop of blood appeared. Adonis dabbed it away and began injecting ink.

Marwa swayed.

"Maybe sit in the waiting room, hon?" Adonis suggested.

♣ ♣ ♣ ♣

She passed through the beaded curtain in a daze, pulled out her water bottle and the old book Desiree had given her as a parting gift.... *George Eliot's Poetry and Other Studies* by Rose E. Cleveland, published by Funk & Wagnalls in 1885. Marwa noted the address on the title page—10 and 12 Dey Street—just three blocks south of City Hall. Walking distance from home.

She flipped to the pages Desiree had underlined in red.

In the essay *"Altruistic Faith,"* Desiree had altered the text, changing masculine pronouns to feminine and clearly casting herself as Cadijah and Marwa as Muhammad.

"Though my Cadijah love me as her own soul... She cannot persuade herself that I can be what I cannot be. She can only perceive me to be what I *can* be. Cadijah is a seer, not a visionary. She wields a diviner's rod, not a wizard's wand."

In the margin she had written, "You. Me. —D"

Further down..."The historical Cadijah was deeply enamored of her young lord. But I am not sure she thought HER a great prophet or spotless priest. She saw HER as a WOMAN of destiny. A WOMAN to beckon and be followed. To speak and be believed. To command and be obeyed."

Desiree had written *prophet—not puppet* in the margin.

At the back of the book, Marwa found another marked passage—this time from the final essay, where Rose Cleveland compared Joan of Arc to a spiritual force.

"Faith! That was Joan's lever. The lever with which that little hand moved the world..."

And, earlier..."I reduce all the miracle, marvel, and mystery of Joan's story to the extraordinary development of one human capacity—*love*—and the extraordinary exercise of another—*faith*."

How much thought Desiree had poured into this gift.

The buzzing of the tattoo machine resumed.

Marwa imagined the red of Judy's blood becoming the red of a flower—an anemone. *The same flower that rhymes with Prix,* she thought.

She slipped the book back into her backpack.

GRTW

Outside, Canal Street pulsed with August heat and noise. The door opened—the chime played—and a rush of thick, boiling air swept in as a gay couple entered.

Like lifting the lid off a steaming pot, Marwa thought.

Then, abruptly, the Romans didn't divide sex by gender. They divided it by *power.* Penetration equaled dominance. Submission meant subordination—regardless of gender.

Homosexuality wasn't stigmatized *if* you were the one doing the penetrating.

But Judy—Judy with her two "drooling mouths"—didn't feel subordinate to Jimmy Wagstaff.

GRTW

Later that day, it was sweltering as Marwa and Judy stood on the deck of the fire-engine-red tugboat *Helen McAllister* at the South Street Seaport. Both girls were sipping cold bottles of water. Judy swallowed and reached out, gently brushing the tip of one of Marwa's newly pierced ears.

"Isn't this against your rules?" she asked. "How do they feel?"

"I didn't mutilate Allah's creation with a tattoo," Marwa replied. "Ear piercing's allowed, technically. The Prophet once told some women to give up their earrings as an offering, so he must've been okay with them."

"And how do *you* feel?" Marwa added.

"The heat's baking it," Judy said, referring to her tattoo, "and I'm sweating so much I hope the boat doesn't just slide into the river. Sweat makes it sting worse. But...I like the hurt."

It startled Marwa how completely she understood what Judy meant.

She turned toward the East River, scanning the horizon beyond Ellis Island into the open bay. A fleeting breeze lifted off the ocean, cooling their damp skin.

"We're crazier than the tourists," Marwa murmured. "We don't have to do this today."

They moved with the rest of the group onboard, which included a British woman who had announced back at the Titanic Memorial Lighthouse that her grandmother had survived the Titanic sinking in 1912.

"My Gran always said God went down with the Titanic," the woman had declared.

Judy leaned over and whispered, "My father always says, 'Follow your blis(s)ter.'"

A tour guide began his presentation, flinging his arms toward tall-masted ships and smaller boats docked at the piers.

"White-maned Walt Whitman once called New York the 'City of Ships,'" he announced. "And in the early 1800s, South Street was famously known as the 'Street of Ships.' Back then, this waterfront was a forest of masts, spars, and jibbooms..."

The crowd chuckled at the last word, and the guide pressed on, describing how South Street had once been lined with "ship chandlers' offices and saloons like *Jip and Jake's* and *Shanghai Brown's*, swarming with tattooed sailors..."

At that, Marwa touched Judy's freshly bandaged shoulder, and Judy instinctively ducked away.

They slipped away from the group as the guide continued, "The odor of rum, molasses, wine, and spices was intoxicating right here..."

GRTV

Marwa couldn't get the image of Judy's blood out of her mind. The last spotting days of her August period—she checked the calendar: August 31st—were a constant, visceral reminder. So much red in the world. Mars was a red planet. So much iron. So much irony.

When she logged into the Stuyvesant High School website, as required before the start of the academic year, Marwa saw the prompt for a yearlong history project. Immediately, she thought of Desiree's parting gift: *George Eliot's Poetry and Other Studies* by Rose Elizabeth Cleveland. It would be perfect.

In a letter written in 1890 to a woman named Evangeline, Rose had confessed.

"Ah, how I love you, it paralyzes me—it makes me heavy with emotion... I tremble at the thought of you—all my being leans out to you... I dare not think of your arms."

Evangeline Whipple had been Rose Cleveland's longtime partner. Rose, a scholar and the unmarried sister of President Grover Cleveland, had lived with Evangeline in Italy after the death of Evangeline's husband, Bishop Henry Whipple. The two women remained together in *Bagni di Lucca* until Rose's death in 1918. During World War I, they devoted themselves to relief work, aiding victims of the conflict across Italy.

Marwa read further about Bishop Whipple—Henry Benjamin Whipple, the Episcopal Bishop of Minnesota (1822–1901). Appointed in 1856 to establish the first Protestant Episcopal Church in Chicago, he counted Union generals like Burnside and McClellan among his parishioners.

What intrigued Marwa most was his advocacy for Indigenous rights. Known by Native Americans as "Straight Tongue," Whipple had condemned unlawful land seizures by white settlers and worked fiercely to protect Native communities in Minnesota. He warned of the impending 1862 Dakota War—a conflict still remembered as the "Indian Massacre"—though Marwa wasn't yet sure whether the aggressors had been settlers or Sioux.

Two years later, on November 29, 1864, at Sand Creek, Colorado, another massacre occurred: over 150 peaceful Cheyennes, many of them women and children, were slaughtered by U.S. soldiers. Marwa noted a pattern: Civil War and Indian Wars overlapping, entangled. The sixth decade of the nineteenth century seemed drenched in blood— a sprawling orgy of violence across North America.

She continued researching President Grover Cleveland, collecting excerpts from obituaries and historical coverage.

One passage stood out... *"Cleveland, against his own will, was morally the founder of the present American imperialism."*

That "present" referred to Berlin, June 25, 1908.

From *The New York Times*, same date, *"MR. CLEVELAND IS DEAD AT 71 Succumbs to a Heart Attack in His Princeton Home After Seeming to Rally. DIES ON THE DAY OF THE VENEZUELA BREAK. Mr. Cleveland's Most Famous Act Recalled to Many by a Coincidence. HIS RINGING MESSAGE It Frightened Many but Raised an Issue That Left the Monroe Doctrine Firmly Established."*

By strange coincidence, Cleveland's death on June 24 occurred on the very day the U.S. severed diplomatic ties with Venezuela—an event that stirred memories of his 1895 message regarding the Venezuelan boundary dispute. In that address, Cleveland had asserted a bold interpretation of the Monroe Doctrine, insisting the United States would enforce its role in protecting the Western Hemisphere from European interference.

Marwa paused, thinking, coincidence and consequence, red lines and red blood, prophetic love and political legacy. All of it—interwoven.

ᏕᎡᎢᎥ

"Cleveland, against his own will, was morally the founder of the present American imperialism."

What did *against his own will* mean? And *morally?*

Unknotting those two ideas could become her senior project, Marwa thought. Grover Cleveland had once been printed on the $1,000 bill, yet he'd died with little money to his name—of any denomination.

She was in her room, reading and printing notes, when Joey burst in, announcing with fanfare, "Is here now— Ositadimma Bem! *'May things be better from today and forever'*—and his last name means Peace!'"

Ositadimma Bem was a former classmate of Joey's, with skin even darker than Lem's (now at Duke—Vivian Cheng had already called Marwa as soon as the yearlong project was posted). Though Osit lived in their building, he and Joey no longer went to the same school. Their mother had moved heaven and earth to get Joey into P.S. 234—*Independence School*—across West Street. It had slightly higher test scores than P.S. 89, and was closer to Marwa's high school, Stuyvesant.

"If Joey gets sick at school," their mother had said, "and I'm at work, you can take him home."

Marwa was about to tell Joey to send Osit away, but the boy at the door—tall, composed—raised a finger to his lips, then held up a $100 bill. He slipped it into his pocket and handed Marwa a small envelope.

GRTΨ

Now Marwa stood in front of Prix's apartment door.

It opened.

Prix—golden curls, tanned skin, green eyes—looked relieved but didn't smile.

"You pierced your ears," he said.

"I thought you were in D.C. or L.A."

"Not today."

She stepped inside. His apartment was larger than her parents', the layout different. The view stretched across the bay, the river, and the northern bridge. Windows were open, screens in place. Sheer curtains would have billowed, but there were none. The air was hot and restless.

"I know this room," Marwa said. "We saw it in a design magazine in art class."

Prix said nothing. He was barefoot, shirtless, and wearing only loose drawstring shorts. No lights were on. Fans hummed softly. The room was full of natural light and drifting shadow. Prix stood in one of the shadows.

"The article said the owner was 'a jewel in a Tiffany setting.' No name, no photo."

"I don't need four bedrooms," he said. "But I have them."

He took her hand—his was cool—and led her down a long hallway lined with masks from around the world. He guided her fingers to one: a lacquered papier-mâché bull head with real horns and a grinning human mouth.

"The Minotaur," he said.

He let go of her hand and pointed to others.

Pan, a giant, goat-eared head with one winking eye. A chimera with curling horns, a lion's nose, fanged mouth, and human eyes.

"These are from India, Japan, Africa...That one's my prize...from Burundi."

"They weren't in the magazine," Marwa said.

"I asked them to leave them out."

They passed a bathroom of brown glass and stainless steel.

"There's no mirror," she noted.

"I know my face."

The bedroom was minimalist, just a wide platform bed and, by the window, a large standing globe.

Marwa walked to it, slowly spun it, thinking, "*With my back to the window, my face is in shadow.*"

Prix still hadn't smiled.

He tossed cushions to the floor, pulled back the bed cover, untied his shorts, and stepped out of them. Naked, he crossed the room and began to undress her in silence.

There were sounds of distant street noise, the soft rattle of screens, the breathy pull of the fan, his breathing as he unbuttoned her sleeveless blouse; and the loudest sound...a zipper.

"I need the bathroom," Marwa said.

"I'll take care of everything."

But she pulled away, slipped through a door she prayed wasn't a closet, and locked it. She didn't understand the sensation—only that something had flooded. Fear prickled her spine. Had her period returned?

She checked. The pad was saturated but colorless.

Her backpack was in the living room. She peeled the pad off, wrapped it in toilet paper, and dropped it into the wastebasket. Then she returned.

Prix was lying on the bed, one arm behind his head, his body angled toward the wood-paneled wall. He wasn't even looking at her.

What followed, Marwa would remember for the rest of her life reliving its details in endless mental loops, connecting it to future thoughts and feelings that could never truly recreate its reality.

Still, it was a luxurious experience. One that almost—*almost*—satisfied even her inner competitor.

Judy may have been first, she thought, *but mine was best.*

Prix moved through that new geography like a seasoned guide. He was patient, then sharp when the terrain called for it. He inspired trust, dissolved her self-consciousness.

Only much later would Marwa come to understand: his disappointment in her eagerness to learn what he wished he did not know had stained the memory, giving that afternoon a color with no name—one shaded by his quiet sacrifice.

It had movements, like a symphony.

At last, he led her into the bathroom, to the glass-walled shower. A wide cedar seat, carved like a natural outgrowth of the wall, held them as the steamy water cascaded down. He washed her gently, showed her how to wash him, poured fragrant oils onto their bodies. Then he directed her onto his lap.

And they joined again.

That was the last time.

All of it—almost all—had happened in silence.

Sublime.

He patted her dry. Gave her cool water to drink.

What followed was rendered in sharp, stone-carved memory.

She saw her blood on his sheets.

PART II

"Forsan et haec olim meminisse iuvabit."
("A joy it will be one day, perhaps, to remember
even this.")

Virgil
"The Aeneid"
Translation by Robert Fagles, 2004

16

SEPTEMBER 2001

Walking to Stuyvesant, Marwa noted it was a bright and sunny morning—not a dark and stormy night. Technically still summer, with ten days to go before the autumnal equinox, it no longer felt like a summer morning. The heavy, amniotic humidity had broken. Ten degrees cooler, and it would feel like October.

A nervous quickening filled the air, and it surrounded her too. Light bounced off surfaces with extra brilliance, and sound struck her ears like timpani beating on bones. The tension wasn't just in the weather—it was the first full week of senior year. This was it: the final, most competitive hurdle before college. Marcus had called it "acute inflammation of the Alpha gland." At most high schools, *senioritis* meant coasting. At Stuy, that was heresy.

Marwa adjusted her heavy backpack and stretched her neck. Walking north on West Street, approaching Murray, the ceaseless traffic reminded her of the waves at that beach Marcus had taken her to—the sculptor swallowed by his own octopus of sand while the real tide claimed the real shore. A taxi horn snapped her out of the memory, and she froze. Then she hoisted the pack higher. *You can never get used to New York. You can never slack off, never let go—because it's always about the shouting.*

Marcus's voice echoed in her mind, *"No one expects the Spanish Inquisition."*

So yes—she admitted it. Marcus was on her mind that September morning. And if Marcus, then Prix.

She had learned that satisfaction doesn't extinguish desire. Quite the opposite. (And thank you, Mr. Haddam, for interrupting the mental spiral to fix her earlier lapse in parallel structure.) Desire expanded in inverse proportion. Each step toward her 7:38 a.m. class whispered, *Again, I want. Him again.* The sidewalk glittered with fragments of granite echoing back: *Again, Prix. Again. And again.*

She tried to swap the heroin-rush of wanting for the methadone of guilt. She had disappointed Prix, somehow, more deeply than he had fulfilled her. He had seen something in her, wanted something she couldn't name—let alone give. And even if she had known, would she have given it? *Would you give up something you didn't understand?* She doubted it. And that made her feel small.

She suspected that what Prix had wanted from her was better—richer—than what she had taken from him. But she knew he would never put it into words. And yet, his mournful expression haunted her. Whether waking or dreaming, whether summoned or not, he returned—a sad, forsaken ghost.

Wake up, she told herself. A block from school. She still had to take the elevator to the tenth-floor art room. Her backpack weighed heavily on one shoulder, packed with the carefully folded white paper for the joint math-art assignment. The challenge was to make a recognizable curve using "computational origami," the result of her married teachers' summer course.

Judy and Marcus had been IMing the night before, rhapsodizing about *origami sekkei*, Marcus lapsing into the high-math dialect of his people. Marwa had found them both annoying.

She had been struggling to finish her Latin homework, trying to get through *Iceland's Bell*, the first novel for AP English, and pulling together notes for her history project on Chicago. Her stomach clenched at the memory—but at least she'd managed five solid hours of sleep after rising at 6:15. She could still taste the hot, sweet coffee she'd gulped at breakfast.

That's when she had noticed the broken-spined paperback on the kitchen counter, splayed open. Her mother's latest obsession was a book about psychics who claimed to have located Alexander the Great's tomb in Alexandria.

"I know by the feel... the older, the colder."

Her mother had also taken to taping Banana's favorite TV show, discussing the psychic's claims in earnest. As soon as Marwa walked into the room, the conversations stopped—as if her skepticism alone could sap their mystic charge.

At last, she was in the elevator, rising through the high school's core. When the doors opened onto the tenth floor, a display case greeted her: a portrait of the first non-Native American settler of Eschikagou—a Haitian who ran a trading and farming business near present-day Michigan Avenue, married to a Potawatomi woman named Catherine.

Catherine? Marwa blinked. *What does Eschikagou mean in Potawatomi?*

She shifted her backpack again. She recalled that the Potawatomi had called Bishop Henry Whipple "Straight Tongue"—the same Whipple who had been married to Evangeline, lover of Rose Cleveland.

Prix's tongue, she thought, *was anything but straight. It had ruched edges and a strange central crack.*

She passed a poster freshly pinned on her new math teacher's back bulletin board.

CLOUDS ARE NOT SPHERES,
MOUNTAINS ARE NOT CONES,
COASTLINES ARE NOT CIRCLES,
AND BARK IS NOT SMOOTH,
NOR DOES LIGHTNING TRAVEL IN A STRAIGHT LINE.
~Benoit B. Mandelbrot

A final jolt of nervous energy propelled Marwa into her assigned seat at one of the art class tables just as the bell rang at 7:38.

Across from her, Vivian Cheng was pulling something large and angular from a shopping bag. It was her homework, a tower-like origami structure with elegant arches, standing nearly two feet tall.

Marwa's heart dropped. It was a near-perfect replica of the model photo they'd been given.

"How did you do that?" Marwa whispered, awestruck.

Vivian shrugged.

"I just copied it."

Their red-haired art teacher shot them a silencing look. She held up an enlarged photograph of a woman clutching a glass jar filled with flies, and walked slowly around the room, making sure each student got a good look. The lid of the jar had holes—just enough for air, not escape.

"There's a psych researcher at Harvard," she began.

Groans rippled through the seniors.

"She uses this fly-in-a-jar demonstration to show how people get trapped by their own perceptions. Even when the lid is removed, the flies don't leave. They can't imagine another way."

A voice from the back piped up.

"Excuse me, Ms. Siegel? Where was that study published?"

Ms. Siegel carried on.

"They've been in the jar so long, they've accepted it. They're free, but they don't act free. They've committed to their confinement."

"Flies commit now?"

"If flies don't fly," someone quipped, "what do you call 'em?"

"Y'know what Picasso said when he climbed out of the caves at Lascaux?" another student offered.

"So now we know what *you* did on your summer vacation."

"He meant humanity didn't commit to living in caves," a would-be defender added.

"Thank you," Ms. Siegel said pointedly. "But Picasso's point was, *'We have invented nothing.'*"

A few students murmured, confused.

"What's that supposed to mean?"

"I thought we were folding paper?"

"Ms. Siegel, did you see Vivian's origami?" Judy cut in.

"May I point out that it's rude to point?" another student deadpanned.

"It's only a point in our limited dimensions," came a reply.

"The point *is...*" Ms. Siegel tried again, but Marwa interrupted her softly.

"Artists fly away."

GRTY

Art class ended at 8:20. Marwa took the stairs down to math with Judy and Vivian. Marcus was already waiting by the classroom door. He took Vivian's towering origami and compared it admiringly to his own—less polished but striking in its originality. Marwa, not interested in the competition, slid into her seat and stared at a new banner hanging above the front board.

THERE IS NO PERMANENT PLACE IN THE WORLD
FOR UGLY MATHEMATICS.

— G.H. HARDY

"How about ugly origami?" Marwa asked aloud.

Mr. Ralph, taking attendance, looked up and noticed her gaze.

"It doesn't take all kinds, Ms. Al-Hal," he said. "There just *are* all kinds."

Mr. Ralph was about the same age as Mr. Spin, but his hair had never settled on a single cut. It was gray, simultaneously curly and straight, flat in some places, cowlicked in others. It distracted his students nearly as much as it fascinated them. Some joked it was an example of topology in motion.

Despite appearances, he was the best math teacher at Stuyvesant. He claimed he could tell a student's grade just by "eyeballing" them. He now wandered the room, scanning origami submissions, and stopped at Marcus's desk.

"What do we have here?" Mr. Ralph asked, picking up Marcus's piece—interlacing concentric domes.

"Paper doesn't stretch," Marcus explained.

"It *tears* and *cuts*," Biren chimed in, waving theatrically bandaged fingers.

"You'll be a comedian before you're a mathematician," Mr. Ralph remarked, still examining the folds.

"I cheated," Marcus admitted. "I looked it up—it's about the pi condition. If a point is surrounded by four creases and you want it to fold flat, the opposite angles around the vertex need to add to 180 degrees. Pi radians."

Mr. Ralph rotated the model.

"You applied that?"

"I don't know what I did," Marcus said. "It was mystical. Like the paper told me how to fold it."

"We know almost nothing about curved creases," Mr. Ralph mused.

"Oh, please say that again!" Biren called out, grinning.

Mr. Ralph turned toward Marwa.

"Your thoughts?"

"Well," Marwa said, glancing at Biren, "aside from him being a pig, and therefore completely non-halal... I thought of protein folding. That's not always pretty."

She nodded at the Hardy quote on the banner.

Vivian added, "It's interesting how math shows up in paper."

"Everything is math," Mr. Ralph said. "Everything affirms the essential unity of mathematics. For all the growing varieties of maths, it's *e pluribus unum* all the time."

Biren asked, "Which came first, the *unum* or the *pluribus*?"

A sharp BANG stopped the banter cold.

It came from above, not like an engine roar, but something different. The time was 8:46:26 A.M.

The lights flickered, then steadied.

The room jolted.

Biren's origami, perched near the edge of his desk, drifted silently to the floor.

"Will you look at that?" he said.

But it wasn't clear whether he meant the falling origami, the trembling lights, or the view out the southern window where students and teacher now gathered.

They stared at the north face of the North Tower.

"What happened?"

"Some idiot flew into the WTC."

Then, without warning, a massive fireball exploded from the black gash—two hundred feet wide, brilliant orange against the sky.

"Holy shit."

"What floor? My mother's on sixty-eight."

And then, whatever had struck the tower, struck them too.

Mr. Ralph swiftly sent the class back to their seats and lowered the blinds. The students obeyed in silence, eyes fixed on him as he walked to the door, spoke briefly to someone outside, nodded, and returned.

He shut the windows behind the blinds.

"Let's move the desks away from the windows. As far back as we can."

A few students were already clutching their phones, trying to call home, but none were getting through.

Eventually, more began lining up requests to use the phone bank in the school lobby.

"I don't think that's a good idea," Mr. Ralph said, his voice calm but firm. "If you've got third period free, you can go then. For now, let's wait. Wait for the bell. Or for information."

The classroom settled into a heavy hush, pierced only by the chaos outside of endless sirens shrieking from every direction, all heading to a single destination. Shouts echoed in the hallways—distorted, unintelligible.

Inside, whispered curses were hurled at useless cell phones.

From beyond the school, a distant rumble, and then a thunderous boom, reverberated five blocks away.

Then they heard it.

A second plane.

Why hadn't they heard the first one?

As if guided by instinct, the entire class leaned in unison toward the shuttered windows—first curious, then recoiling as the sound surged past them, Dopplering south.

"Oh my God," a girl whispered, catching her breath. "Not the Statue of Liberty—"

But the roar veered back north, directly toward them.

The class shrank inward, huddled in their tightly packed seats. Mr. Ralph stood between them and the windows, his body instinctively shielding them.

9:02:54 A.M.

There was no flash of lightning—only the thunder, a single, deafening crack. Heads ducked, hands shot up to cover ears, and even through the explosive sound, a low, drawn-out moan escaped from the room. Not a scream. Not a sob. A human vibration of fear pressed through clenched teeth.

The lights flickered. The building trembled.

When the students opened their eyes, they saw Mr. Ralph leaning forward behind his desk, hands flat on the surface, arms locked, holding himself steady. All eyes turned toward the sealed windows. The heat in the room was growing.

Mr. Ralph met their gazes and shook his head slowly, as if confirming what no one wanted to believe.

"The South Tower, I guess."

A moment later, the Principal's voice crackled through the PA system at the front of the room.

"Please remain calm and stay in the building. There are currently no trains or buses running in Lower Manhattan. If you leave, you won't be able to get home. There is nowhere safe to go. The streets are dangerous due to falling debris. Stay in the building. Stay away from any south-facing windows. Those are the ones near the Statue of Liberty. We have school security, and federal agents are already here. If someone asks for ID, please show them your program card or school ID. Stay calm. Go to class if you can. The second period bell will ring at 9:07 as usual. Go to your third period class. If you linger in the hallways, we don't have the space for movement. If you have a free period and want to sit quietly, the theater is open. I'll try to give you an update before 10:30. Thank you."

Time seemed to stop.

No one noticed the five minutes pass. Then, automatically, the bell melody sounded.

And, just as automatically, the students rose and filed out.

Judy and Marwa clasped hands briefly in the corridor. Then Marwa went to Latin with Vivian. Marcus disappeared into his third-period class.

In the hallways, there were scattered tears, but some sounded theatrical, like younger girls imitating emotion. Elsewhere, a few boys postured with low, bravado-laced curses.

Marwa and Vivian stepped into the Latin classroom. Their teacher, Ms. Margolis, greeted them at the door.

Three years ago, Marwa had thought she sounded like the witch from *Hansel and Gretel*. But now, Ms. Margolis's fluent Latin felt like a balm, like a connection to something ancient and eternal. Above the chalkboard, the familiar posters displayed phrases translated long ago. Their meanings floated in the air now, strangely soothing.

QUOT HOMINES, TOT SENTENIAE.
(There are as many opinions as there are men.)

HOMO SUM: HUMANI NIHIL A ME ALIENUM PUTO.
(I am a man: nothing human is alien to me.)

Marwa's favorite was, *PROXIMUS SUM EGOMET MIHI...* I am closest to myself.

The door opened, and the electronic melody played.

Marwa was struck by a sudden, frantic realization.

Joey—I have to get Joey!

"Ms. Margolis," she said, turning but unable to move toward her seat, "I have to get my little brother. He's across the street at 234, at Independence."

"So's mine," Vivian added, her expression sharp and focused like a drawn sword.

"I understand," Ms. Margolis replied calmly. "Sit down, ladies. Now."

They obeyed.

More students trickled into the classroom, though many seats remained empty.

At her desk, Ms. Margolis lifted their text, the Terence play *The Woman of Andros*.

"We'll skip the rest of the Prologue today. Let's begin with Act I," she instructed.

The moments that followed felt dreamlike, disconnected. A classmate read aloud, stumbling through a translation.

Ms. Margolis supplied the line smoothly, "Of surpassing beauty and in the bloom of youth."

She then called on Vivian.

Vivian's voice was steady, cutting the silence like her fencing saber.

"Percussit ilico animum. Attat! hoc illud est."

She translated, "This hit me at once. Oh no! This is it—"

Her breath caught. "*Hinc illae lacrimae—*"

She looked up at the teacher.

"Hence these tears," said Ms. Margolis.

"Hence these tears," Vivian echoed.

Marwa whispered the next line to herself, '*Quam timeo quorsum evadas!'— 'I dread to think where this is leading.'*

But she was interrupted.

The PA speaker at the front of the room crackled to life. This time, it was the Assistant Principal.

"A bell will ring shortly. All students are to report to Homeroom, which will be extended until further notice."

Marwa and Vivian exchanged a look.

The next thing Marwa knew, she and Vivian were on the marble staircase, weaving through the crowded lobby packed with grim-faced men in uniforms. Stuy security, teachers, and dozens of students all headed toward the exits onto Chambers and West Streets.

Outside, they were hit by light, smoke, and the sharp wail of sirens. White police vans. Wooden barriers. Uniforms everywhere—NYPD, and massive, rifle-carrying military personnel. Their familiar corner—West and Chambers—had transformed into something resembling a war zone. A new Wall Street, dividing those allowed to pass south from those who were not.

The two girls joined hands so as not to be separated in the tide of urgency pushing them east on Chambers. They were surrounded by clamor and confusion, but in her mind, Marwa heard the voice of her Latin homework.

Urbs vias latas habet. Per vias urbis contendimus. The city has wide streets. We hurry through the city streets.

Ash. Powder. Timber Wolf. Shadow. Charcoal. Char. Sere. Payne's Gray. *Pain.*

Marwa tasted the smoke—gray and black—and saw the gash in the tower, fires flaring orange, red, yellow. White beams slashed up like chalk against a clear blue sky. Towering. Terrible. Stunning. *Irresistible.*

Looking south—south was all that existed now—they saw debris erupting, falling, flying.

They were falling.

Men and women stood in the black wound of the North Tower, waving jackets and shirts for help. The faces were on the north and west sides.

A man in a white shirt and dark slacks, no jacket, dark hair, arms pinned to his sides by the force of descent, fell. His legs were crossed as if mid-dream on a bed. He plummeted like a figure in suspended sleep.

He must have kept his arms stiffly at his sides, because many others fell like ragdolls...twisting, flailing, perhaps unconscious or already dead.

"Oh, don't—"

"NO! NO, NO!"

But there was no stopping it. No stopping them. The people falling. The people moving. It was as if they themselves had crossed West Street without noticing, swept through traffic, through crowds—minute particles in a catastrophic Brownian motion.

Then the earth shuddered. Marwa and Vivian were thrown into each other, steadied by the arms of others, equally off-balance.

And then—a sound.

Low, deep. A rumble.

From above.

Cries broke out around them as the crowd momentarily froze in place. And then...

The South Tower.

It was falling.

Cloaked in billowing smoke—oh, might that smoke cushion it? Might it soften the impact? —

But no. It was collapsing. Folding into itself.

Its furious roar gave rise to something worse...a monstrous volcanic cloud, racing north, veering west.

Straight toward them.

Somehow...randomly, reflexively...they had made it inside the elementary school.

In the rush, Marwa lost sight of Vivian. She was too focused, scanning the halls for Joey's classroom, momentarily forgetting that Vivian's brother was in the same class. Remarkably, neat lines of small children were already filing past her, led by teachers whose faces bore a calm, solemn focus. Marwa recognized Mrs. Shapiro, Joey's teacher—and there he was, eighth in line behind her.

Joey.

Was that the moment the pain started in her chest? A sharp, unfamiliar ache that made her wonder if she had been shot? Was Joey in danger of being shot? Or was it something else, a physical echo of what she'd seen outside—when her mind had instinctively, insanely, calculated the math of falling bodies? $V = g \times t$ (velocity equals gravity times time). The impact. The leaping, tumbling, still-living bodies.

All she knew was that it hurt to breathe.

Mrs. Shapiro recognized both girls. Vivian was already in the line, quietly holding her little brother's hand. And then Marwa realized, so was she. Her hand was clasped tightly around Joey's.

They followed another group outside, heading west on Warren Street toward the river. At the end of Warren stood P.S. 89, which they joined in evacuating to a nearby cove marina. Fireboats were moored there, waiting to ferry the children across the Hudson to New Jersey. A Circle Line ferry curved toward a slip, and their fireboat appeared to be lining up for the same path.

They were aboard.

Joey gripped Marwa's hand tightly and looked up at her. "Your eye is bleeding," he said.

Marwa touched her face with her free hand. It came away sticky, wet with blood. She hadn't noticed. The sight jogged a memory of injured people walking north past her on West Street, faces and shirts streaked with red.

Maybe, she thought, it had been *their* blood that got on her.

"It's just the lid," she said gently. "It doesn't hurt at all."

How lucky, she thought, that the children were distracted. The dark, roaring storm of smoke behind them was momentarily forgotten in the presence of yellow-striped, black-slickered firefighters—towering figures in hard black helmets, like a swarm of human wasps—guiding the tugboat through the splashing, sunlit Hudson. It plowed forward, slicing white foam through silver water, leaving a broad wake behind.

Joey was still talking.

"Eschikagou means *Stinkland*," he said. "Onions grew in the swamp. The Black man who started Chicago married a Potawatomi lady named Kittihawa, but what does *Potawatomi* mean?"

Marwa shook her head, smiling faintly.

"The Hudson River has lots of native names," Joey continued. "It depends which tribe is telling the story."

"*Shawnatawty, Cahohatatea, Shatemuc*," recited a little girl in braids, hand-in-hand with her buddy.

Joey beamed.

"*Mahicanituck*—the river of the Mohicans!"

"What was the name of Hudson's ship?" Mrs. Shapiro asked, gently encouraging the group.

"The *Half Moon!*" a student called out.

The teacher nodded, then turned to Marwa and Vivian.

"On September 13, 1609, on a clear day like this..." she stopped, caught herself. "Hudson sailed from the Narrows into the Upper Bay. Twenty-eight log canoes came out to meet them, bringing oysters and beans, and the welcomers smoked tobacco in big pipes of yellow copper. Hudson called it 'the noble, nameless stream.'"

She looked back over her shoulder, toward the burning city.

Then she saw it.

The North Tower, groaning, roaring, collapsing.

Mrs. Shapiro covered her mouth in horror as another enormous plume of black smoke surged into the sky.

⚶⚶⚶

Marwa didn't remember the landing. Didn't remember disembarking in New Jersey. All she knew was that she had returned to herself later, still holding Joey's hand, seated beside him on a metal folding chair.

Vivian sat nearby with her brother. Mrs. Shapiro and other teachers remained close.

Marwa had no idea where they were.

The overhead fluorescent lights buzzed coldly, even though it was still bright outside. Her right eye had been bandaged. She could only see from the left. The injured side throbbed, hot and swollen, and reminded her of when she'd had her ears pierced.

That had happened in the past.

If there had been a past, then maybe there could be a future.

Maybe.

But for now, there was only *now*.

A cluster of teachers stood talking nearby.

Marwa noticed, through her one good eye, that Vivian was leaning slightly toward them, eavesdropping with fierce attention.

"What exactly did he say?" Mrs. Shapiro was asking one of the kindergarten teachers.

"'Giant towers will fall down, will fall down, will fall down, giant towers will fall down, my fair lady!'" the teacher replied. "Fawaz didn't say it. He sang it. And his whole group danced along."

"And *when* exactly did he sing that?" a third teacher asked.

"Last Thursday, I told you," the woman said, shaking her head, hands covering her face in a gesture that bordered on a keening. "I asked him what he meant, and he pointed right at the Twin Towers."

Her voice dropped.

"He said, 'Those two buildings won't be standing there next week, and you shouldn't go on a bus.' Then Abdel told him to shut up and pushed him, so I had to give them both timeouts. I wrote it all down. Reported it to the new principal, but she was overwhelmed with the first week of school. And really, how seriously can you take something a five-year-old says?"

Marwa sat nearby, her mind fogged, as if the black billows now blowing south and east from New Jersey to Long Island had veered direction and filled her head instead. She thought she could smell smoke and was *horrified* to be filtering through her lungs the cinders of souls incinerated above her city.

But there was no real smoke in this building. Only memory.

"Where is Daddy?" Joey asked quietly.

Marwa looked down at his curls, his wide dark eyes.

"I tried to call Ummee," she said. "The phones still aren't working. We'll go home soon."

Vivian's brother suddenly let go of her hand.

"You're shaking," he said. "Stop shaking."

Vivian looked at Marwa and in that instant, Marwa knew. Vivian's father worked there. *Had* worked there.

Marwa took out her cell phone. It was connecting.

Everyone stilled.

Then, a breath on the line, "Joey?"

"Ummee, Ummee," Marwa whispered. "I've got him right here. He's safe."

She handed Joey the phone.

Joey snatched it from her.

"Ummee, I'm in New Jersey," he said quickly. "Marwa cut her eye. She's okay. How is Daddy?"

The smile that bloomed on his face changed everything.

Marwa didn't look at Vivian.

Joey handed the phone back.

"Ummee said you."

Her mother's voice came through, scattered, but urgent. They couldn't return to Battery Park City. The apartment was contaminated or something. Her father was making arrangements for them to stay somewhere in Brooklyn. Don't meet at Masjid Salam, the one on 116th near Columbia. And absolutely not Masjid al-Farah, downtown. Not there either. The call dissolved into static, then cut out completely.

Marwa stared at the phone, as if her mother were still inside it.

"Try yours," she told Vivian.

Vivian's phone was dead. No signal. No hope.

Her face flushed red with fury.

"Did you know?" she hissed. "Did you all know? Are you happy?"

Marwa absorbed it without flinching.

Vivian is scared, she thought. *Scared, and hurt, and furious.*

And I...feel nothing at all. Only protective. Of Joey.

"No," Marwa said quietly. "I'm not happy."

She might have added *"either" but* didn't.

GRTW

How strange it was, living through something and remembering it only in fragments. Shreds. Images torn from sequence. The past refused to line up. She couldn't remember when they crossed the river again—by boat? Daylight or night?

When did she hear about the other planes?

The Pentagon. The field in Pennsylvania.

When had she learned two jets took off from Boston? DC to LA—*that* one chilled her. But Boston to LA—no memory of that.

Only one detail stayed sharp.

Denim Prix was the ninety-third passenger on American Airlines Flight 11, which left Logan International in Boston at 7:59 A.M.

It crashed into the North Tower at 8:46 A.M.

The exact moment Biren had been asking, "Which came first—the *unum* or the *pluribus?*"

17

A DIFFERENT NORMAL

Marwa was blind in one eye. Not a single New York City schoolchild died that day. The *New York Times* reported that "just minutes after the first plane struck the World Trade Center, the full sense of chaos and panic had yet to reach the PATH station below the Twin Towers." But the dispatcher on duty already sensed something was terribly wrong as he directed the arrival of thousands of commuters during the morning rush.

"Rich," the dispatcher radioed to Richie Moran, the PATH system's train master, "What are you going to do with us? I just unloaded."

Moran, supervising train traffic from his office in Journal Square, Jersey City, gave a clear directive, "We want people out of the station, not in. Load the train back up and get it out of there."

Over the next 20 minutes, PATH supervisors made swift decisions. Several trains en route to the World Trade Center were rerouted. One train that had just arrived was ordered to keep passengers aboard and reverse course. Another was instructed to loop through the station without stopping and return to New Jersey.

Their efficiency saved lives. Port Authority officials would later credit these actions, captured in dispatch transcripts, with saving hundreds.

"Take those passengers with you," Moran told a conductor whose Hoboken-bound train was carrying an estimated 1,000 people.

"I will not open my doors," the conductor replied. "I'm taking them with me."

Passengers who had already disembarked were quickly evacuated by police, and the station emptied rapidly.

But one last train, manned only by a conductor and an engineer, was dispatched from Jersey City to pick up a dozen or so PATH workers who were still in the station.

"We're going to use you as an evacuation train," Moran told the crew.

Then a complication arose. A man who had been sleeping on the platform refused to board.

"You'll have to get the passenger on board," Moran instructed. "If he won't come, you'll have to leave him."

The crew asked if a police officer could be dispatched, but Moran responded gravely: "We have an extreme situation at the World Trade Center."

The final train left at 9:11 a.m., 48 minutes before the South Tower collapsed. No passengers were stranded in the tunnels. Even the sleeping man was safely evacuated.

⚚ ℜ ☥ ⚚

Marwa never cried—not even when she finally saw her father again.

He greeted her the way he did in prayer: fingertips touching, palms open, inclined. A posture of penitence. Gratitude. Plea.

Among the first obituaries to appear in *The New York Times*, some with photographs, some without, was a section on page A25, dated September 13, 2001.

William Feehan, Fire Dept. Leader, Dies at 71
William Feehan, the Fire Department's second-highest official, whose knowledge and cunning in battling fires himself made him the stuff of legend to his firefighters, died Tuesday when the south tower of the World Trade Center collapsed on his command station.

Peter J. Ganci, 54, Fire Chief,
While Leading Tower Rescue
Peter J. Ganci, the New York City Fire Department's highest-ranking uniformed officer, died on Tuesday in the collapse of the World Trade Center towers.

Barbara Olson, 45, Advocate and Conservative Commentator
Barbara K. Olson, who was killed on Tuesday on the commercial jetliner that was hijacked and flown into the Pentagon, was well known to television viewers across the nation as a combative and confident political commentator representing the conservative Republican point of view.

Mychal Judge, 68, Chaplain for Fire Dept.
The Rev. Mychal F. Judge, a chaplain with the New York City Fire Department since 1992, died amid a rain of debris at the World Trade Center on Tuesday as he ministered to victims. He was 68 and lived in a Franciscan friary across West 31st Street from a firehouse. His head was struck by debris, according to friars at the Holy Name Province of the Franciscan Friars

Lisa J. Raines, 42, a Lobbyist for Biotechnology
Lisa J. Raines, one of the earliest and most prominent lobbyists for the biotechnology industry, died on Tuesday in the crash of the hijacked airplane that hit the Pentagon.

Ace Bailey, 53, Hockey Scout and Player
Garnet (Ace) Bailey, a scout for the Los Angeles Kings of the National Hockey League and a former player in the league, was among the passengers killed when the hijacked United Airlines Flight 175 crashed into the World Trade Center on Tuesday.

Berry Berenson Perkins, 53, Photographer Known for Fashion. Berry Berenson Perkins, a photographer and eclectic fashion plate of the 1970's before she settled into marriage with the actor Anthony Perkins, was killed on Tuesday, a passenger on American Airlines Flight 11, which was the first jetliner to strike the World Trade Center, a spokeswoman for the family said.

Robert Doucette, 23, Times Square Billboard Model
'Grand Prix' Robert Doucette (Prix Freeman), nicknamed 'Grand Prix' as the international fashion world's highest paid male model, died Tuesday in the crash of American Airlines Flight 11. His magnified face and form (often photographed by Berry Berenson Perkins, seated beside him on the jetliner) looked down at the Crossroads of the World in Times Square and in similar intersections worldwide.

The *New York Times* editor chose a photo of Denim Prix taken by Berry Berenson Perkins to accompany his obituary. The image seemed to embody the contradictions of the modern world, contradictions that would have been incomprehensible to the medieval mind.

Television commentators and *Letters to the Editor* quickly began to conflate Prix's photograph with the images of the ravaged Towers. Somehow, it was less painful to display his face, his mixed heritage, than to revisit the horrors of that September morning.

For Marwa, it was surreal to see Prix not only rendered two-dimensionally in the media but also filtered through her own altered perception. Her world had flattened. Everything looked off, like lamps that were unplugged.

She looked strange to herself, too, with the black patch covering her right eye.

She didn't mind the Stuy students, now attending split-session classes at Brooklyn Tech ("*Eck!*"), calling her "Popeye" and jokingly offering her spinach. Nothing really bothered her anymore—and it didn't bother her that *nothing mattered*.

Well, one thing mattered. Joey was safe. Joey was okay.

GRTψ

For the time being, they were living in a borrowed apartment in Brooklyn, vacant while its Egyptian owners stayed in their primary home in Alexandria. The connection came through the family of Sharif's fiancée.

Marwa's father had also relocated his office to Brooklyn, moving from the Deutsche Bank–Bankers Trust Building, which had directly faced the South Tower from Liberty Street. That forty-story skyscraper now stood shrouded in black, like a Muslim woman in full burka, concealing the deep, twenty-four-story gash torn into its north face.

In Brooklyn, Joey began attending a nearby private elementary school. Marwa's mother commuted to Columbia three times a week—without her headscarf. Even Banana had resumed her afternoons with Joey, tuning in faithfully to her psychic's television show (now dedicated to "reading" the families of WTC victims).

When would they be allowed to return to their apartment in Battery Park City?

No one knew. And Marwa didn't care.

She had recently learned that the entire neighborhood of Battery Park City had been built on landfill—land that was excavated to make way for the World Trade Center itself. She also discovered that the place she was born—southern Queens—shared geological roots with the Brooklyn Flatlands, where they now lived. Both were part of the same Jamaica Bay wetlands, shaped by a sandbar that once linked Far Rockaway to Long Island's massive barrier island.

To make sense of it all, their father brought home a Hagstrom atlas to help them orient themselves in their new environment—what Joey proudly called their "refugee haven."

Joey quickly claimed the atlas as his own. His favorite place on the map? Big Muck Creek, nestled above Silver Hole Marsh in Jamaica Bay.

Except he believed Big Muck should flow *out of* Silver Hole—an observation he found endlessly hilarious, his own private joke blending geography and toilet humor in equal measure.

GRTW

At Brooklyn Tech, the Stuyvesant students began their split-session school day with first period starting at 1:30 p.m. and the final bell ringing at 6:23 p.m.

One of Marwa's first-period art classmates organized the painting of two large murals in Greenwich Village, scheduled for Sunday, September 16. In class, nearly everyone offered imagery or ideas to be part of, or inspire, the murals' themes. Marwa didn't. Instead, she found herself absorbed by the obsessive sketches of a younger classmate, who kept drawing the same face over and over again—the face of someone he'd seen while fleeing toward the Staten Island Ferry. It was a face without a body.

Some sketches were clearly of a young woman—no facial hair, no shadows. Others resembled someone Asian, perhaps even his fraternal twin.

177

"I can't get it right! I have to get it right!" the boy hissed before breaking down in tears.

A classmate walked him to the nurse's office, where school psychologists had set up temporary stations.

On Sunday, under the same piercing blue skies and sharp autumn light as the Tuesday before—with shadows long and deeply black—over 400 Stuy students gathered at Washington Square Village, where Judy lived. It was September 16.

Their first mural depicted a tree growing from rubble, its branches sprawling across twelve-by-eighty-foot lengths of tarp. "Tree of Life" was painted above it in over thirty-five languages. Students daubed green paint on each other's faces as often as they did on the mural itself.

"War paint," someone joked.

"Peace paint," another corrected.

The second mural was a montage. A city skyline, an American flag, a police badge, a Red Cross armband, and an upside-down firefighter's helmet with a sapling sprouting from it. At the bottom, a crumbled brick wall bore a spray-painted message.

NEW YORK THANKS ITS HEROES

From a second-story apartment window, someone snapped a photo of the students. Marwa, looking around, noticed that many were smiling—some even raising their arms as they sang a Beatles song from the '60s. Because the photo was taken facing the sun, students were shielding their eyes, laughing, and telling Marwa how lucky she was to have her black eye patch.

A long-haired boy from her math class stood with his boyfriend, both holding up peace signs. Marcus, in a black T-shirt, turned his head away from the camera. Judy had her hands on her hips and was peering downward through her glasses.

Marwa closed her good eye.

In the dark, she saw the face again, the one from the sketches. The headless face she had at first mistaken for a mask.

GRTY

In September, a flurry of instant messages began circulating—many initiated in art class but quickly spreading beyond. The topic: the architectural influences on the downed Twin Towers.

BEKInd: do u c Islamic correspondences/influences on...

BEKInd: Japanese architect Yamasaki in designing the...

BEKInd: WTCs as a plaza similar to mecca w/2 minarets?

Ram84: i c 2nd gen Japanese American +

Ram84: pointed arches like tuning forks

Mars429: Romanesque arches evolved into gothic ones when...

Mars429: crusaders were impressed by arabesque design

Ag47coff: crusaders?

Mars429: infidels

Ag47coff: thought a Martian had taken over your body

BEKInd: stay off her body, we're talking art & arch, mathboy

Ram84: well-built is well-built, bones are bones

Mars429: "The innovation known as the Gothic (pointed) arch emerged from intercultural contact between Europeans and Muslims during the Crusades. It became popular in religious architecture because it allowed structures to soar higher—like early skyscrapers. Romanesque cathedrals, with rounded arches, were limited in height."

BEKInd: u r the fastest cut & paster in the west!

BEKInd: "Yamasaki was a leader in merging modernism with Islamic influence. He was favored by patrons of the Bin Laden family, including the Saudi royal family."

Ram84: he designed the Dhahran airport in the 50s

Mars429: he intended the plaza as a...

Mars429: mecca-like retreat from wall street's narrow streets

Mars429: "Yamasaki's plaza echoed Mecca's sacred ensemble: (1) the Kaaba, (2) the burial sites of Hagar & Ishmael, (3) the holy spring."

Ag47coff: you know sugar cubes aren't actually perfect cubes?

BEKInd: I found this...

BEKInd: "Yamasaki wrapped the Towers in a shimmering skin that also functioned as a massive truss. It followed Islamic tradition—enclosing geometric power in intricate filigree."

BEKInd: wasn't it blasphemy to build a mecca to mammon?

Mars429: the shimmering filigree is the mark of the holy

Ag47coff: filigree is full of holes...

Ag47coff: someone's religion is someone else's mythology

Ram84: Gaudi designed a 1908 plan...

Ram84: for a skyscraper hotel on the WTC site, taller than the Chrysler

BEKInd: found it. looks phallic. very barcelony.

Mars429: it's deco

Ram84: not gaudy?

BEKInd: punny. Gaudí the Barcelonian rhymes w/...

BEKInd: alexander's father the Macedonian. discuss!

Ram84: not. Alex doesn't look Greek.

Marwa signed off. She wanted to return to reading *Iceland's Bell*, the novel she'd set aside when her class was given a new assignment: to bring in—or write—a poem expressing their feelings.

An ice island. That, Marwa thought, best expressed how she felt.

She felt more at home within the pages of that book—set in 18th-century Iceland, two centuries in the past—than anywhere or anytime in Brooklyn. According to the introduction, the events of the novel unfolded around the same time Lewis and Clark were being guided to the Pacific by Sacagawea.

Marwa especially appreciated being able to understand enough Latin that she didn't have to rely on the endnotes to decipher the scholarly passages. The narrator, immersed in the preservation of decaying Icelandic literature, lingered reverently over every fragmented finding.

"Membranum," (Parchment) he said, glancing at his friend the bishop.

Together, they examined several sheets of calfskin, sewn at the spine, the thread long since torn or rotted away. The surface was black and grimy, but the Gothic script was still discernible. They handled the brittle pages as if they were the delicate flesh of a skinless embryo, muttering Latin words like *"pretiosissima," "thesaurus," "cimelium"*—most precious, a treasure, a jewel.

"The script dates to around 1300," said Arnas Arnaeus. "My guess is that this is a page from the *Skalda* itself... It's come to this, Reverend Thorsteinn, the people who once possessed the most distinguished *litteras* in the northern world now walk on calfskin, or eat it, rather than read the words written upon it."

Marwa wanted to finish the final section, *Fire in Copenhagen*, where the lovers—separated for twenty years— meet again.

He waited just beyond the threshold until the maidservant passed him. Then he stepped into the room.

She said nothing, only closed the door behind her, stepped forward, and greeted him with a kiss. She wrapped her arms around his neck and pressed her face to his cheek. He stroked her long, fair hair, now streaked with pale threads. She stayed there for a while, her face buried in his chest, before looking up.

"I didn't think you would come, Arni," she said. "Yet somehow I knew you would."

"Some come late," he replied.

"I have a book for you," she said.

"That's like you," he said.

"It was my blessed father's dearest book."

He began unwrapping it slowly from its silk cover.

She waited eagerly for that telltale gleam, the one his eyes always held when encountering a new old book.

But suddenly, he paused, looked up, smiled, and said, "I've lost my dearest book."

"Which one?"

"The one we found together."

Then he explained, casually, with resignation, how he had lost the *Skalda*.

"It's a terrible loss," she said.

"Most terrible," he agreed. "When a man loses his love for precious books."

"I thought a man could love a lost treasure as long as he missed it."

"A man doesn't know precisely when the longing disappears," he said. "It's like a wound that's healed, or like death. You don't know when the pain stopped, nor exactly when you died. Suddenly you're healed. Suddenly, dead."

Marwa kept reading, rushing to the heart of their dialogue.

"As long as we are sitting here together, we have everything."

She leaned back, repeating the final word softly.

"Everything."

"In any case," he said, "only one thing exists in our lives."

She whispered, "One thing."

"Do you know why I've come?"

"Yes," she said. "So that you will never part from me again."

Then Marwa turned to her favorite passage, the one she reread again and again, the one where they imagine their perfect future together.

"We'll build palaces," she said, "no less grand than those Governor Gyldenløve built in Denmark, funded by taxes from Iceland."

He replied, "A splendid courthouse will rise at Thingvellir, and we'll hang another bell there, larger and more melodious than the one the king demanded from Iceland, the one the hangman ordered Jón Hreggviðsson to tear down."

"...And we'll ride throughout the land on white horses," she said.

Governor *Golden-Love*, Marwa thought, smiling to herself. *A more melodious bell.*

"And we'll ride throughout the land on white horses," Marwa whispered aloud.

⁂

Marwa's patched eye itched. The ophthalmologist's examination had revealed delicate, branching tributaries of blood vessels slowly returning vision to that eye. Meanwhile, her uninjured eye ached intermittently from overuse—but she was strictly forbidden from even touching it.

Her mother, relying on folk wisdom, kept used tea bags chilled in a glass in the refrigerator. She would gently place the cool squares over Marwa's strained eye. Marwa protested, skeptical of these old remedies—but the chilled compress felt soothing. And more than that, the gesture—her mother's quiet care—felt even better.

One day, a thick envelope arrived, forwarded from their old address to their temporary exile in Brooklyn. It was from Desiree Lipshitz, now living on Long Island.

"Please just let me know you're okay," Desiree had written. "I didn't email because I didn't want to upset you. My AP English teacher (yes, I know you Stuy kids do AP in junior year) handed out this poem, and I grabbed an extra copy for you, just in case you haven't seen it.

"I thought John Hollander (he teaches at Yale) was the best concrete poet I'd ever come across. Until this.

"No one's really thinking about college stuff right now—except my mother...

Love, Desiree."

Enclosed was a copy of *Manhattan*, a poem by Howard Horowitz that had appeared on the *New York Times* Op-Ed page on August 30, 1997. The poem doubled as an image of a topographical map of Manhattan Island, drawn entirely from lines of poetry. Where bridges and tunnels extended beyond the landmass, the lines of verse followed suit—stretching out from the northern end of Manhattan.

> *the George Washington Bridge. Walk east*
> *toward the Bronx across High Bridge;*

to 125th Street,

> *Kids splash around a hydrant as lovers embrace on a*
> *Riverside Park bench and rush-hour traffic is stalled on the Triborough Bridge.*

Marwa quickly scanned down Manhattan Island, but there were no words for Battery Park City, so she looked a few blocks north in the poem where Stuyvesant caught her good eye, and she read the poem to its end at the tip of Manhattan.

> *delicatessen sells good chicken soup; enjoy zuppa di*
> *pesca at the Festival of San Gennaro, or bird's nest*
> *soup in Chinatown. Marchers to City Hall cross the Brooklyn Bridge*
> *to demonstrate, as tourists at South Street Seaport*
> *eat lunch with a view. The Fulton Fish Market is*
> *mobbed before dawn. Precambrian stocks bond the*
> *upper crust with solid foundations below the*
> *Trade Towers, Trinity Church and Wall Street.*
> *Ferryboats to Staten Island, Ellis*
> *Island, the Statue of Liberty,*
> *and Governor's Island*
> *depart from wind-*
> *swept docks*
> *at Battery*
> *Park.*

Marwa emailed Desiree, thanking her for giving her "her

first happy moment since," though she left out the fact that Desiree had also saved her from a homework dilemma.

Thanks to the poem Desiree sent, Sunny wouldn't have to stress about using Adonis's *The Funeral of New York* for the assignment—though Marwa knew she herself could never have read aloud Adonis's *A Mirror for Khalida*, the one that shook her to her core:

"The bed forgets the fire / of its past and dies. / Pillows are only pillows / now."

Her eye was dry and burning. She wanted it to cry, but it wouldn't.

She wandered into the kitchen of the unfamiliar apartment, took a teabag from the glass in the refrigerator, and returned to the room she shared with Joey. She lay down on the bed and let the cool tea bag draw out the fire behind her eyelid.

All the everyday sounds of the apartment buzzed around her, but nothing was as real, as searing, as the image burned into her mind: the jet. She was beside Prix. Screaming metal. Doom. The crush. The heat. The pain. And then, the wall of ice.

"You're making that sound again, Marwa."

Joey's small hand shook her shoulder, jostling the tea bag from her eye. Afternoon light spilled into the room.

"Stop making that sound," he said. "You wake me up all the time at night."

In an instant, Marwa saw the dream from the night before: a mirror. Her ow face, but not her own. A stranger. She was speaking to Judy. Awake now, she realized something—she had never before *known* she was lying in a dream.

"I want my room back," Joey said.

"Everything will get back to normal eventually," Marwa replied, because that's what you were supposed to say to kids.

"A *different* normal."

"What?"

"That's what my new teacher said. I liked my Independence teacher better. She's older."

Marwa opened her eye and sat up.

"You're funny," she said.

"I'm *hungry*," Joey corrected.

"You're always hungry."

Joey let out a playful growl and transformed into a hungry bear, pouncing on the bed and gnawing on Marwa's arm with bear cub teeth.

She tried to fend him off, then attempted to lift him off the bed—but he squirmed free, bolted from the room, and beat her to the kitchen.

He roared in victory.

She let him win.

18

SEPTEMBER 2001 - JUNE 2002

Sunny began to read Adonis's poem.

> *"New York,*
> *you are a woman standing in the wind's archways,*
> *a figure remote as an atom,*
> *a mere dot in the numbered sky,*
> *one thigh in the clouds, the other in water.*
> *Tell me the name of your star.*
> *A battle between grass and computers is coming.*
> *The whole century is hemorrhaging.*
> *Its head adds disaster to disaster.*
> *Its waist is Asia.*
> *Its legs belong to nothing...*
> *I know you, O body, swimming in the musk of poppies.*
> *You bare one nipple..."*

Sunny's voice caught.

> *"...and its twin—..."*

She coughed.

"…to me.
I look at you and dream of snow.
I look at you and wait for autumn."

She sat down. Judy followed, reading next.

Caw, caw, caw, crows shriek in the white sun over
gravestones in Long Island.
Lord, Lord, Lord, Naomi beneath this grass—my half-life,
and my own as hers.
Caw, caw, my eye be buried in the same ground where I
stand, in Angel.
Lord, Lord, great Eye…"

Judy glanced at Marwa's patch.

"…that stares on All, moves in a black cloud.
Caw, caw, strange cry of
Beings flung up into sky over the waving trees.
Lord, Lord, O Grinder of Giant Beyonds,
my voice in a boundless field, in Sheol.
Caw, caw, the call of Time rent out of foot and wing,
an instant in the universe…"

Judy stopped briefly.

"Lord, Lord…"

She took a breath.

"…an echo in the sky, the wind through ragged leaves,"

It was hard.

"...the roar of memory.
Caw, caw, all years, my birth a dream.
Caw, caw, New York, the bus,
the broken shoe..."

She looked up, faltered, the teacher nodded.

"...the vast high school—caw, caw—
All Visions of the Lord.
Lord, Lord, Lord.
Caw, caw, caw.
Lord, Lord, Lord.
Caw, caw, caw.
Lord."

Judy had chosen Ginsberg's *Kaddish*. When she finished, Marcus stood and began reciting lines from the Jewish mourner's prayer—words Marwa remembered hearing at the cemetery.

Yis'ga'dal v'yis'kadash sh'may ra'bbo... v'imru Omein.

Several classmates murmured, *"Omein."*
Then a boy protested, annoyed.
"You can't say that. It doesn't count. We don't have a *minyan*. Girls don't count in the ten."
The Orthodox boy's remark stirred anger among the Jewish girls—until they realized Marcus wasn't reciting scripture. He was reading *his own poem*. He waited out the stir, then continued.

"Blessed are those that mourn, for they will be comforted.
Jets in the sky—
I force myself to look up at them.
"226 years ago, NYC fell
to the British,
at the start of the Revolutionary War;

this was taken as a sign that democracy couldn't win.
We'll tell our kids…"

Marcus paused.

"They said back then,
there wasn't much more to NYC in 1776
beyond Vesey Street.
Greenwich Village was country.
But Washington returned here in triumph,
as the first President of the R'pub-lic.
"New York's the heart—
systole… diastole—
of America.
"History
has many atrocities to tell us.
New York, New York,
lub dub, free dom."

A voice piped up, "*Of the R'pub-LICK?*"
"*Lub dub,*" another mocked. "*Free dumb?*"
"You're dumb. It's *free DOM,*" someone shot back.
"Marcus is serious."
"I hoped someone might laugh," Marcus said evenly.
"Yeah, that's exactly what you were going for, Silbercoff,"
the boy muttered.
Later that week, Biren read last. His piece was a rhythmic,
meditative chant.

"Monks, the All is aflame. What All is aflame?
The eye is aflame. Forms are aflame.
Consciousness at the eye is aflame.
Contact at the eye is aflame.
"And whatever there is that arises in dependence
on contact at the eye—
experienced as pleasure, pain,

or neither pleasure nor pain—
that too is aflame."

His voice was flat and trance-like. Marwa slipped into a strange, almost altered state as he continued.

"Aflame with what?
Aflame with the fire of passion,
the fire of aversion, the fire of delusion.
Aflame, I tell you, with birth, aging, and death,
with sorrows, lamentations, pains, distresses, and
despairs..."

Marwa's mind wandered, focused and unfocused, like the eye exercises she had to do. Her patch had just been removed that week.

She thought, *all words are imprecise generalizations of reality—but they're also lenses. Through them, sometimes, reality becomes clearer.*

Biren's chant went on.

"Seeing thus, the instructed noble disciple grows
disenchanted with the eye,
disenchanted with forms,
disenchanted with contact at the eye...
And whatever arises from that contact—
pleasure, pain, or neither—
he grows disenchanted."

For the first time, Marwa was genuinely impressed by Biren.

He paused, as if reading her thoughts. He looked straight at her.

She looked away.

"Disenchanted, he becomes dispassionate.
Through dispassion, he is fully released.
With full release comes the knowledge, "Fully released."
He discerns, "Birth is depleted. The holy life fulfilled. The
task done.
There is nothing further for this world."

It took courage to step back into the bull's-eye that was New York City. Before September ended, Liza Minnelli stood at Shea Stadium during a Mets-Braves game and belted out her signature song, *New York, New York*. The crowd roared. Her rendition was no longer a show tune—it had become, in her words, "a fight song... a call."

Marcus went to a Yankees game with his father, a lifelong fan, when the team reached the World Series. The Bronx Bombers lost, but it didn't matter. Just being there—thinking about baseball, about New York—was a win. The city could once again be imagined not only as Ground Zero's gray grave, but as Yankee Stadium's green diamond.

Classes resumed at Stuyvesant in mid-October. Marwa commuted from Brooklyn back to southern Manhattan for two weeks before her family was finally allowed to return to their apartment in Battery Park City—just in time for Joey's birthday during the first week of November. He rejoined his elementary school soon after.

The only thing Marwa missed about being a Brooklyn refugee was the split-day school schedule. Waking naturally in morning light had felt like a small grace. Now she was back to pre-dawn alarm clocks at 6:15 a.m. Her father still had to work in Brooklyn. Her family was quietly relieved that Sharif remained in Alexandria since New York was no longer a safe place to be a young man easily identified as Muslim.

Her senior classmates were deep into Early Admission applications, due for review by November first and final submission by November fifteenth. Ramadan would begin the sixteenth.

Marwa's guidance counselor grew impatient with her detachment, reminding her that if she didn't apply, *someone else*—a classmate with ambition, if not more merit—would take her place. Marwa didn't argue. She just repeated to herself, silently, fragments of two poems they'd read in class.

Once out of nature,
I shall never take
my bodily form from any natural thing...
I was neither living nor dead,
and I knew nothing...
I had not thought death had undone so many.

All she told the counselor was, "Find me someplace my father doesn't have to pay for."

She couldn't remember if she'd said thank you. *These fragments I have shored against my ruins.*

GRŤ

The old fourth-floor clique—forty or so juniors and seniors, Jewish, Christian, Sikh, Jain, mostly Hindu and Muslim—still met behind the escalator. The custodial staff had scrubbed it to first-day-of-school gleam.

Noticing the almost eerie cleanliness, one junior said, "We breathed in jet planes. We breathed in buildings. We breathed in people."

At that moment, Marwa knew her tight-knit group would never again walk up to the 23rd Street halal diner for lunch together.

GRŤ

The Stuyvesant Peglegs are prevailing in boys' soccer," *The Spectator* chronicled, "despite shuffled athletic schedules." Football less so, but New York Giants wide receiver Amani Toomer had visited and coached the October 23 practice. In another show of sportsmanship, a rival girls' cross-country team brought cupcakes to the Stuy team before their October 10 meet. Vivian Cheng returned to school and led the fencing team to a "pointed" saber victory over her Long Island nemesis.

Vivian applied Early Admission to Stanford. Marcus, to Harvard. Judy, to Columbia. Sunny, to NYU. Biren, to Berkeley.

Although Marwa's eye had clinically healed, some classmates who asked her about Princeton or Yale whispered behind her back that she seemed to look *through* them—or right past them.

Her guidance counselor suggested Fordham was likely to offer a full scholarship. Marwa shrugged, and the harried woman took that as a yes.

To the extent that Marwa focused on anything, it was her independent social studies project. Her thoughts were scattered—like spores, like shattered bits of self. *Sparagmos*, Mr. Haddam had taught them last year, borrowing from Northrop Frye. The literary quality of Irony: explosive fragmentation. Biren had illustrated it with a Bronx cheer. Mr. Haddam's raspy laugh had sounded like sandpaper.

GRTY

Marwa returned to the book Desiree had given her in August: a collection of letters by Rose Cleveland. She became absorbed by the correspondence between Rose and her lover, Evangeline Whipple, and by Evangeline's late husband, The Right Reverend Henry Whipple—Bishop of Minnesota, known as "Straight Tongue"—who had issued early warnings of the 1862 Minnesota Massacre.

Marwa's brain was active, but she felt absent. She studied the events of 1862 from multiple vantage points—as if time and space themselves could be observed from without. Apparently, Cartesian coordinates no longer located her.

But research helped. It got her out of the classroom. It gave her time alone. And it gave her something to hold on to.

In 1862, the Sioux Nation extended from the Big Woods of Minnesota to the Rocky Mountains. It comprised seven tribes—three in the west, known collectively as the Lakota, and four in the east, known as the Dakota, who lived in Minnesota and the eastern Dakotas. Approximately 7,000 members of the four Dakota tribes resided on a reservation that bordered the western frontier along the Minnesota River in southwestern Minnesota. The Dakota Conflict—also called the Dakota War or Sioux Uprising—primarily involved the two southernmost Dakota tribes: the Mdewakanton and the Wahpekute.

A decade earlier, the Minnesota Territory, stretching from the upper Mississippi to the Missouri River, was still largely Indigenous land. In 1851, however, the Dakota signed a treaty ceding most of southern Minnesota to the U.S. government in exchange for two reservations, each twenty miles wide by seventy miles long, along the Minnesota River, along with annuity payments totaling $1.4 million over fifty years. Then, in 1858, the Dakota ceded roughly half of this reservation land in return for increased annuity payments.

These treaties, in practice, sowed the seeds of conflict. They weakened traditional Dakota leadership, centralized discontented factions, and entrenched a corrupt system of Indian agents and traders. By the summer of 1862, annuity payments were delayed, and tensions reached a breaking point.

On August 15, 1862, at a meeting with Dakota leaders, Indian Agent Thomas Galbraith, and several white traders, Galbraith was urged to distribute emergency provisions stored in agency warehouses. The Dakota were starving. The traders refused.

One of them, Andrew Myrick, responded bluntly, *"So far as I am concerned, if they are hungry, let them eat grass."*

On August 16, a keg containing $71,000 in gold arrived in St. Paul for annuity distribution. It was sent immediately to Fort Ridgely, but it came just hours too late to prevent violence.

That same night, a group of young Dakota men brought news of bloodshed to Chief Shakopee's camp. Big Eagle, a Dakota chief, later recounted the events.

The tale told by the young men created the greatest excitement. Everyone was awakened and listened. Shakopee took them to Little Crow's house, two miles above the agency. Little Crow sat up in bed and heard their story. He said war had now begun. Blood had been shed, the payments would be stopped, and the whites would seek dreadful vengeance— especially since women had been killed...

My village was near Little Crow's, up on Crow Creek. I had only thirty or forty fighting men. Most weren't for war at first, but almost all joined in eventually. Many others were the same—uninvolved at first but later swept into the conflict. The next morning, when the force moved to attack the agency, I went along. Most of the killing had already happened by the time I arrived.

Little Crow was on the ground directing operations. I saw the bodies. Mr. Andrew Myrick, the trader who had refused to offer credit to starving Indians, lay dead on the ground—his mouth stuffed full of grass.

The Indians said tauntingly, "Myrick is eating grass himself."

Events escalated quickly. On the first full day of violence at the Lower Sioux Agency near Redwood, 44 Americans were killed and 10 taken captive. Over the next few days, nearly 200 more settlers died as the Dakota attacked isolated farms, Fort Ridgely, and the town of New Ulm.

On August 23, a second attack on New Ulm left much of the town in ruins. Roughly 2,000 refugees—mostly women, children, and the wounded—fled to Mankato, thirty miles away.

Three days later, Governor Alexander Ramsey appointed Colonel Henry Sibley, a former governor, to lead the military response. Sibley advanced from the east with 1,400 soldiers and arrived at Fort Ridgely on August 27, lifting the siege. This marked the beginning of the second phase of the Dakota Conflict: a formal American military campaign to suppress and punish the Sioux.

The war's final act came four months later.

On December 26, 1862, 38 Dakota men were hanged in Mankato—the largest mass execution in U.S. history. The executions followed trials in which over 300 Dakota and mixed-blood participants were sentenced to death. Only the intervention of President Abraham Lincoln, deeply unpopular in Minnesota at the time, spared 265 others from execution.

That mass hanging closed the first chapter of a long, brutal history of American-Sioux conflict—one that would not truly end until the massacre at Wounded Knee, South Dakota, by the Seventh Cavalry on December 29, 1890.

Marwa heard the same talks that roving psychologists and social workers were giving to all Stuyvesant students— about disinterest, anger, isolation, changes in habits. She minimized her "at risk" behaviors by doing something simple. She paid attention when she crossed paths with Vivian Cheng.

Vivian was in full lecture mode.

"It was a fundamentalist spasm," she declared about the Protestant Reformation. "The Enlightenment emerged in Roman Catholic and Jewish centers. The Renaissance and Scientific Revolution contrast with jihad—not with America's Protestants, who are our rabid fundamentalists now. The pendulum is swinging reactionary, globally—"

"Reactionar-*ily*?" Marwa interrupted.

"What?"

"How it's swinging—the pendulum. It's an adverb. '-ily.'"

"I meant *where* it's swinging. Like north or south."

Vivian kept talking, but Marwa wasn't listening anymore. Her thoughts drifted to Shakespeare—*Methinks I see my father*, something about a bunghole...the noble dust of

Alexander stopping a bunghole. Mr. Haddam had called it "like a beer barrel cork."

Meanwhile, Judy and Marcus were paying more attention to Marwa than she wanted.

Judy acted like a mourning expert—her mother had died, after all. Marcus kept sending Marwa poems and pressing her to read them. He even asked if she was still emailing Desiree. When Marwa said no, he encouraged her to reconnect. He told her his mom had asked about her.

How was she?

Fine. Turning in all her assignments. Retaking the SATs (finally matching Vivian's perfect Verbal score). Breathing, digesting, bleeding.

Prix had been better than good—in word and deed. Better than anyone. And now: silence. Plenty of blood. But no Denim Prix.

A massacre. A mass grave.

In December, Marwa visited Ground Zero for the first time.

She stood in the cold, watching the crater fill with snow. White flakes fell from a gray, churning sky—a stark contrast to the warm blue skies of September, when debris had blown downward. Now, snow softened the sharp edges of wreckage, blurring them into curves—shoulders, hips, knees.

All my graves are not in Egypt anymore, she thought.

Cleanup crews kept working through the storm. Giant machines groaned. Men breathed steam. Even in the darkness, they operated under Klieg lights, in shifts. The only thing that finally sent them home—briefly—was the blizzard.

Marwa, too, left. She was shaking. Her teeth chattered.

Because she was alive.

Later, Marcus called her.

"The Eskimos don't have hundreds of words for snow," he said.

"Who said they did?" Marwa asked.

"You sound so interested."

"Well, not all of us got into the college of our choice."

"As if *you* care."

"Like the universe," she said, "I'm going through the motions."

"Did you know Indiana once tried to legislate the value of pi to be 3? House Bill 246. In 1897."

"Your social studies project has *devolved* to this?"

Marcus warmed to the subject. Numbers always did that to him.

"No, no, listen. It's amazing. Some amateur convinced a legislator he'd solved angle trisection, cube duplication, and circle quadrature. The state's House actually passed the bill. But the Indiana Senate, at least, realized math shouldn't be a matter of law. They postponed the bill—and it's stayed postponed ever since. What I'm researching, Princess Going-Through-the-Motions, is how history functions. How nonsense perseveres."

"And the Eskimos?"

"That whole idea's a myth. The claim was such that since snow played such a big role in their lives, they had tons of words for it. But it started in 1911 with Franz Boas—founder of American linguistics. He said they had *four* words for snow. Then in 1940, Whorf bumped it up to *seven*. By 1984, the *New York Times* claimed *a hundred*. Total nonsense. Now we know, turns out, they have about as many snow words as we do. A dozen or so. 'Blizzard' included."

"Worf was a Klingon raised by humans," Marwa said.

"Klingons aren't my favorite," Marcus replied. "All that 'honor through violence' stuff—it's just the primate pecking order, dressed up in human language. Jihad. Bullies with books."

"Your book says *an eye for an eye. Do unto others as they do unto you.*"

"Nope. That's Hammurabi's law. The actual quote is *as you would have them do unto you*, Marwa. Big difference."

"*Turn the other cheek. Forgive your enemies. Blessed are the meek.* All is illusion. Maya. The gospel according to Hindu Biren?"

Marcus didn't say how great it was to hear Marwa sounding like herself again—arguing, teasing, challenging him.

What he did say was, *"It's the multitudes versus the beatitudes wherever you go."*

Then, on Friday, December 14, as her guidance counselor had predicted, Fordham University accepted Marwa. With it came a full scholarship.

Marcus had been pestering her all week about Muslim "winter solstice holidays."

"When do you give and get presents?" he'd asked.

Ramadan had ended that year nine days before Christmas. In 2001, December followed the same calendar layout as September—except it had a 31st, a Monday, which would be New Year's Eve. Id al-Fitr, the holiday marking the end of Ramadan, fell on Sunday, December 16. That weekend, Marwa's family celebrated both her college news and the holiday.

Her father was the first to congratulate her. He brought her the gilt-edged family plate, handed down from mother to daughter for generations, heaped with dates for iftar.

As he handed it over, he said warmly, *"Atyab at-tihani bi-munasabat hulul shahru Ramadan al-Mubarak,"* putting special emphasis on the phrase: *"The most precious congratulations on the occasion..."*

Their home gleamed with silvered holiday banners. Marwa's mother chattered happily as she set out food and drink on colorful plates ordered from a new Muslim-American online shop. For her, Id al-Fitr was their real Thanksgiving.

Joey wasn't interested in conversation. He was all about presents, but he dutifully handed out gifts to his mother and sister before opening his own.

Then Marwa opened a CD.

"The Silbercoff boy?" her mother said, raising an eyebrow.

Marwa looked over at her father.

"It seems Marwa has received many interesting envelopes," he said, clearly enjoying himself. He handed her one, already opened, with a business envelope marked *Counselors at Law* in raised black lettering. The return address was an uptown Fifth Avenue firm.

Marwa read the letter. Then she froze.

Her heart pounded. Heat rushed to her face. Dizzy, she fled to her room.

The letter stated she had been named in the will of Denim Prix.

"...A key..."

"...safety deposit box..."

She felt half-blind again.

The CD from Marcus was still in her hand. She slipped it into her Walkman, clumsily adjusted the headphones, and lay down. She closed her eyes as the sound of the Beatles filled her ears, warm and old and distant. Marcus had been ranting for weeks about George Harrison's death in November. How he'd never get to hear Harrison play some ukulele song live. He said he might take up the ukulele in college—less cliché than a guitar. Biren had made a joke about the sexual symbolism of small instruments.

People celebrated Christmas that year, too.

The day after, on December 26, Marwa said nothing to anyone. But she remembered: it was the 139th anniversary of the largest mass execution in American history—December 26, 1862.

By the time June arrived, the Stuyvesant orchestra played a Beatles song at the Class of 2002 graduation ceremony. George Harrison's son, Dhani, had recently produced *Brainwashed*, the posthumous album that Marwa and Marcus gifted each other as graduation presents.

After several jokes about *great minds thinking alike*, Marwa explained that she had bought it for Marcus because of the ukulele track, *Between the Devil and the Deep Blue Sea*. It wasn't necessary for Marcus to mention the instrumental piece *Marwa Blues*—but they both knew.

After graduation, Stuy's art students reunited to paint a mural along the wall leading to the high school. The theme: the ability to dream of peace in the face of violence.

Neither Marcus nor Marwa participated.

Marcus had returned to Brookhaven for the summer. Marwa left for Alexandria before starting her freshman year of college in New York.

Part III

Thought is the thought of thought.

James Joyce, Ulysses

19

AUGUST 2004

O n the last day of August, 2004, Marwa al-Hal was arrested during a demonstration outside the Republican National Convention in New York City. She was about to begin her junior year as a Presidential Scholar at Fordham University. She was arrested alongside another Presidential Scholar—a senior, her boyfriend, James Beekmans.

During the slow churn of interrogation, detention, and her unexpected early release, Marwa replied to her interrogator— the one she silently called *Iblis*, the Muslim name for Satan— with dry conviction.

"I'm definitely not an idealist," she said. "I don't have illusions. I'm one of those people who see through to nothing."

The line came from a Flannery O'Connor short story, where a Ph.D. student has her wooden leg stolen by a Bible salesman lover who leaves her stranded in a barn. Marwa had quoted the character, and she thought of her often—Joy Hopewell, who had renamed herself Hulga because it sounded uglier. Marwa's synesthesia hadn't returned with her eyesight. If her mother's favorite TV psychic was right—that death was only an illusion, a test—then it was one you took blind. She still felt acutely colorblind.

Her boyfriend, and most of the other demonstrators, had not been released as quickly as she had.

Everyone called him James-Beekmans. He was tall, Black, and often mistaken for a Fordham basketball player. But he wasn't brawn—he was brain. He'd grown up in Belmont, the Bronx's Little Italy.

"Just west of the Bronx Zoo," he said once. "I thought my grandfather owned it because he took me there like, daily, when I was little."

"You were never little," Marwa replied.

He grew up fighting and defeating white boys who saw him as an intruder in their neighborhood even though, as he explained to Marwa, his people had been owned and buried in New York since the early 1700s.

"You know South Street Seaport?" he had asked on their first date, back in January. "Beekman Street? That's us. We're Beekmans. Dropped the master's apostrophe three centuries ago. We moved north into the woods and swamps of Manhattan before Olmsted terraformed Central Park, and we got pushed again when the land became valuable. But once we hit the Bronx, we bought land—and kept it. My mom's grandfather photographed the Italians when they first arrived. He delivered mail to the ones who could read."

ᏩᎡᏔᏤ

James-Beekmans and Marcus got along fine when they met, on a hot Sunday at the start of August. Marcus was visiting from "Cambridge."

"Why don't you just say Harvard?" Marwa teased.

Marcus had a copy of the September *Scientific American* in hand. The cover read, *Special Issue: BEYOND EINSTEIN.*

"Was anything?" James-Beekmans asked, nodding at the headline.

"Isn't the title a double entendre?" Marcus replied.

Marwa took the magazine from him, flipped to a dog-eared page, and read aloud:

"Any an imprint on the shape of space-time... The Earth's mass makes time pass slightly more rapidly for an apple near the top of a tree than for a physicist working in its shade. When the apple falls, it is actually responding to this warping of time."

They stood on the esplanade at Battery Park City, looking west over the Hudson. Marwa turned, briefly, toward the emptiness where the Towers once stood. Both men caught the glance. Marcus quickly filled the silence.

"I'm hoping to do grad work with one of the article's authors at Berkeley," he said.

Later, Marwa mistakenly assumed that James-Beekmans liked Marcus because he always answered questions with more questions. In truth, it was because Marcus had, in that moment, gently pulled Marwa away from the memory of falling bodies.

She handed the magazine back.

"James-Beekmans is going to the real Cambridge," she said, "on a Gates magic carpet. All expenses paid."

Marcus raised his eyebrows—impressed. The Gates Cambridge Scholarship was Bill Gates's response to the British Rhodes.

"I'm applying for one," James-Beekmans clarified.

The three walked toward the construction site of the new Teardrop Park. They stopped at a fenced overlook to watch hard-hatted workers pouring concrete, arranging boulders, and planting young trees and shrubs.

Leaning against the fence for a better view was Joey's friend, Ositadimma Bem. He spotted Marwa and grinned—then craned his neck upward, impressed by the height of James-Beekmans.

"Hey, Marwa, this park is gonna be so great!" Ositadimma Bem called out.

"Watch you don't fall in before it even opens," Marwa replied.

Marcus stooped to pick up a few loose stones near the boy's feet. Without a word, he began juggling, gradually drifting away from the fence.

Following him, Ositadimma asked, "Can you do more?"

"Try me," Marcus said, angling his palm expectantly.

Ositadimma handed him more stones. Marcus was juggling six when one slipped. He cursed under his breath.

Ositadimma quickly picked it up and tossed it back. Marcus caught it, kept the other five aloft, and this time maintained all six—up and down, left and right—for several minutes.

Ositadimma let out a low whistle.

"How d'you *do* that?"

Marcus caught the stones and gently tossed one to the boy. "You can do that, right?"

Ositadimma juggled it hand to hand with ease. Marcus slipped three stones into his pocket and resumed tossing two in a steady rhythm. He tossed one to Ositadimma, who mimicked him.

"Watch this," Marcus said, calling back the two and juggling three. "You watching?"

"Gimme."

Ositadimma kept practicing the arc and rhythm.

"You want to try four?" Marcus asked.

"For later," Ositadimma said, focused now.

He paused, gathering the stones in one hand, then held out his other hand for the remaining three. Marcus handed them over.

"Try using balls instead," Marcus advised. "Same size and weight. Much easier."

Ositadimma nodded.

"There's a lot more to this than I thought."

"Just stay clear of the fence," Marcus warned. "Don't lean on it."

The three of them—Marcus, Marwa, and James-Beekmans—watched the boy walk away, juggling as he went.

"He'll have Joey doing that by next week," Marwa said. "So… something you picked up at Harvard?"

"The masters are actually at Caltech," Marcus said. "It's not really how many you can juggle, it's the throwing sequences that matter. Only one rule…no matter the tempo, a hand can only throw one object at a time."

As they headed toward their separate uptown and Bronx-bound subways, they talked movies on the way to the reopened Chambers Street station.

"I just rewatched *Norma Rae*," Marcus said.

"How's your ukulele?" Marwa teased.

Marcus began to sing.

"So, it goes like it goes,
Like the river flows,
And time it rolls right on…
And maybe what's good gets a little bit better,
And maybe what's bad gets gone…"

"Acapella group?" James-Beekmans asked, amused.

"Oh, he knows all the Academy Award-winning songs," Marwa said. "What year was that one?"

"1979," Marcus replied.

"*To Kill a Mockingbird* was 1962," James-Beekmans offered. "Only one I know."

"*Days of Wine and Roses* was also '62," Marcus added. "I only remember the songs."

"He knows them in order. From 1934," Marwa said. "Please don't get him started."

That night, after returning from meeting Marcus, Marwa and James-Beekmans had dinner at his parents' house in the Bronx. Inside, the row house was cool and air-conditioned against the heavy August humidity. But the two of them sat outside on the back steps, overlooking a small, neatly planted garden and a shared driveway that connected rows of garages and gardens behind the attached homes.

Marwa's hair was twisted up, pinned with a barrette. James-Beekmans gently brushed sweat from the nape of her neck, then pressed his thumb and forefinger together to feel the dampness. The sensation drew an involuntary, purring sound from her throat. Startled, she dropped the draft of his Gates Scholarship personal statement she had been reading.

She bent to pick it up and cleared her throat.

"What's wrong?" James-Beekmans asked.

"Nothing," she said quickly. "*The Hobbit and Goliath* is a great title."

She flipped to a page and added, "I love how you tie it to the blond mummies in China with tattoos. I didn't know anything about those hominid migrations. The Cherchen Man...fascinating."

She read aloud, "A tattooed woman with red yarn earrings over six feet tall, and he was 6'6" with ten hats. *Ten hats!*"

She paused.

"Do you have to go to med school to be a geneticist?"

"You ask my mother that question," James-Beekmans said, "but wait until I'm out of earshot."

He mimicked her voice, *"Your father and I haven't commuted our asses to 23rd Street to that VA Hospital for three decades just so you can turn your back on...!"*

Then, in his own voice again, he added, "Spelling our last name without that slave apostrophe was a big deal."

"My last name is my father's," Marwa said. "But I like how they do it in Norway. I think girls take their mother's name with *dottir* at the end, and boys take their father's with *son*..."

She trailed off, then groaned, "Ugh, I'm so hot!" and tugged her damp skirt away from where it was sticking to the backs of her legs. She blushed.

James‑Beekmans stood up, pulled her gently into his arms, and kissed her.

20

JANUARY - MAY 2004

Their first kiss had been back in the coldest January in a decade, when ice lay inches thick on suburban streets, and Arctic blasts slammed into New York City pedestrians caught at crosswalks like steel. But on Mars, Opportunity—the second robotic rover—had landed safely just two weeks earlier, avoiding the strong winds that had troubled its twin, Spirit. Spirit was now stuck, immobilized by a computer crash brought on by excessive multitasking.

Dating in NYC that January hadn't been for the faint of heart. Some blamed global warming for the bitter cold. Marwa did.

She and James-Beekmans were exploring the Museum of Natural History, wandering from beneath the looming blue whale to the Rose Center for Earth and Space inside the Hayden Planetarium.

"See," Marwa said, gesturing, "weather is pumped—like blood in our bodies."

The word *bodies* derailed James-Beekmans' attention from the stony asteroids on display. His sudden focus startled her, but she continued.

"Cold water sinks in the North Atlantic," she explained, "which pushes warm Gulf Stream water north. But now, with polar ice thawing and heavier rainfall freshening the ocean surface, that cold water isn't sinking as fast. If the warm water stops flowing north, and the North Atlantic just freezes—boom, another Ice Age."

James-Beekmans looked intrigued.

"But isn't that going to happen anyway? Eventually? So... why not now?"

Marwa smiled. She loved knowing the answer.

"Past Ice Ages happened when the Earth's tilt changed toward the Sun. But we weren't due for another one anytime soon. Since the 1950s, though, the deep-water pump in the Atlantic—between Iceland and Scotland—has already slowed by twenty percent."

"Not so hot," he said, grinning, "and we're not even tilting."

The conversation left Marwa feeling slightly off balance.

"You want to sit down?" he asked.

"Where?"

They looked around the tall glass cube of the planetarium's ground floor, crowded with asteroids and weekend visitors. Above them, the illuminated Cosmic Pathway curved around a suspended white sphere—the Hayden Planetarium theater.

Nearby, an older woman, visibly tired and trailed by grandchildren and an exasperated daughter, rushed toward what she thought was a wire stool. Before Marwa, James-Beekmans, or a horrified guard could stop her, she sat—squarely into a model of a black hole. Her screams startled the crowd (was it a terrorist attack?). Then the daughter and the guard rushed to help her, and the Rose Center echoed with wild, relieved laughter—especially from the grandchildren.

Inside that very white sphere, under a projected sky full of stars, James-Beekmans had kissed Marwa for the first time.

The Bronx Zoo had been another great winter date. Its 85 acres sat catty-corner from the University. James-Beekmans loved the Gorilla Forest. In frozen January, the Congo natives were kept indoors, where the warm humidity made Marwa's wavy hair swell, much to her dismay—and to his delight.

They spotted a De Brazza's monkey—loud, white-bearded, and fur-turbaned.

"He looks like a tyrant imam," Marwa said, pressing her hands to her ears.

Her eyes tracked the monkey's palette: a flat orange-red turban crest and a dull bluish scrotum.

Scrotum Blue—now that would be a new Crayola color.

Marwa emailed Judy Yamaguchi at Columbia. *I'd heard boys on campus joke about monkey blue balls. I didn't know DBM was their mascot.*

Over dinner one evening, Marwa sat across from James-Beekmans and thought briefly of Prix—remembering Valentine's Day with him. This time, she rambled on about her summer in Alexandria after high school graduation, obsessed with finding out where Alexander the Great had been buried.

James-Beekmans rambled back with a story about Mama Cass, how the folksinger supposedly sang better after being knocked unconscious by a lead pipe in the Virgin Islands.

"Anywhere near the brainy Island of Reil, below the fissure of Sylvius?" Marwa teased, tapping her head and trying to flatten her curls. "That sounds so apocryphal, James-Beekmans."

"Oh, ye of little faith," he said.

"Religion's not the opiate of the masses," she countered. "It's the steroid that incites war."

In February, as daffodil bulbs pierced the frozen ground, the fate of the forty-story, black-shrouded Deutsche Bank building—where Marwa's father had worked—was announced.

"The grim remnant of the trade center attack will become the site of a new park... The Deutsche Bank property will be incorporated into the sixteen-acre Trade Center complex..."

Fate was something Marwa brought up with her psychiatrist, Dr. Homer Rawi.

She didn't mind the long subway ride from Fordham in the Bronx to his office near Penn Station. His green-walled office, lined with tall windows and full bookshelves, felt like a portal. Dr. Rawi was her father's age—short, round, waddling like a thoughtful penguin.

They first met in October 2003, after the hospital visit that had sent her to the ER. He had introduced himself as originally from Alexandria.

At each visit, he stood when she entered, closing a book mid-sentence. One day, he lent her a rare volume from his collection: an 1885 edition of *1001 Arabian Nights*. In its foreword, she read that *"The Rawi"* meant *"a reciter."*

By March, they had traveled together to ancient Alexandria—at least in the imagination. They explored it through the *Odyssey*, through Banana's strange book about a psychic locating Alexander's tomb, and through texts of real historians.

"Have you read Strabo on Alexandria?" Dr. Rawi asked her one day.

"Have *you?*" Marwa shot back.

He opened a book to a silver bookmark etched with his initials.

"'The shape of the city is like a chlamys. The Sema is a part of the royal palaces.'"

"Strabo wrote about Alexander's body in Alexandria," he said, savoring the classical language. *"Chlamys... plethrum... exedra."*

"I had to look them all up."

Marwa nodded.

"*Soma*—not *Sema. Soma Street.* That's where the tomb was."

Holding her hands like intersecting blades, left vertical and right horizontal, Marwa moved them to demonstrate.

"This—'Soma,'" she said, lifting the vertical hand. "And this—'Canopic,'" moving the horizontal. "Here, where they cross—that's where Ptolemy probably built Alexander's *soma*. His tomb. *Tomb Street.* Not what it's called now. I walked it. Noise and traffic, just like—" she gestured toward the window, "—NYC."

"Because we have *eyes*," Dr. Rawi replied, smiling at her pun.

"Ptolemy probably assassinated Alexander," Marwa said. "Caesar's Cleopatra was Ptolemy's last royal heir. By the fourth century, after the Roman Empire went Christian, a woman mathematician was running the Library like a university president."

"Hypatia," Dr. Rawi said.

"She was skinned alive by the Bishop of Alexandria." Marwa paused. "Homer wrote about Eidothea, a woman of Egypt."

"And also, about a sea goddess who 'deceives her father blind,'" Dr. Rawi added.

"She deceived her father? I didn't remember that part." Marwa frowned. "Menelaus was becalmed for twenty days in what would become Alexandria. Eidothea helped him escape."

"As Ariadne did for Theseus in the labyrinth," Dr. Rawi said.

Sometime between October and February, Marwa stopped resisting the sessions. Dr. Rawi had prescribed medication, and once her dreams became less violent, she could finally sleep. She told him that the world looked different now.

"It's like those old black-and-white movies—when they colorize them," she said. "I used to be able to *smell* colors. Now I just feel unplugged."

"Ah, synesthesia," Dr. Rawi said thoughtfully. "I had a patient once, an artist who lost his color vision in a car crash."

"A teenager?" she asked. "What happened to him?"

"No, he was an adult. It changed the way he painted. He had to stop driving because shadows on the road looked like deep pits. When you lose color vision, contrast sharpens. Animals see that way—less color, more contrast. Better night vision."

"So, I see like a dog now?" Marwa asked, only half-joking.

"More likely," he said, "you see within the standard range of human color vision, without synesthesia. But if you *were* totally color-blind, you'd have been quite valuable during World War II."

"Seriously?"

"Yes. As a spy. Color-blind operatives were better at spotting camouflage, like netting over tanks in reconnaissance photos that others wouldn't see."

"What happened to the artist?"

"He took taxis instead of driving," Dr. Rawi said. "And his paintings changed. His later work became more valuable."

In March and April, Marwa began to remember.

"In Alexandria," she told Dr. Rawi, "I stayed with my fat Auntie Fatima, my mother's oldest sister. I shared a room with my two cousins. One of them snored louder than the air conditioning. No one told me to wear hijab. My cousins wore theirs or didn't, depending on their mood. It was like fashion.

"At night, if I got up and walked into the living room, there was no air conditioning there. Just the night noises of Alexandria—not as loud as New York, but still, people were out, moving around. I had this irrational idea: *if the dead can't rest, then neither should the living.* I thought if I could find where Alexander had really been buried—if I could *know*—"

She stopped, staring past Dr. Rawi, out the window.

"—If... then what?" she said softly. "What did I think I'd know?"

She took a breath.

"I kept falling asleep. On buses, in the new Library. My brother took me. The Reading Room columns looked like the base of the Towers. They had a planetarium. My cousins introduced me to their friends, and we walked along the Corniche, along the shoreline, just like the esplanade at Battery Park City. Or uptown, where Marcus lives—Carl Schurz Park. The walkway by the East River. Near the mayor's mansion. Which the mayor doesn't actually live in."

She paused again.

"My uncle, Auntie Fatima's husband, is a doctor. That's why I stayed with them, not my grandparents. I see that now."

She looked down, then back up.

"When I got back to New York, I started to feel... real again. Like I was materializing. Like the Cheshire Cat, but in reverse. Reappearing. In Alexandria, I felt transparent. We're mostly empty space anyway—atoms are mostly space. But there, I felt like a window screen. Like anyone could see right through me."

Dr. Rawi didn't try to fix it. He just listened—looked at her differently than anyone else had, like the question itself was a valid answer.

She didn't feel love for him, or reverence. She just felt... relaxed.

After more nightmares of Alexandria, of James-Beekmans, Marwa finally retrieved Denim Prix's letter from the safety deposit box. She brought it to Dr. Rawi's office.

But she hadn't been able to bring herself to open the small jeweler's box that held the diamond.

"Do you want me to read this?" Dr. Rawi asked gently.

"No one else has," Marwa said.

August 31, 2001

Dear Marwa,

If you're reading this, something bad has happened to me, so please—don't be upset.

Also, don't expect too much from this letter. I'm not one of your Stuyvesant genius friends. But I didn't want you to misunderstand the diamond. It's not like *Titanic*, and it's not an engagement ring. If you're reading this, then I was right— I couldn't see myself getting engaged. But I wanted you to have a diamond big enough to do that experiment you mentioned. I know you'll think of some way to use it better than I could ever justify what it cost.

Please don't think of it as payment—for anything—except maybe in the good sense: for your effect on me.

I tend to have the *effect*—yes, with an "e"—of being a drug on people. They get physical around me in different ways. So mostly, I put up a wall. I walk around wearing a mask. But behind that mask, I hadn't been drawn to anyone for a very long time. Until you.

Not that you were into me. But that was okay.

It took me a while to figure out what I liked about you. You knew so much, and you had so many questions. That was like a drug to me—someone who *knew* things. I didn't think life could make sense, but with you, I saw that maybe it could. Not necessarily for me, but for someone. And maybe that was enough. That's why I'm going to California. To try something new.

I hate modeling. A model should be an example, not a puppet. But I've always been treated like a mannequin, like I had no thoughts or feelings of my own. Maybe I didn't. I never got the chance to learn how to do anything besides walk, pose, take direction.

You once said how Muslims turn to Mecca five times a day. My whole life, I've turned toward a camera.

The most dominating camera is someone else's eye— *their* idea of what you have to be. You said that. A real model is like Jesus. Or Alexander. Or you, for me.

When you disobeyed your father to come to my birthday party, I knew—I'd never done anything like that for someone. When you came to my apartment for sex, I knew it was a big deal for you. I didn't think it could still be a big deal for me— but it was. Because it was you.

I don't know if I can go from model to actor—from someone who poses to someone who *acts.* I don't know what I can learn. I never really went to school. I don't trust gurus, and I don't know if I could sit in a library. Who knows how soon you'll read this. Hopefully not for a long time. But if I get there— wherever *there* is—I'll think of you. And the diamond.

People need something to hold onto.

You made me want to know things I didn't even know I didn't know.

Be yourself. That's the hardest thing. But I think you can do it.

Don't blush too hard.

Love,

Robert (my real name)

He misspelled *effect*," Marwa said softly.

Dr. Rawi looked at her.

"And Mecca. What was the experiment?"

Marwa stared at the floor.

"So, I killed him. He was on that flight to L.A. because I was such a *terrific* model. Now maybe I'll be the death of James-Beekmans."

She counted the silence between them.

"James-Beekmans?" Dr. Rawi asked.

"Shouldn't I tell him about Prix?" she said, all at once. "Can a psychiatrist prescribe birth control? Is that how it works now? One person's truth becomes the next person's lie? How can anyone be true—to anything? To *anyone*? To God? To yourself? Do either of those even *exist*?"

She inhaled sharply.

"I'm afraid even to *look* at the diamond. If you put it on your tongue, it's supposed to cool it. Like ice."

"Ice," Dr. Rawi said quietly, "costs a lot less. And it melts."

He paused.

"It reminds me of the coal placed on Isaiah's tongue by the angel."

"What do I dream about Alexandria?" Marwa echoed. "I'm in Alexander's tomb. Like Juliet waking up and seeing Tybalt. All her dead. Romeo. I'm in the plane. I'm in the Tower. I've found Alexander. But I can't get out. I *can't bear it!* But they had to. And they did."

Her voice dropped to a whisper.

"Why would an angel do that? Burning bushes. Lion's dens. Furnaces. Diamonds on the tongue?"

Her voice rose without volume, like a string pulled taut, "Who's responsible? Who's accountable? Shame on them! That woman—she was *right!* 'SHAME!' she shouted, and she was right."

"What woman?" Dr. Rawi asked.

Marwa waved the question off.

"At the hearings. When Rice testified about the August 6th warning memo. That woman's mother died in the North Tower. Where Prix—" she stopped. "She went to the hearings. They had *so much* information. Enough to *do something.* And by going there, she was saying to her mother: 'I'm swinging back for you now.' She said, 'Knowing what they knew changes the rest of my life.' And she couldn't help it—she shouted *SHAME!*"

Marwa leapt from her chair, screaming, "I AM FURIOUS!" She ran around the room, touching the desk, the chaise, grabbing a toy from the top shelf.

Then she turned, eyes wild, and said softly, "Joey's going to kill himself with his friend Osit one of these days, bouncing off walls—imitating those stupid teenagers who run up buildings and backflip off ledges. Tracers, Joey calls them."

She began tossing the toy from hand to hand.

"*Parkourists,*" Dr. Rawi said. "I've seen them in Central Park. Catapulting themselves through space."

"They climb up alcoves in Battery Park City."

"Very gymnastic."

"They—think—they—can—defy—gravity," Marwa said, falling heavily back into her chair. She covered her face. "I can't—breathe," she gasped, though she was breathing, hard. "Fire."

☧ℜ☥☙

When she came to, she was lying on the chaise. Her forehead felt cool and damp. A cold compress. Dr. Rawi sat nearby.

"Coal," she whispered. "Not diamond."

Then, almost inaudibly, "Will I ever be better? Will I get well? Will I get over it?"

"So, it wasn't a mountain?" Dr. Rawi asked gently.

It wasn't a mountain.

Marwa, the doctor, and Time itself—they were all moving together now. In waves. In fractals. Beyond her current understanding.

"Was it ever whole?" she asked softly. "Was it ever One?"

"Golf?" Dr. Rawi replied, then added with a half-smile, "Or before the Big Bang?"

He handed her a referral to a gynecologist, for the birth control prescription she'd requested.

ᏨᏒᎢᏤ

In late April, the window in James-Beekmans's dorm room was open to a damp breeze that carried the scent of lilacs like an offering. He sat in a plastic desk chair; Marwa sat cross-legged on his neatly made bed. He had been listening to her for some time. Then he stood, walked to the window, and turned his back to her.

She said, "When those planes hit the Twin Towers, it felt like they hit *arkan al-Islam*—the Five Pillars. And when the Towers fell, the Pillars fell. I was on the Hudson, on a Fire Department boat, holding Joey's hand. They were evacuating children from the city. The Towers collapsed. Black clouds, shot through with shades of white and gray. I didn't know Prix was on one of the planes. That he was inside those clouds."

"I had two classes that Tuesday," James-Beekmans said. "I don't even remember if they were cancelled. There were sirens all day, but no jets overhead. You could see the smoke all the way up here. 'Pillars of cloud by day, fire by night,' someone said. I started walking west, off campus, when I heard. Not easy to reach the Hudson from here.

"Girls always worry about rape. But if you're Black, you worry about *everything*. 'You're a neighborhood of one,' my uncle told me once. When I saw those blurry security videos of Atta and the others at the airport, you know what I thought? I thought—of course they got through. They didn't have African faces. Any of *us* get stopped all the time. Even by our own. At airports, on the street, by cops, by screeners. But not that day. That day, I walked all the way to the Hudson—this side of the train tracks. Nothing was running. Everything had stopped. Except the sirens.

"I sat down on a curb. Other people did the same. Like we all just... ran out of energy. Just sat there. Overwhelmed. The weight of all the hurt in the world. From monster microorganisms under microscopes to the mess of *us.*"

"*Lex Talionis,*" Marwa said.

"Exactly. Law of the jungle. Tooth and claw."

He turned to face her. Backlit by the open window, he looked tall and shadowed.

She squinted to see him.

"When you first started dating me," he said, "and told me you had color blindness, I thought...maybe that's why. Because you couldn't see what color I really was."

"Oh, James-Beekmans," Marwa whispered.

She rose to her knees on the bed and reached out for him.

⚕ 🍄 ✞ 🍄

Later, she woke in the golden hush of late afternoon. The rain still fell. She lay beside him in the dorm room, the Bronx campus just beyond the window. He was sleeping. She turned her head and studied his face.

He stirred, shifted slightly. Though their bodies were no longer joined, she still felt him inside her. His scent was in her lungs, his taste in her mouth, the milk of him within her.

"Hmmm," he murmured as he woke, smiling. "What're you thinking, Beauty?"

Marwa whispered, "Do you have all three of your Gates letters lined up?"

He sat up, looking at her. "Yes. In fact, I do. Why—are you offering to write me one?"

GRTV

After completing their original three-month mission, the two Mars rovers continued exploring. Opportunity was now en route to a 430-foot-wide crater called Endurance. Along the way, it struck something unexpected: a volcanic rock unlike anything yet seen on Mars.

NASA called it *Bounce Rock*—it had been hit during Opportunity's airbag-cushioned landing. About the size of a football, the rock was rich in pyroxene, a mineral. Incredibly, it resembled a meteorite found in India in 1865—also filled with pyroxene and containing gas bubbles with Martian-like atmospheric signatures.

Talk of life on Mars—past or present—was everywhere. In bed and out, Marwa and James-Beekmans speculated.

"You think the meteorite in Mecca's Cube came from Mars?" he asked.

"No one can get close enough to study it," Marwa replied.

He nodded. "*Nature* just published a report—some bacteria seem to survive by pulling electrons straight from metallic iron."

"In heaven as it is on Earth?" Marwa mused.

"They better be careful what they bring back on those rovers," she added. "It's not like passing through Earth's fiery Admissions Office. Imagine—if the most significant thing about our entire era ended up being what came back from Mars in a modern Trojan Horse."

"If they even remember what Troy was," James-Beekmans said.

GRTV

Do you remember me? Desiree had written, attaching a note to a spring poem titled *Atmosphere*.

The air is everywhere here
the thing we cannot see.
The wind's so slim it fits
between the new green leaves
and moves them so we also see
them separate and again as one.
Without this invisibility, the words
we speak would be utterly still.

Marwa showed the poem to James-Beekmans but didn't respond to Desiree.

In May, as they walked down the cobbled hill from the Cloisters—having just wandered through medieval galleries of saints and unicorns—James-Beekmans asked, "What are the Pillars of Islam?"

A soft wind carried the scent of spring lilacs, blowing Marwa's long hair into his face. He raised his hands to swat it away, and when she turned to face him, he looked like he was surrendering.

"The Five Pillars," she said, "are the five official acts all Muslims must perform."

She gestured for him to lower his hands, then raised her right, pointing to each finger with her left:

"One, *shahadah*, the declaration of faith: the oneness of Allah and the prophethood of Muhammad. Two, *salat*, the five daily prayers. Three, *zakah*, giving to charity. Four, *sawm*, fasting during Ramadan. Five, *hajj*, the pilgrimage to Mecca."

Marwa closed her fingers into a fist, then slowly opened her hand and cupped his cheek. As they walked downhill into Fort Tryon Park, James-Beekmans picked stems of lily of the valley. Their delicate bells chimed faintly in the breeze, releasing their perfume.

21

JUNE – SEPTEMBER 2004

In June, Marwa finally responded to Desiree's instant message.

Mars429: there are mockingbirds in the bronx

D3sir33: wow, at long last reply...

D3sir33: hello... mockingbirds?

Mars429: kept awake last night...

Mars429: 3rd night in a row by car alarm

Mars429: today heard it again—with chirps

Mars429: saw gray bird on oak tree singing car alarm cycle

D3sir33: u still on campus?

Mars429: BF & I working at Dem HQ...

Mars429: gotta hold back the night

D3sir33: keep the faith

D3sir33: 3 things people talk about: things, other people, ideas

D3sir33: i think the universe is made of whole cloth

Mars429: shreds and patches

Mars429: or julia sets—repetitive iterations of the same
D3sir33: signifying nothing? nah…
D3sir33: warp & woof, cruel & kind
D3sir33: down threads & up, weaving whole cloth
Mars429: cloth sags, rips, rots
D3sir33: calling all tailors!
Mars429: metaphor is useless
Mars429: action is the cornerstone of better government
D3sir33: they're laying the cornerstone
D3sir33: for the Freedom Tower—July 4
D3sir33: 20 tons of Adirondack granite, full of garnets
Mars429: i'll be working at slick willie's Harlem office
Mars429: starting next month. IM'ing a friend there now
(Marwa lied)
D3sir33: fly away!
Marwa reddened—guilt and relief in equal measure.

⚭⚮⚭⚮

On June 29, after seven years of travel, the *Cassini* spacecraft neared its destination—soon to become the first robotic explorer to orbit Saturn and study its thirty-one known moons. During its four-year mission, the spacecraft would perform 157 trajectory maneuvers and 45 flybys of Titan, the moon scientists called a window into Earth's primordial past.

Marwa thought about the geometry of space—dimensions in which parallel lines might, impossibly, intersect.

She IM'd Desiree again over the Fourth of July weekend.
Mars429: BF & I finally saw the DiCaprio *R&J*
D3sir33: my GF is a Red Sox fanatic
Mars429: BF is a Yankee
D3sir33: see jeter fly into the stands?
D3sir33: make that catch?
D3sir33: thought he'd lose teeth!
Mars429: we were there. perks of politics
D3sir33: i hope Boston finally wins it this year

Mars429: i hope we win in November. check your email

Desiree opened her inbox to find a forwarded joke.

A woman in a hot air balloon realized she was lost. She lowered her altitude and spotted a man in a boat below.

"Excuse me," she called down. "Can you help me? I promised a friend I'd meet him an hour ago, but I don't know where I am."

The man checked his GPS and replied, "You're in a hot air balloon, approximately 30 feet above ground elevation 2,346 feet above sea level. You're at 31 degrees, 14.97 minutes north latitude and 100 degrees, 49.09 minutes west longitude."

The woman rolled her eyes.

"You must be a Democrat."

"I am," he said. "How did you know?"

"Everything you told me is technically correct, but completely unhelpful. I'm still lost, and now it's your fault."

The man smiled.

"You must be a Republican."

"I am," she admitted. "How did you know?"

"You don't know where you are or where you're going. You rose to where you are by a lot of hot air. You made a promise you can't keep. And now you expect me to solve your problem. You're in the same place you were before, but suddenly it's my fault."

GRTV

At the end of July, Marwa and James-Beekmans were working as unofficial gofers on the floor of the Democratic National Convention in Boston. They stayed in Marcus's apartment in Cambridge while he visited his parents in Manhattan.

"Nice," James-Beekmans said, taking in the space.

Marwa adjusted the thermostat to cool the rooms, then began making coffee with Marcus's elaborate machine. Meanwhile, James-Beekmans turned on the flat screen above the fireplace. Convention coverage dominated the news.

Marwa handed him a mug.

"It looks different on TV," he said.

"So... what are we doing?" Marwa asked.

James-Beekmans pulled himself up from a fatigued sprawl in a leather club chair.

"Go out or order in?"

"No," Marwa said, sitting down. "I mean what are *we* doing? Together."

Her khaki skirt was chafing at the waist. She tugged at her tucked-in polo shirt, then gave up and pulled it free altogether.

"Hierarchy. Politics. This coffee."

She picked up her cup and took a sip.

"This coffee?" he asked. "Didn't you want to make it?"

"Did it occur to you to make any?"

"I didn't want any."

"Did it occur to you that I might?"

He raised his hands.

"I sit convicted."

"Oh, funny," she said. "So, you were doing me a favor by letting me serve you."

"'As I would not be a slave, so I would not be a master,'" James-Beekmans quoted Lincoln. "'This expresses my idea of democracy. Whatever differs from this to the extent of the difference, is no democracy.'"

Marwa kicked off her sandals and put down the coffee. She lay back on the couch and closed her eyes.

James-Beekmans hoped she might fall asleep and wake up less tense. But when she opened her wide Egyptian eyes, they were sharp with anger.

"Order out?" he offered.

"It's *all* bosses," Marwa said. "Jay Gould said in 1886 that he could get one half of the working class to kill the other half."

"'Hire,'" James-Beekmans corrected. "'I can *hire* one half to kill the other.'"

"Bullies," she muttered. "I'm not surprised when Beijing censors a novel about peasants rising up against corrupt local officials. Not when the doors are closed tight at Kissinger's Bilderberg bash—excuse me, 'international economic policy conference.'"

"Rankism sucks," he agreed. "So, what *did* surprise you?"

Marwa stood and walked to the bay window. She looked down at the narrow Cambridge street below.

"We're volunteers," she said. "Not slaves. Not groupies. But today a woman shrieked orders directly into my ear. We're in the *same* party."

"In, not at," James-Beekmans said.

⸎⸎⸎

That night, in Marcus's apartment, streetlight filtered through the mini-blinds. One second before, Marwa had been dreaming, watching Princess Leia's holographic plea to Obi-Wan Kenobi and somehow *being* her at the same time.

I was the bully, Marwa thought. *I bullied Prix. I wanted Beauty. To possess it, to flatter myself. I knew what he wanted from me. I made him sacrifice his belief in Innocence for my hunger for Beauty.*

"What?" James-Beekmans murmured groggily.

"Beauty. Innocence. *Star Wars,*" Marwa whispered.

"Are all illusions," he replied. "Dream about me."

"The universe is a hologram," she said softly.

"Obi-Wan Kenobi, help me," James-Beekmans groaned.

"Any fraction of a hologram contains the whole. Information escapes black holes. Nothing is ever truly lost. You can run the film backward and get back to the beginning. When you finally untie a knot—it's gone."

She yawned loudly.

"Yoda say, 'That a good thing sounds like,'" he mumbled.

He turned and draped his heavy, warm arm over her waist. Beyond gravity, beyond thought, they drifted together into sleep.

230

In July 2004, solar blast waves from the storms of autumn 2003 continued to ripple through the solar system, past Mars and out to the outer planets. One wave damaged the radiation monitor on *Odyssey*, the spacecraft orbiting Mars (not to be confused with *Opportunity*, which was still roving the surface). When the blast reached Saturn, *Cassini* recorded similar effects.

On Earth, public outrage simmered ahead of the Republican National Convention in New York City. On August 31, Democratic protestors—especially those opposing the war in Iraq—were confined to a fenced pen on Manhattan's far West Side, far from Madison Square Garden. Out-of-town GOP delegates could pretend New York had welcomed them.

Marwa and James-Beekmans were among the 1,806 protestors arrested after stepping outside the restricted zone. Marwa was released without even being fingerprinted, well within the legal 24-hour holding limit.

James-Beekmans wasn't as lucky.

He was detained for 49.5 hours, along with more than 200 others, including a 73-year-old carpenter from Massachusetts

"I make chairs and tables," he said. "Don't call me a furniture designer."

The police used orange netting to corral the protestors, zip-tied their wrists, and loaded them into vans. They were processed at a makeshift facility on a Hudson River pier—photographed, searched, and held. In the end, the Manhattan District Attorney's Office dropped all charges against all but a few.

When Marwa asked James-Beekmans about his confinement, he answered matter-of-factly, "We were only handcuffed for about three hours, but I'll never use a plastic tie on a garbage bag again... I don't know how some people managed to keep their phones after the searches, but they were sharing—calling parents, lawyers. The cell was too small for all twenty of us to lie down, so we slept in two-hour shifts. We all stank. There were awful voices doing great Dylan impressions...and the only cameras were personal handhelds. But they'll show we didn't resist arrest."

Marwa didn't explain why she had been released so quickly. They'd started the protest near Ground Zero, beneath the absent shadow of the North Tower, and were arrested as they crossed Church Street onto Fulton.

She also didn't explain that August 31st had become, in her mind, the *mawlid*—the anniversary—of her blood tie with Prix.

(*Mawlid al-Nabi*, the Prophet's birthday, typically falls in May or June on the lunar calendar—the twelfth of Rabi al-Awwal. In popular usage, *mawlid* could also mean a commemorative date for someone deceased. In 2002, Marwa had considered observing a Mawlid al-Prix on August 31st instead of September 11th. But neither then nor the year after could she imagine a proper ceremony—especially not at Ground Zero.)

So, when she found herself *there* on August 31st, 2004, walking in protest, Marwa understood this *was* her Mawlid al-Prix.

ᎬᏒᎢᏇ

By the end of September 2004, Marwa was a junior in a political theory seminar. A fellow student was speaking, "All history is psychology. The current retro-metro wars between fundamentalism and modernism in the Middle East—and the zero-sum game here at home, too. If sunrise gives you sunburn, you prefer the night."

"You think the Renaissance was sunrise?" another student challenged.

"You don't?"

"Did the enemies of modernity agree with Lipsius's antiquarianism?"

A girl next to Marwa leaned in and whispered, puzzled, "Is he talking about the traditionalists—like Guénon?"

Instead of answering quietly, Marwa raised her voice, "Leaving aside all the blather about neocons engineering the invasion of Iraq—"

"That's *some* aside!"

"—Aside," she emphasized, "I'm less surprised that sixteenth- and seventeenth-century Western rulers believed Greco-Roman antiquity offered solutions, than that they relied on an intellect like Lipsius."

"He was totally against the state tolerating religious dissent, Ms. al-Hal," said a familiar, combative voice—Flaherty, known for his Islamophobic barbs.

"I translated Lipsius last semester, Mr. Flaherty," Marwa replied evenly. "And what he did first was distinguish between *public* and *private* dissent. Then he compiled the views of Cyprian, Augustine, Seneca, Cicero, and Justinian—pagan and Christian, legal and oratorical. Lipsius concluded that all wise men, across time and tradition, agreed on suppressing *public* dissent, but not necessarily private belief."

Then, turning back to the girl beside her, she softened.

"Guénon believed the twentieth-century West was the last phase of the final age. To him, the Renaissance wasn't a rebirth but a death. He saw rationalism, science, and democracy as delusions. The cure was a return to primordial truths, unified beneath a religious elite. And of course," she added, "he saw himself among the elect."

The professor, a clerical scholar, added, "Guénon was born Catholic, trained in mathematics. He turned to theosophy, Freemasonry, medieval Christianity, Hinduism, and finally Islam. He moved to Cairo and lived in solitude, fearing sorcery."

From the back of the room, a student chimed in, "That's what I meant—history *is* psychology."

The professor ignored the interruption and addressed Marwa directly.

"Are you familiar with Lipsius and the Family of Love? A curious sect from mid-sixteenth-century Europe. They believed all organized religions were equally useful for instilling discipline in the masses—and equally irrelevant to spiritual truth. Their members claimed direct, inward access to the divine. They joined churches for political survival, interpreted scripture as allegory, but still advocated for enforced unity—especially against the mob. You might consider writing your term paper on them."

Marwa frowned.

"There is no religious truth," she said quietly. "There is no truth *in* religion. Religion *is* the Hydra-headed mob."

The girl beside her asked softly, "How do you know?"

In that moment, Marwa caught a brief glimpse of her unconscious self, its ego peeking through, and then, just for a second, color returned. A silvery gray shimmer, like snow in a dream. The sensation reminded her of those seconds before waking up, when everything is still suspended and weightless.

GRTV

On September 28, 2004, *The New York Times* reported that the Mars rovers had received a new lease on life. After a period of disrupted communications, both machines had resumed partial operations. NASA extended funding for six more months—if the rovers could hold out that long.

22

OCTOBER 2004 - JANUARY 2005

"Does it seem like Spain at all?"
How gaudy Barcelona Gaudi is, whose Hotel Attraction he
long before designed to rise where our Towers fell.
What wild dreamscape is this now we call The City?
Upsprang the aboriginal name,
Mannahatta!
City nested in bays! my city!
More Oz than Oz, this is the world's alter ego & other home.
In Kansas City, they've gone about as far as they can go,
but, Toto, I don't think we're in Kansas anymore.
Autumn in New York, why does it seem so inviting?
Autumn in New York, it spells the thrill of first nighting...

If James-Beekmans would agree to see a play Marwa
wanted to attend, she promised she'd go with him to the
Yankees–Red Sox game on Wednesday night, October 20th.

"You don't seem to understand," James-Beekmans said, holding out the precious pair of tickets, "what *these* mean."

"Then translate," Marwa said.

He sat down heavily in her desk chair, staring at the tickets. He shook his head a few times in disbelief.

"What play are we talking about?" he finally asked.

"NINE PARTS OF DESIRE," Marwa said. "It's by a blond Catholic woman from the Midwest with family in Baghdad. The title comes from a hadith a few generations after the Prophet: 'God created sexual desire in ten parts; He gave nine parts to women and one to men.'"

"You sure that's translated right?" he asked, raising an eyebrow.

"I'm sure."

James-Beekmans sighed, shrugged, and nodded.

"Okay. We'll go. No big deal."

But he kept looking down at the tickets.

Then he looked back up at her.

"In the previous 100 postseasons, 138 best-of-seven series, no team has *ever* come back from a 3–0 deficit to force a Game Seven. This is *that* game."

"It *is* a big deal," Marwa said quietly.

"That's all I'm saying," he replied. "So... why are you shaking your head?"

ᎦᏰᎢᎤ

On October 28th, Desiree forwarded her girlfriend Bess's email from Boston to everyone in her address book.

THEY WON IT! THEY WON IT! THEY WON IT! It's a *great* time to be in Boston! Last night we joined neighbors pouring into the streets—jumping for joy, high-fiving, hooting into the night! What *collective joy*—an entire city thinking the same thought at once, savoring the moment and remembering the suffering, the years of *so close*, *almost*, and *maybe next year!* But no more! Today, God rubs our Red Sox tummy!

Marwa read it, smiled briefly, and did not share it with James-Beekmans.

We'll have Manhattan, the Bronx, and Staten Island, too,
It's lovely going through the Zoo...
Even in a hurricane, New Yorkers don't stay home.
Fast-forward movie motion like maggots on a carcass.
I don't have any reasons. I left them all behind. I'm in a New
York state of mind.
But at dawn in Bryant Park, a businessman stops before
work to play his bagpipe,
Amazing Grace, the Ode to Joy, and the Marine Corps hymn.
'I get a lot of thank you's,' the bagpiper says.
After 20 years, he'd found an instructor on the Lower East
Side,
and asked, Teach me.
The great big City's a wondrous toy –
We'll turn Manhattan into an isle of joy.

James-Beekmans once explained to Marwa that his mother kept a boomerang on their fireplace mantel because she insisted it originated in Africa, not Australia. To her, it symbolized her life philosophy.

"Which just 'shows to go ya,'" James said with a grin, mimicking his father's favorite malapropism, "that there's always an *irrational* explanation for everything."

"Like pi?" Marwa teased.

It was a golden October day, sycamore leaves skittering along the sidewalk in a crisp breeze, perfect for walking home from school. And that's exactly what they were doing: walking back from Fordham to James's parents' house for dinner.

It was plaid skirt and leather jacket weather. Marwa wore the former, James the latter—his brown leather darker than his skin.

At the Beekmans' dinner table, his mother declared, with light exasperation, "No politics, please. I don't cook with stomach acid."

Then, turning to Marwa, she added, "Just call him James."

"Leave Marwa alone," Mr. Beekmans chimed in. "She can call him anything *they* like. It's a free country, with free speech."

Laughter followed, warm and full.

When it faded, Mrs. Beekmans asked, "James, did you mail your Gates application?"

James gave a mock salute. "Yes, Mom. A whole week early."

New York, New York, it's a wonderful town! The Bronx is up and the Battery's down...
East Side, West Side, all around the town,
The tots sing 'Ring-a-Rosie, London Bridge is falling down.'
Boys and girls together, Me and Mamie O'Rourke, tripped the light fantastic on the sidewalks of New York.
If I can make it there, I'd make it anywhere.
A little Muslim girl from Queens called 'her most beautiful skyscraper' (the Chrysler)
'the Jesus Building'--
Autumn in New York, it lifts you up when you're run down,
Jaded roués and gay divorcees who lunch at the Ritz will tell you that 'it's divine!'
Autumn in New York, you'll need no castles in Spain.

In Japan, October 2004 brought the tenth typhoon of the year to Tokyo. Airlines canceled 937 flights, and bullet train service between Tokyo and Osaka was suspended. At least sixty-six people died, and over 300 were injured in mudslides and flash floods. As the storm churned through the capital, members of Greenpeace Japan held a defiant outdoor press conference in front of Shibuya Station, urging the country to honor its commitment to reduce greenhouse gas emissions. The number of typhoons that year was the highest since Japan began keeping records in 1551.

That same day, Marcus sent Marwa an instant message.

Ag47coff: Happy Halloween!

Ag47coff: You should've seen our Math Dept...

Ag47coff: Costume party. Beauty pageant—for equations.

Mars429: What'd you go as?

Ag47coff: 1 + 1 = 2. Printed it on a T-shirt.

Ag47coff: Tell Joey I won.

It made Marwa smile.

Joey had written a story back in second grade called *"The Power of Plus One."* It was short, as the title suggested.

Once upon a time there was a boy named Joey. He counted all his fingers and toes, his ears, eyes, nose, and mouth, his belly button and more. Then he couldn't count anymore. Then he said, "1 + 1 = 2!" And then all he had to do was add 1 more, and no one could stop him from counting ever again. The End. Plus 1.

Lovers that bless the dark
on benches in Central Park
greet autumn in New York,
it's good to live it again.
Aphrodite promised Adonis,
There shall be an everlasting token of my grief,
and every year an imitation of your death will complete
a reenactment of my mourning;
the blood of Cinyras will be changed into a flower,
but enjoyment of it is brief,
for lightly clinging and too easily fallen,
the winds deflower it, whereby its name,
windflower, anemone.
Brevis est tamen usus in illo;
namque male haerentem et nimia levitate caducum
excutiunt idem, qui praestant nomina, venti.
These things that happen in the particle of time
we have to be alive,
these violations which almost more than any
altar, ark, or mosque
embody sanctity by enacting so precisely

sanctity's desecration...
Autumn in New York, it's good to live it again.

On a chilly mid-November morning, Marwa emerged from the subway into a low cloud of fog that clung to the pavement. This wasn't the Bleeker Street of the Paul Simon song—it was Wall Street, where a stockade had been erected 400 years earlier to shield European settlers from the native Lenape of Mannahatta. The fog mingled with the ever-present steam rising from underground vents across the city.

Marwa tilted her head to gaze at the gleaming new building on the north side of Wall Street, where her father now worked. It reminded her of something Joey might've built a few years back out of blue and gray Legos. One block north, on Pine Street, looming over the ghost of the old wall, stood a miniature Empire State Building — the American International Building. In high school, she and her classmates at Stuyvesant had taken joy in tricking wide-eyed freshmen from the Outer Boroughs into believing it *was* the real Empire State Building. A rite of passage: to torment or be tormented.

A snippet of memory surfaced without context, like a displaced stanza from a forgotten poem...*these violations...more than any altar, ark, or mosque / embody sanctity by enacting precisely sanctity's desecration.* Oh, right—that class right after 9/11. They'd all been told to bring in a poem. C.K. Williams. Someone had joked—cruelly, absurdly—about the poem being "hot off the presses" or "still smoking," when Ground Zero itself still was.

Marwa entered the building, the Lego-like tower with its high white arches, postmodern Romanesque, and heard the echoing *k* sounds in her mind: *arK – mosKque – sanKtity – enaKting – deseKration.*

Her father's secretary greeted her.

Marwa took a seat in a cushioned chair facing his desk and the window beyond. A new school photo of Joey as a sixth grader sat beside the computer.

"He looks so old!" Marwa said. "Ummee says he's grown four inches since June. He looks more like you than Sharif does."

Her father glanced at the photo.

"Yes, as you do. Sharif takes after your Aunt Fatima."

"Without the fat," Marwa quipped.

Mr. Al-Hal smiled faintly, then said, "I didn't expect you."

"I'm not home for the weekend," she said. "Ummee doesn't know I'm here. I wanted to see you before I meet Dr. Rawi. He rescheduled our appointment—maybe someone needed him more after the election. I'm grabbing lunch with some Stuy teachers, then heading uptown to see him. After that, back to Fordham."

"You wanted to see me...not at home?"

Marwa took a deep breath.

"It's about the diamond. I dreamed about it. Dr. Rawi and I discussed it. I think...it's time."

"It needs an appraisal."

"And then it should be sold. The money should go toward something redemptive. It's a waste to let it sit in a safety deposit box, like that ridiculous ending in *Titanic* when she throws the blue diamond into the ocean."

"I hope you have a child like yourself someday."

She caught the shift in his expression, a flicker of emotion like a passing dream. The momentary change delighted her.

"I'm sorry," he said quietly.

"What did I do?"

"This diamond, this *shabka*, from a naked Colossus in Times Square. I don't know what to make of it."

He stood, turning to the window.

"I had no talent for religion. But I thought your mother—"

"He wasn't naked, Daddy. And it wasn't an engagement ring. Not really."

He faced her.

"Then what was it?"

"It was...alchemy. A way to turn something taken from him into something given to me."

"That doesn't make sense."

"It's what Prix believed. When does belief ever make sense?"

"You say you believe, but you don't."

"Oh, Daddy, neither do you."

He sat down heavily.

"My failure shouldn't become yours."

A warm, rose-colored light seemed to wrap around his shoulders.

Marwa saw it, felt it.

"I could always see they were fairy tales," she said. "The bubbles in one religion rise just like the bubbles in another. And they all burst—physics, not faith. Stories might hold truth, but not *the* truth. Will you go back to Egypt when you retire? I can't."

"You don't even know where you're going."

"Please," she said. "Help me with the diamond."

"And we'll dance at Sharif's wedding next summer," he said, his voice suddenly weary.

"Oh," she replied, "so he gave her the *shabka*."

She stepped back out into the brisk November air. The scent of chestnuts roasting on a street vendor's cart reached her. Hungry, she pulled her coat tighter and walked uptown.

As she walked, her dream returned—Prix's face, the diamond in her palm, Dr. Rawi's office. She thought of the Lenape looking up at the first wooden wall erected by settlers on this land. She could almost hear James's voice narrating, *"Think of it, the first humans who ever walked here. Did they cross from Jersey in the south, or ford the Hudson in the north, ten to thirteen thousand years ago?"*

Then Dr. Rawi's voice, *"What do you think?"*

And she was back in the dream—Prix pressing the hard diamond into her palm in a moment of deft intimacy. Marwa continued up West Street, her heart huge and pounding. Prix had given her what she desired.

Now, she would return his innocence.

*Peace, peace! he is not dead, he doth not sleep – He hath
awakened from the dream of life –
He is a portion of the loveliness which once he made more
lovely…The soul of Adonais, like a star,
beacons from the abode where the Eternal are.
On the rim of the Bethesda Fountain in Central Park, Prior
Walter's "favorite place in NYC. No, in the whole universe.
'This angel. She's my favorite angel.
I like them best when they're statuary. They commemorate
death but suggest a world without dying.'
For a ruined Heaven of bureaucrats, the playwright invoked
San Francisco, but for 'More Life,'
New York is the Angel you wrestle to win your name,
well worth a lifetime of limping thereafter.
'You will always have to make choices, and finally all life can
offer you in the face of these terrible decisions is that you
can make the choices freely.'"
Recognize Hamlet's 'interim'? That's New York.*

Marwa and James sat in a downtown café, sipping strong espresso. Marwa had just finished reading a Tom Wolfe story titled *Monday*, about a contractor renovating a Brooklyn apartment free of charge.

"Her husband was in the south tower," the father said quietly. "He didn't get out." Then he turned and went after his daughter, walking stiffly down the stairs, like a crane.

"No charge?" James scoffed. "That's why they call it fiction."

Marwa dropped the lemon peel she'd been licking. She stared out the café window at the Village shops lighting up in the early November twilight.

"I loved that story," she said. "I hate you."

Then she took too big a sip of the hot espresso and burned her tongue.

That year, the last day of Ramadan fell on Sunday, November 14th. On *Id al-Fitr*, an animated film titled *Muhammad: The Last Prophet* opened in ninety-three theaters nationwide. Marwa's mother wanted Joey to see it.

"I'm not a baby," Joey shouted toward the kitchen.

He was bothering Marwa, home for the holiday, by weaving around her with a pair of miniature blue Nerf footballs, the only kind allowed indoors.

"Baby," he said again, using it as a rhythmic chant as he tossed the balls in the air.

Marwa lowered her newspaper. Joey caught the balls midair and dropped one directly onto her head. She snatched them all, walked to the window, and threw them outside. They tumbled down, caught and lifted by cold November gusts.

A week later, Marwa was pacing in the common area of James's dorm suite. His two roommates were tucked away in their rooms, preparing for finals.

"My father left Egypt," she said, circling the room. "People can move. We're not trees."

James looked up from his reading, confused. "What?"

Marwa stopped pacing. "I don't know if I want to live in this country."

"People move for different reasons."

"That's a content-free statement," she shot back.

James tapped the book he was reading.

"Not really. It's packed with content. Think about it. Why would anyone go live in a place called *Iceland?* Or *Lýðveldið Ísland.* That's how you really say it. With Nordic T's called *thorns.* Imagine having a lisp in Iceland— 'EyeTHland.' Must be brutal." He lisped the last few words deliberately.

"I'm not joking."

"You could try."

"We could leave this country," Marwa said quietly.

"They believe in elves in Iceland."

"You wouldn't leave?"

"This is my city. *We the People.*"

"I'm afraid."

"You're angry."

"Don't tell me how I feel."

"Okay," James said, eyes returning to his book. "I won't."

Marwa turned and walked out.

> *Chestnuts roasting on an open fire,*
> *Jack Frost nipping at your nose,*
> *Yuletide carols being sung by a choir,*
> *and folks dressed up like Eskimos.*
> *City sidewalks, busy sidewalks,*
> *dressed in holiday style.*
> *In the air there's a feeling of Christmas.*
> *Children laughing, people passing,*
> *meeting smile after smile,*
> *and on ev'ry street corner you'll hear,*
> *silver bells, silver bells,*
> *it's Christmas time in the City.*

After their breakup, Marwa and James communicated only by email. There was no discussion of what had happened. Between semesters, they were off-campus and out of each other's lives.

Marwa wrote, *I knew this year's Siemens Westinghouse winner when he was a freshman at Stuy.*

James replied, *What is that, $100,000? What'd he win for?*

Yes, $100k. He invented a gyroscope that converts ocean wave energy into electricity, she responded.

⚛⚛⚛

The day after Christmas, the floor of the Indian Ocean shifted, slipping beneath the Pacific plate. The Earth's crust released centuries of built-up tension in one violent moment.

Huge Quake Spawns Tremors and Tsunamis in Southeast Asia

A massive earthquake rocked Southeast Asia on Sunday, setting off tsunami waves that sent residents fleeing to high ground in Indonesia. The surge reached the Indian city of Chennai and the Thai tourist island of Phuket...

Thousands Die as Quake-Spawned Waves Crash Onto Coastlines Across Southern Asia Measuring 9.0 on the Richter scale, the quake triggered tsunamis that raced at speeds of up to 500 miles per hour.

A THIRD OF THE DEAD ARE SAID TO BE CHILDREN

Toll Soaring, Survivors Face a Second Terror: Disease

January 7*th* Tsunami's Ripples, Unnoticed, Washed Along Atlantic Coast

The tsunami that devastated countries around the Indian Ocean also touched the eastern U.S. Though imperceptible to people, the surge registered on tide gauges as far as the North Atlantic. The waves had traveled around the world within 36 hours, jostling instruments from Russia's Pacific coast to the Caribbean.

In Kenya, a baby hippopotamus swept out to sea by the waves washed ashore alive. Rescued by rangers, the calf was placed in an animal sanctuary in Mombasa, where it formed a bond with a century-old tortoise. The 100-year-old male seemed content—maternal, even—toward the orphaned hippo.

Elsewhere, a nanotechnology researcher reported a strange musical discovery: yeast cells vibrate at about 1,000 times per second. When amplified, the vibrations create a soft, harmonic hum. He theorized that, in the future, doctors might diagnose cancer by simply listening—each type of cell giving off its own sound signature.

Marwa paused at that idea.

What would malignant cancer cells sound like? she wondered. *Like clapping? Like crying?*

She kept reading. In the *New York Times* Science section, a report dated January 10th from the American Astronomical Society meeting in San Diego caught her eye.

Vestiges of Big Bang Waves Are Reported

Astronomers say they've detected the remnants of sound waves echoing from the Big Bang, preserved in the pattern of galaxies scattered across the sky.

GRTW

Later that day, Marwa walked through the biting cold toward the subway, heading to meet Judy Yamaguchi for lunch in the Village. Wind knifed through the street corners. She tried to summon warmth from a distant memory—the heat of their impulsive tattoo and earring day at the South Street Seaport, late August 2001, just before her first time with Denim Prix.

A sudden flush of arousal spread through her, cutting through the cold. She dodged dirty snowbanks, descended the icy subway stairs, and disappeared underground.

Sexy ladies from the 80's, who are indiscreet.
They're side by side, they're glorified, where the underworld can meet the elite,
42nd Street. Naughty, bawdy, gaudy, sporty, 42nd Street!

Hot town, summer in the City, back of my neck getting dirty and gritty.
Take the "A" Train. There is a rose in Spanish Harlem.
Me and Julio down by the schoolyard. I like New York in June, how about you? I like a Gershwin tune, how about you? Come on along and listen to the lullaby of Broadway, the rumble of a subway train, the rattle of the taxis,[1]

---

[1] From the epic poem *Marwa* by Desiree Lipshitz.

23

JANUARY 2005 – APRIL 2005

To exchange a few post-breakup belongings, Marwa arranged to meet James for lunch before heading to a matinee of Shaw's *St. Joan*. She scheduled it for 12:30 at a luncheonette near the basement theater, intentionally limiting their time together. Since she arrived early in the lower Chelsea neighborhood, she ducked into a Barnes & Noble to escape the bitter cold. From a kiosk of New Arrivals, she bought a green paperback: *Under the Glacier* by Icelandic writer Halldór Laxness.

At the luncheonette, they traded their bagged artifacts of history. Marwa talked too much and too fast, sharing thoughts about Dr. Rawi and her recent reading about Mecca.

"'Even a woman can demand. Why do we look only to the past and not the future?'" she quoted. "It's attracted people for over 1,400 years."

"But non-Muslims aren't allowed in," James said.

"I hope you win a Gates next year," she offered quickly, changing the subject.

James focused on his hot food.

"I got called for the Annapolis interview next week. What time's your play?"

"Soon," Marwa said, glancing at the clock behind the counter. "Annapolis? That means you got it!"

James shrugged.

Marwa recognized the meaning behind his shrug.

Later, in the theater's bathroom, Marwa cried and missed most of *St. Joan*. She made it back in time for the Epilogue.

The Executioner, "Her heart would not burn, and it would not drown. She is up and alive everywhere."

Joan, "And now tell me, shall I rise from the dead, and come back to you a living woman?"

On the frozen street outside, the sky had darkened into the early rush-hour twilight. Marwa joined the crowd making its way to the subway. She wondered if Prix had asked Joan's question, would she have wanted him to return to her, a living young man?

To avoid spiraling into that thought, she headed toward Battery Park City. Her parents were still at work. There was no Mrs. al-Banna babysitting today. Eleven-year-old Joey was horsing around, almost literally, with his friend Ositadimma Bem. They were galloping around the living room, pretending to be centaurs from the world of *Harry Potter*.

"Followers of Firenze! Muggle alert!" Osit shouted when Marwa walked in.

Joey, reverting to bratty little brother mode, demanded, "What are you doing home on a Wednesday? Does Ummee know?"

Marwa ignored him, retreated to her bedroom, and began reading Susan Sontag's introduction to *Under the Glacier*.

"There are special places in the universe where familiar laws that govern identity and morality are violated," she read, flinching. *"These are places where wisdom accumulates... a*

place of secret pilgrimage... The question is not survival but what one can know, and if one can know anything at all... the little village at the foot of a glacier is in full spiritual molt... The utopia of erotic transformation was only a dream, after all. But it is hard to undo an initiation."

Secret pilgrimage. Erotic initiation. Marwa shut her eyes.

GRTV

Her parents expressed no surprise at her unexpected presence, nor at her rambling reflections on *St. Joan.*
"She was condemned on my birthday in 1431," Marwa said.

"April 29th—553 years before you were born in 1984," Joey chimed in, showing off his math skills.

Her parents remained silent when she mentioned considering an *umra* to Mecca before Sharif's wedding in the summer.

Because they didn't ask, Marwa explained anyway.

"It's not a hajj. Not an anti-hajj. It's a *meta*-hajj. I enter Mecca through Ground Zero, in full spiritual molt."

She struggled with the words.

"I mean, not submission. I share celebration."

Her mother replied gently, "Yes, with all Muslims."

"No," Marwa said, still searching, "with *All.*"

Her father said, "You don't expect us to understand."

His voice was quiet, but something in its clarity reminded Marwa of a cleansed blue sky—*After Blizzard Blue.*

Her colors had returned.

GRTV

Later, she wandered into Joey's room. He was sitting on his bed, arranging striped red, white, and blue Cracker Jack booklets into piles.

"These are Ballpark Legends. One in a series of ten collectible prizes," he said. "I got Cy Young, Ty Cobb, Honus Wagner, George Sisler, Walter Johnson, Thurman Munson,

Satchel Paige, Roy Campanella, and Lou Brock. Nine outta ten. I'm missing Joe Jackson. *Shoeless* Joe Jackson. 'Say it ain't so, Joe.'"

"That you're missing his card?"

"His glove was the place triples went to die. He's the Judas of baseball, don't you know? The 1919 World Series?"

"That what they're calling homework these days?" Marwa teased.

"Infidel!" Joey shouted. "Get outta my room!"

Marwa returned to her bedroom. Someone she used to be had once lived there, but she didn't anymore.

That night, she dreamed of a pyramid tomb. The Opening of the Mouth ceremony played out like a cartoon. A kaleidoscopically-colored Osiris-Prix, Lord of the Underworld, was gathering his scattered body parts. Isis, played by the same actress who had portrayed St. Joan, was putting him back together like Humpty Dumpty.

Marwa wondered if her Divine Box was still hidden in her bedroom.

Then she was Hagar, searching for water for newborn Ishmael between the two mountains, Marwa and Safa.

A voice-over, sounding like Desiree, intoned, *"Truly, Safa and Marwa are among the landmarks of God; therefore, anyone who performs the hajj or the umra does no harm if they circumambulate them both...The pilgrim leaves the courtyard of the Kaaba and enters the lane that runs between the two points right outside... The starting point is from as-Safa... The pilgrim walks back and forth between these two points seven times... This ritual ends at Marwa..."*

⸎⸎⸎

When Marwa woke the next morning, she understood something clearly: You can't go home again. So, she went back uptown to Fordham.

⸎⸎⸎

In early March, her Presidential Scholar advisor scheduled a meeting to discuss her summer and senior year plans. That same week, the university newspaper published a photograph of James alongside a color image of Christo and Jeanne-Claude's *The Gates* installation—7,500 bright orange fabric panels fluttering in Central Park.

The headline read, FORDHAM WELCOMES THE GATES.

April, as always in the northern latitudes, was the iconoclast. Mawlid al-Nabi, the Prophet Muhammad's birthday, fell that year on April 21st. Fierce winter storms had stripped the trees bare, but now April's greening was slowly stitching them back to life.

A week later, Marwa unwrapped an unexpected birthday gift: the new Edith Grossman translation of *Don Quixote*. The book was unsigned, but she recognized the handwriting both on the page and off the wall. James Beekmans had quoted Sancho Panza:

To Marwa, "I'd like to send your grace something, but I don't know what to send, except some very curious tubing for syringes that they make on this insula to be used with bladders; though if my position lasts, I'll find something to send to you, one way or another." (p. 796) "Let us go slowly, for there are no birds today in yesterday's nests." (p. 937) Happy Birthday, every day, always.

April 29, 2005

A bird sang lustily outside Marwa's dorm window. She opened it wider.

So, she'd been sent an enema, promised a future gift, and wished lifelong happiness.

Outside, a student passing by looked up at the smiling, dark Rapunzel leaning out the window, letting her long, wavy hair fall down.

http://sakina.wikidot.com/the-black-stone

24

CODA...TEN YEARS LATER

It was mid-May in Berkeley, just after his graduation, when Joey turned to his older sister and asked, "Marwa, what happened in Mecca?"
Marwa sidestepped the question.
Joey recognized her evasions. He always had. Not even the lift of her brows or the widening of her almond-shaped Nefertiti eyes, which once signaled teasing approval, could distract him now. He also understood her synesthesia, the way she saw the world in colors, not as a distortion, but as a different, truthful register. He wondered, *What color was his question to her?*

"Funny you should ask, Joey," Marwa said. "This morning, I read about the world's largest hotel being built in Mecca. The Abraj Kudai—twelve towers, forty-five floors, 10,000 bedrooms. Seventy restaurants, a shopping mall, even helicopter pads. Five floors reserved for the Saudi royal family. Cost? Three and a half billion dollars. Supposed to be finished by 2017. Another monument rising to overshadow the Grand Mosque. People are praying in the wrong direction now because they can't even find the mosque. And Khadijah's house? It's been turned into a block of toilets."

His question was Crayola Vivid Tangerine.

Joey stopped walking.

He took her hand gently and said, "You never let go of mine that whole day."

He meant September 11th.

He was in third grade. She was nearby at Stuyvesant High School, which had trembled when the planes struck the Towers. Now, at twenty-two, he stood at least six inches taller than her 5 feet 8 inches. She had to look up to him.

"Ummee's gone back to Alexandria," Joey said. "Dad won't leave New York. His 'Mansion of the Sistrum' is being performed this weekend. You're the only one who stayed. I was in China last summer, and now I'm going back. But you never went back. So, I need to know what happened when you went to Mecca."

Instead of answering, Marwa began reciting from the libretto of the symphony their father had composed at Juilliard, now premiering at Lincoln Center.

"I am Praise; I am Majesty; I am Bat with Her Two Faces; I am the One Who Is Saved, and I have saved myself from all things evil."

She lifted his hand and kissed his palm. But still, she didn't answer.

GRTW

Marwa was nine years older than Joey and had preceded him at Stuyvesant. Both had refused their father's generous offers to pay for college, choosing instead to rely on scholarships and loans, which they secured quickly. In 2005, before her final year as a Presidential Scholar at Fordham, and before her elite summer placement in Mecca at the age of twenty-one, Marwa had realized she might be a pawn. That realization had come during a meeting with her advisor in a Fordham office—a memory shaded, in her mind's palette, Blue-Violet.

That March day had been crisp and wind-whipped. Crossing campus, she noticed the first crocuses pushing through crusted earth, the blackened snowbanks beginning to shrink. The air still carried winter's chill, but it was softened by the first threads of spring. At her advisor's office, she knocked gently.

A low, musical voice replied, "*Entrez!*"

Madame Professor Erisa Toto looked up from behind a desk crowded with paper and books. Above her loomed precarious shelves that Marwa often feared would collapse and knock the professor senseless. Professor Toto, over six feet tall and very thin, never stood to greet students. On a wall adjacent to the window hung a curated arrangement of African masks from Burundi, where the professor's family had roots.

"Ah, Mam'selle Al-Hal, *bienvenue, asseyez-vous,*" she said.

Marwa sat and pulled her Presidential Scholars folder from her backpack.

"'02, '03," said Prof. Toto, scanning a form. "Planning to return to Alexandria for a third summer?"

"I'll be in Alexandria for my brother's wedding in July," Marwa said, "but I hope to go to Mecca before, and maybe after, with your help. There's a high school there—Mawhiba. They see themselves as a counter to extremism. If I could teach—science, Latin, even the U.S. Constitution... My mother's cousin teaches in the program in Jeddah. She recommended it."

Professor Toto raised an already arched eyebrow.

"But you wanted a position at the New Library in Alexandria."

"I did."

Professor Toto pursed her dark, glossed lips.

"I see."

She paused, then added, "There is interest in your plans. The Alexandrian Library is encouraged. A fellowship has been offered."

Marwa frowned.

"When we were arrested at the end of August, after the GOP convention, was that why I got released so quickly?"

Professor Toto exhaled audibly.

"You're fluent in Arabic. You have family in Egypt. The State Department's Bureau of Educational and Cultural Affairs oversees Fulbright and other exchanges. An Egyptian-born woman has just been appointed director."

"No one told me."

"And I am not telling you."

"I can't believe anyone cares whether I go to Alexandria or Mecca this summer."

"I can never believe anyone cares about my modest tax contributions," Professor Toto said with a slight smile, "and yet, every year, they are emphatically collected. Between belief and..." she shook her head, "...reality, is a chasm."

"So, this director, she can't *make* me go to Alexandria, can she?"

"Mecca may even be preferable. I will find out."

Marwa glanced at the African masks on the wall.

"Why can't I see what's really going on?"

"You would prefer if the placement in Saudi Arabia were arranged smoothly?"

Marwa zipped her folder into her backpack and grabbed her coat from the back of the chair. Her hand was already on the doorknob when Professor Toto stood to her full height.

"We still need to discuss your fall fellowship applications..."

"Not now."

After Marwa left, Professor Toto remained standing, gazing into the hollow eyes of one of her masks.

ᎶᎡᎢᎺ

When Marcus IM'd Marwa later, she said nothing about the meeting. She had a creeping sense that *they* might be monitoring her laptop—right out of Orwell's *1984*, the year she was born.

Marcus's message distracted her.

Ag47coff: check out Friendster and see Biren come out! She clicked the link.

There was Biren Ramanathan, three years older than she remembered, bulked up, wearing a sleeveless black tee with a green three-dollar bill printed across the chest.

Ag47coff: u know he was gay?

Mars429: he was always flirting with me

Ag47coff: Judy said you're going to Mecca

Mars429: did she say why?

Ag47coff: don't u know?

Mars429: that's why

Ag47coff: congrats on JB's Gates

Mars429: we broke up

Ag47coff: geez…

Ag47coff: did Archimedes drown in the Eureka bathtub?

Mars429: cicero found Archimedes' tomb in Syracuse

Ag47coff: Hadron Collider comes online in 2007…

Ag47coff: God particle exists or it's the toilet…

Ag47coff: down which bad theories will flush…

Ag47coff: I guess if u don't seek, u can't find

Mars429: I guess

ᎶᎡᎢᎺ

The Berkeley graduation had been windy and cloudy, but at least it didn't rain. The weather and the ceremony served as small talk inside the large SUV Joey's girlfriend's parents had driven down from Seattle. There were seven people in the car. Joey and Jennifer sat in the middle row with her younger sister, June. Dr. Lily Cheng drove, her husband in the front passenger seat. Marwa, perfectly content, had the upholstered rear bench to herself.

They were headed to lunch at a San Francisco restaurant called Benefit, opened by a young owner from Rhode Island. The exterior mimicked an 18th-century Providence street, but the interior was a surprise, like climbing aboard a restored whaling ship. The lighting was all Unmellow Yellow.

"I feel seasick," June said.

"We're not in California, or Kansas, anymore," her father agreed.

"Have you ever been to Rhode Island?" Dr. Cheng asked Marwa.

"I went to a wedding in Newport. I've been going to a lot of weddings lately. One in L.A. last year—my best friend from high school. Another coming up in upstate New York in August."

"Maybe I'll go to Brown in two years," June said, "and get you and Daddy to fly east."

"First you have to get in," her father replied.

"Maybe by then you'll float to a college in the Cloud," Jennifer teased, referencing the CEO guest speaker at graduation, some Silicon Valley guru.

As they passed a full-wall mural of whaling ship anatomy, June read aloud, "Buntline, bellyband, jib of jibs, fore sky sail, fore royal, fore play..."

"There's no foreplay," Jennifer snapped.

"So you say," June shot back.

"Siblings," Dr. Cheng warned with mock severity.

The hostess led them up wooden steps to a raised area like a ship's quarterdeck overlooking the main dining room.

Dr. Cheng leaned in and squeezed Marwa's elbow.

"Family can be cloud cuckoo land, can't it? What a shame your parents couldn't make the trip."

"Well, my mother looks after Sharif's kids so his wife can keep working; and my dad, after he retired from banking, finally took a class in composition. Now his musical success surprises him more than anyone else."

They were seated and ordered drinks.

As if uninterrupted, Dr. Cheng continued, "Are your parents separated? Joseph never mentioned a divorce. Not that he says much. But I didn't raise boys, so I wouldn't know."

Across the table, Joey met Marwa's eyes.

In unison, Jennifer and June hissed, "Mom!"

"Marwa doesn't mind," Dr. Cheng said. "Do you, dear? Your brother married an Egyptian girl? Your mother returned to her family?"

"This is all because I'm also going to China," Jennifer explained. "But not with Joseph, and not to visit family. I say it over and over, in English and all seven Chinese dialects I study. He's going to Fudan in Shanghai. I'm going to Zhejiang in Hangzhou."

Marwa finished her glass of prosecco.

"My best friend in high school was Jewish and Japanese-American. Caltech astrophysicist Judy Yamaguchi. Joseph and I take after our father, I think, more than our mother or Sharif. We emphasize the *American* side of the hyphen."

Mr. Cheng polished off his daiquiri.

"I'm not driving," he said, refilling Marwa's glass.

She raised it in salute.

"Don't Muslims abstain?" June asked.

Marwa took a long, unhurried sip, then said, "Even the most devout believe their religion is the one true way, meaning they disbelieve all the rest. Atheists just go one god further."

June blinked.

"So, what *do* you believe in?"

The waiter returned with another daiquiri for Mr. Cheng and a new bottle of prosecco for the table. Marwa lifted her glass in a toast to Joey and Jennifer, echoing the graduation speeches.

"Go Bears!"

The next evening, en route and waiting at LAX, Joey couldn't stop apologizing. They stood together in a long check-in line. The vast terminal space reminded Marwa of Misty Moss, one of the muted tones in Crayola's Silver Swirls 24-pack.

"Dr. Cheng is hardly my first Tiger Mom," she assured him. "I doubt she'd even make the cut for Stuyvesant's PTA. I keep thinking of Vivian, another Cheng, no relation, my nationally ranked, saber-wielding classmate. Her parents were probably from Taiwan. Vivian got a perfect SAT Verbal score in eighth grade. We worked together on the Intel project. She had synesthesia, like me. Dr. Cheng wouldn't stand a chance against *her* mother."

"She'll do," Joey said. "Wasn't Vivian's brother in my class? I can't remember his name. But weren't we all on that tugboat crossing the Hudson, giant firemen in black helmets all around us? It felt wider than the Nile that day, but maybe that's just memory. Or maybe that's just Alexandria. I was eight. Your hair was long, like an open, waving fan. We ended up in New Jersey, but I don't remember getting home. The wind was blowing..."

He paused, seeing it again in his mind's eye, an immense dark cloud shifting low across the water.

"Southeast, toward Brooklyn and Long Island. So the wind must've been from the northwest. Your eyelid was bleeding."

The line inched forward. He rolled her upright carry-on as they moved.

Joey's memory had stirred Marwa's. She was thinking of a movie set in this airport, or maybe only pretending to be. After fifteen years, LAX had changed too much. Or maybe it had been shot on a soundstage. The California sunset poured through a massive window wall, casting a three-dimensional block of orange light onto the concourse floor. Several people were wearing sunglasses indoors.

"The *Langoliers!*" Marwa blurted.

"Stephen King! You're right. The jet lands here at LAX just ahead of those monsters that eat the past. They looked like vagina-dentata Pac-Men. Dean Stockwell was in it. *Quantum Leap.* March 1989 through May 1993. The year I was born. He spent a year at Berkeley, you know. I streamed it all on Hulu. I'm a sucker for time travel stuff."

"Ummee was forty-seven when you were born."

"Thirty-three for Sharif, thirty-eight for you. So, you've still got time," Joey said. "Anyone in mind?"

"I spend most nights in the lab. Jennifer reminds me of Mei Li," Marwa said, referring to Joey's high school girlfriend.

"Don't tell Jenn that."

"She actually lived in Chinatown, right?"

"And lectured me about how Chinese is the best language for math," Joey smiled. "It only has nine number names. English has over two dozen. The trouble starts at eleven. English gives it a unique word, while Chinese just says 'ten-one.' That makes place value easier, and the base-ten system clearer."

He glanced at her.

"You're never going to answer me, are you?"

"I'm a scientist. You're a mathematician. Define *answer.*"

"The Hudson is one mile wide. The Nile's average width is 1.7. A mile equals 0.62137 kilometers."

ᏳᎡᎢᏤ

On the return flight, Marwa had a window seat. She felt fragile, like an egg in a carton. Lowering the shade made more sense than keeping it up; since takeoff, there had been nothing to see but clouds and darkness as they headed east. Night, without her synesthetic colors, was calmer, more neutral. She leaned away from the man beside her and shut her eyes.

Her mind lit up—a neural map firing memories from the weekend with Joey.

They had once lived in Battery Park City, their apartment overlooking the Hudson. Chinatown was nearby, Greenwich Village just uptown. Before 9/11, there had been Denim Prix, the international model who'd lived in their building. Prix had lost his battle for innocence to Marwa, who'd wanted to surrender hers more. He'd been on the Boston-to-L.A. flight that crashed into the North Tower. Marwa had been five blocks away, in math class at Stuyvesant.

She thought of ecstasies.

The Prophet Muhammad's 766-mile one-night flight, from Mecca to Jerusalem and then up through the heavens, returning before dawn. *Sura 17:1: Glory to Allah, who took His Servant by night from the Sacred Mosque to the Farthest Mosque, whose precincts We blessed...*

The Buddha beneath the Bodhi tree, *I will not move until I have solved my problem.* And when he did, as the morning star rose, the earth trembled, the heavens sang, and flowers rained from the tree. He surrendered to what had always been.

Wasn't that Islam? *Submission*?

Moses, too, in the dual-authored *Exodus 3:5*, told to remove his sandals, God manifesting through a pun: *Sinai/seneh*, the burning bush. Angel or Adonai, Elohist or Yahwist, the shepherd was afraid to look upon the divine.

And Jesus. Not just his human despair—*Why hast Thou forsaken me?* —but the transcendent forgiveness: *Forgive them, for they know not what they do.*

Those were their ecstasies.

What of her own?

Her body had been wise to choose Prix first. It wasn't romantic. It was fine. It was fierce. What had she learned?

That orgasm, though sublime, was not God.

Her clitoris tightened in memory, and she shifted slightly, again leaning away from the man beside her. Was she releasing pheromones? She peeked at him through barely opened eyelids. He was still focused on his laptop, bathed in the narrow beam of his reading light.

He could be gay, she thought.

Relief softened her muscles. She closed her eyes again.

James came next in her memory. Tall, commanding James. Black, brilliant, another Presidential Scholar at Fordham, and a year ahead of her. They'd been arrested together at the 2004 GOP convention. She had been released within hours. He had been cuffed and held for three days.

Marwa had never forgiven Mayor Bloomberg for that.

After they broke up, James had sent her a birthday gift, a copy of *Don Quixote*, the new Edith Grossman translation, inscribed with Sancho Panza's words.

"I'd like to send your grace something, but I don't know what to send, except some very curious tubing for syringes that they make on this *insula* to be used with bladders. Though if my position lasts, I'll find something to send you, one way or another...Let us go slowly, for there are no birds today in yesterday's nests."

Happy Birthday, every day, always.
~*Dr. James Beekmans*

Now with Doctors Without Borders and married.

How entirely James, she thought. And well deserved, to send her an enema.

"Good thoughts?" her seatmate asked, startling her.

Marwa opened her eyes.

"I'm sorry, were you dreaming? You were grinning," he said.

To avoid any further conversation, or smiles, Marwa turned away and opened the window shade. A cloudless night sky stretched out beside them, scattered with more stars than she could count. Below, the Midwest translated its dreams into luminous hieroglyphs etched on black papyrus.

They were flying at least 30,000 feet up, speeding east at 600 miles per hour over the invisible curvature of the Earth. Marwa wondered, how many degrees of longitude separated her from her mother, her brother, and the rest of her family in Alexandria? Could there be Cartesian coordinates for the space between her past and present, those four intense years from high school to college?

In New York City, on the hottest day of late August 2001, she and Judy had gone to the Seaport. Judy got a tattoo; and Marwa had her ears pierced. Four years later, on an even hotter day in August 2005, Marwa left Mecca behind.

It had been a decade of departures.

She thought of Roger. After her first post-grad year at Rockefeller University in New York, she spent the next two years in Cambridge, working in a genetics lab with the Englishman she believed she would marry. They looked, she'd once thought, like the perfect contrast. His straight, white-blond hair and pale blue eyes beside her "Nile waves" and Egyptian skin, as he'd called them. For a while, they felt magnetic, polarities in balance, until career ambitions flipped those poles and pushed them apart.

She returned to Rockefeller.

Roger stayed in Cambridge.

And then, perhaps, she drifted into sleep as the jet glided east. Because suddenly she was back, seated on a bench in Battery Park City, facing the Hudson. She was still in college then. There had been a moment, a seizure or something like it, on that very bench. She'd been taken by ambulance to a nearby hospital. The memory glowed Ruby in her mind, the color from the Gem Tones 16-pack she'd loved at ten years old.

After that, she'd begun riding the subway from Fordham to see a psychiatrist midtown. She had cracked in his office, spoken, for the first time, about Prix's plane. About Muhammad's night flight. About Siddhartha's roar. About Moses and the incandescent acacia bush.

Her body tensed involuntarily. Marwa shuddered, and the movement jolted her seatmate—just in time for him to catch his laptop before it slipped off the tray.

"What happened?" he sighed, shaken but calm.

"I'm so sorry," Marwa murmured.

But he was not her younger brother.

Another August. It had been exactly a year since Marwa last saw Judy, when she'd stood as maid of honor at her best friend's wedding in Pasadena. Now, Edward stayed back in California with their five-month-old daughter, Eleanor, while the two reunited for another celebration: their Stuyvesant classmate Biren's wedding, this time in upstate New York.

They began the weekend in a Catskills motel, more decrepit than quaint, where Marwa satisfied some, but not all, of Judy's curiosity about Joey's recent graduation from Berkeley. The two friends wandered the town, a one-street village called Thebes along Lenape Creek, part of the watershed that fed New York City 125 miles south. As always, time with Judy tinted the world Granny Smith Apple green.

Their original lodging, Lookout Lenape, sounded scenic but proved otherwise—a misnomer born from what had once been a line of garages, now converted into ant-infested, curtainless rooms with no air conditioning. A last-minute cancellation let them escape to Dawn Star Lodge, one of the guest houses at the Munsee Mountain Resort, west of Woodstock, the site of yet another fabled August, the muddy love-in of 1969. This August of 2015 was cloudless and blistering.

"If we dance the night away," Judy said as they unpacked, "we'll get a perfect view of the Perseids before dawn."

"What?" Marwa shouted over the music thumping through the paper-thin wall.

Judy banged on it, and moments later the door opened.

A handsome, bearded man appeared, lowering the volume on his iPod.

"Sorry," he said, "That was *I May Be Wrong, But I Won't Be Wrong Always*—Ten Years After. They played it at Woodstock. Though, technically, that was Bethel. Legend says it's a Count Basie cover. I'm making a playlist for Biren and Charlie. Last-minute, as usual. I'll keep it down."

He disappeared just as quickly.

"Who was that, Rumpelstiltskin?" Judy asked.

"You remember when Mr. Haddam had us bring in our family fairytales?"

"And you brought in the lusty Joseph and Potiphar's wife story..."

"No, that was Sunny's. *Yusuf and Zulaikha.*"

"Oh, right! And I said it sounded like Adam and Eve, only Yusuf was the apple, the snake, and the tree all in one. A trinity! And Zooley was like Job, suffering until she figured out how to get back to Paradise."

"I got mad because you called her *Drooling Zooley.*"

"No, you got mad because Yusuf was Prix and you were Zulaikha."

"Mr. Haddam's supposed to be at the wedding with his husband," Marwa said.

"I heard Sunny's on Long Island. Very religious now. Married. Kids. Works at Whole Foods or maybe Trader Joe's."

"Sounds more like gossip than fact."

"She always followed you like a disciple."

"And look where that led her," Marwa muttered, turning toward the dresser to unpack.

She stood still, her back to Judy.

"Where are you now, Marwa, under the Bodhi tree again? I remember in tenth grade, you said you wouldn't move until you found a reason. Your bladder, unlike Buddha's morning star, eventually gave you one."

Judy was on her bed, naked, pulling on the bottom half of her bikini.

Marwa moved her gaze from Judy's frontal view to the tattoo on her shoulder.

"That was another hot August," Marwa said. "Did you ever tell Edward about Shakespeare Jimmy Wagstaff?"

They had met up years ago between Greenwich Village and Battery Park City, at Adonis Piercing & Tattoo on Canal Street. Judy had an appointment to get a boat inked onto her right shoulder. A brief chime sounded as they entered.

A muscular Black man with a shaved head emerged through a doorway of hanging beads.

"I'll be right with you, Ms...?"

"Yamaguchi," Judy said.

He checked his schedule, then glanced at Marwa.

"I'm not sure yet," Marwa said.

"Never let anyone talk you into something you don't want to do. That's the mark of a bad shop. I'm Adonis. You can choose from the wall or just sit and hang out."

He slipped back behind the beads.

The girls examined framed tattoo samples of flowers, animals, names, and a gallery of vehicles: rockets, motorcycles, jets, and boats.

Judy pointed to a miniature yacht with a high prow.

"Shakespeare and I rode around Baltimore harbor in one just like that. It's what he had tattooed on *his* shoulder."

"Why are you getting one?"

"To make a blood memory," Judy said quietly. "My mom took me to get my ears pierced when I turned thirteen. I thought it was a birthday gift. I didn't know she was dying. Shakespeare got his tattoo afterward."

"After the boat ride?"

"No."

"You didn't."

"We did."

Marwa's head spun.

"Stop calling him *Shakespeare*! He's giraffe Jimmy Wagstaff!"

"Keep your voice down! So, he's not on billboards like your Prix. His eyes are pale as vodka."

"Vodka? *Amantes sunt amentes*," Marwa muttered. "He's not my Prix."

"You wish he were. And hey, who're you calling a *sunt*?"

"Lovers are lunatics. You're in love with him," Marwa said.

"I am. He leaves for college in three days. It hurts."

"Did it?"

"What?"

"Hurt?"

Judy whispered, "You know how your mouth waters when you see or smell something delicious? It's like that. Women have two mouths. The better to eat you with."

Marwa swatted at her. "You are *awful.*"

Adonis reappeared with an androgynous client whose forearm was wrapped in fresh gauze. They waved goodbye. Adonis ushered Judy and Marwa to the back, which resembled a beauty salon. Two other tattoo artists were already at work.

Judy showed Adonis her chosen design. He seated her in a barber chair and prepared the field. The tattoo needle buzzed like a dentist's drill. At its first touch, a bead of blood rose. Adonis dabbed it, then began injecting ink.

Marwa swayed.

"Take a breather in the front, hon," Adonis suggested gently.

Marwa drifted through the hanging beads.

Later, the girls stood sweltering on the deck of the fire-engine-red tugboat *Helen McAllister* at South Street Seaport, sucking down cold bottles of water.

Judy reached out to touch one of Marwa's newly pierced ears.

"Isn't it against your rules?"

"I didn't mutilate Allah's creation with a tattoo. Ear piercing's fine. The Prophet once told women to give up their earrings as alms, so clearly he was okay with them."

"How do *they* feel?"

"Fine. How about you?"

"It's burning in this heat. I'm sweating so much I hope the boat doesn't float away. Sweat makes it sting. But...I like the hurt."

That scared Marwa, how much she understood.

"You're drifting again," Judy said now, years later, ready for the pool.

"Did you ever tell Edward the tattoo story?" Marwa asked again.

"He didn't want to hear it. Said, 'No one gets out of life without scars. They're medals.'"

"What a guy. What would we have called him back in ninth grade? Remember how we used code initials for our boy band crushes?"

"Oh, definitely LB. He looks like Lance Bass!"

"What zealots we were. You'd think we could've picked better demigods than *NSYNC*."

"Wolf pack or sheep herd, it's in our genes. Culture teaches conformity, especially to kids. Remember Joey calling us *Muggles*? Now quit resisting and come swim."

"It's a free country," Marwa said. "You're not the boss of me. Whatever happened to individuality?"

Judy paused, then asked quietly, "Did you ever answer Joey's question?"

GRTV

Dinner was served in a vast, renovated barn. The next morning, breakfast was in the basement café of the main lodge. A banner stretched across a knotty pine wall read: LOVE CONQUERS ALL. Couples, fluidly defined, posed for photos beneath it with plates of eggs, bagels, or juice in hand.

Marwa and Judy snapped a selfie together.

Mr. Haddam and his husband posed with Biren and Charlie.

The wedding was set for early evening, following an afternoon of swimming, hiking, reminiscing, and new connections. The outdoor ceremony took place under a Maize-colored sunset, followed by a musical cocktail hour with drinks and tables spread across a broad lawn. Everyone was sun-kissed, happily buzzed, and high on the day.

Under the reception tent, as chamber music gave way to reggae and rock between dinner courses, Marwa led when she danced with Judy and followed when Mr. Haddam tapped her shoulder.

An elderly woman called out to Biren's parents, "I always hoped we'd dance at his wedding, and here we are!"

Well before dawn, Judy found Marwa.

"Come see the Perseids! No moonlight to outshine the shower tonight!"

They were both exhausted and a little drunk as they slipped out from the tent into the country night. Crickets and frogs made up a living chorus, wings of owls and bats brushed the air. But it was sight that ruled—the night sky erupting with meteors streaking across the Milky Way.

Marwa tilted her head back.

"It's like a cosmic brain scan. Meteorites as divine thoughts."

"Except you feel them scrape your chest and sink into your stomach," Judy replied.

"How could ancient people have made sense of this?" Marwa wondered. "The sky literally falling. Chicken Little with fire. Was it a gift? A warning? Judgment? And if they found one, cool and shiny, maybe obsidian…"

"Tektites," Judy nodded. "Possibly Libyan desert glass. There are at least six recognized tektite fields on Earth. Mecca falls in the path of one."

Marwa looked away.

"The shock of it," she murmured. "The shock of it."

Judy gazed upward like it was her personal sky.

"Those are fragments from Comet Swift-Tuttle. The Perseids appear to originate from the constellation Perseus."

She pointed northeast.

"There's Capella. Aldebaran. And Perseus, holding Medusa's severed head."

A fiery streak cut across the heavens like a match struck by an unseen giant.

"Perseus," Marwa echoed. "Son of Zeus. *Per-Zeus.* Son of God. And he kills the Goddess—turns her into myth, her power into symbol."

"Turned men to stone," Judy teased. "Made them hard, you mean."

Unamused, Marwa pressed on.

"A celestial chronicle of patriarchy overtaking matriarchy. In Arabia, Allat became Allah, and her shrine became his. In Ireland, St. Patrick drove out the sacred snakes that coiled around the arms of Minoan priestesses."

"Same old story," Judy said. "What happened in Mecca, Marwa?"

Marwa shut her eyes and rubbed the ache in her neck.

"Is there somewhere to sit?"

They had wandered beyond the resort grounds, but Judy spotted a cluster of Adirondack chairs. They settled into the damp wood, the cool dew a relief in the warm August air. A nearby pine tree sighed in the breeze.

Marwa closed her eyes. Everything was shifting—light, color, memory.

"I didn't actually live in Mecca. I was assigned to a high school in Jeddah. Placed in a women's dorm. My mentor wouldn't take me to the Haram right away. First, she brought me to my namesake, Safa and Marwa. We walked between them. It's all indoors now, air-conditioned. However hot it gets here or in Pasadena, it's nothing compared to August in Saudi."

"The walk you do for Hagar," Judy said.

"Yes. It's marble, columns, thousands of voices. Like birds at dawn. But the 'mountains', they're just rocky mounds behind glass. Smaller than you imagine. Like seeing the Stock Exchange for the first time. So much significance, yet so small."

She paused.

"We should've brought champagne."

"We can't think of everything," Judy said. "The universe started from twenty pounds of matter. Inconceivable conception. We morons came from an oxymoron."

"You're still drunk."

"Entirely possib—probable—*probable*," Judy murmured, eyes half-closed.

Marwa went on.

"When I finally entered the Haram...you begin the *tawaf* from the eastern corner of the Kaaba, where the Black Stone is set. The Hajar al-Aswad."

Judy startled awake.

"What?"

"The Black Stone. Not inside the Kaaba, but on its corner, five feet up in a silver collar. It was venerated long before Islam. The Kaaba once housed 360 idols. The stone's said to have fallen from heaven, a guide for Adam and Eve. In 930, it was stolen and broken by the Qarmatians. Later, the fragments were returned, sealed in pitch, held by silver wire."

Marwa cupped her hands to show its size.

"Less than twelve inches across. If you can't kiss it during the seven circuits, you just point. I wasn't on *hajj*, just a random *umrah*. But I got close enough."

She closed her eyes again.

"A semicircle of pilgrims sat on rugs nearby, praying. Above them, the Royal Clock Tower loomed, like a skyscraper-lingam. The Kaaba, eternal yoni. You walk counter-clockwise. When I saw the Black Stone...the people around me were in a state of near-ecstasy. I was terrified. I thought I'd have another seizure, like the one on the bench in Battery Park that sent me to the hospital. I was terrified I'd lose my colors again."

"Like after the Towers fell," Judy said softly.

"I thought you were asleep."

"It's okay," Judy whispered.

"I was so relieved when my synesthesia came back...after I saw Dr. Rawi."

"It was the opposite for me," Judy said. "I saw my mother."

"We never talked about this."

"No one did. You moved to Brooklyn. We had split sessions at Tech. Chaos. I don't even know where my sister went to school. Jody was in third grade. Joey in second."

"He went to private school in Brooklyn, then we moved back."

"We were all in shock. Remember all the psychologists at school? Always asking if we were okay. Then came the World Series in October. Liza Minnelli sang the anthem. Everything felt surreal."

Judy looked up.

"All that time, I thought I was seeing my mom. Not hallucinations. More like…sensing her. I could smell her perfume. *Shalimar.* I knew it was common, but it felt like her. Holding me. I was only afraid I'd lose her again."

"Did you?"

"Of course. Jody followed her boyfriend to Silicon Valley. My dad lives with a woman now, in the same NYU building. And your father became a composer. What happened in Mecca, Marwa? What *color* was it?"

A brilliant meteor flashed across the sky and silenced them.

When the moment passed and fainter streaks followed behind like straggling sheep, Marwa finally answered.

"The nausea hit me. I nearly collapsed. Two women, fully veiled, had just been stroking the exposed, what did you call it in ninth grade? 'Pud'? —trying to kiss the stone. Then they saw me falter and rushed to help. They moved like enormous black-winged birds. They thought I was overcome by religious ecstasy. They led me to a wall of water fountains, made me drink, bathed my face and wrists in Zam Zam water."

"Bam Bam," Judy murmured.

"I wasn't even speaking Arabic anymore. I was rambling in English about *The Flintstones.* Thankfully no one understood me. The school in Jeddah had already worn me down. I had to censor everything I knew. Outside of school, at first I liked being called 'Sister' or 'Daughter' by strangers. But eventually even that felt suffocating. The climate mirrored the claustrophobia. *Crayola Burnished Brown.* Unconstitutional confinement, in a crowd."

She paused.

276

"I stayed till mid-August, like a zombie. When I left, I knew I couldn't go back. To any of it. Meaning drained away. Words became sound. Like birdsong. Receptive aphasia."

Judy was fully awake now. She studied the sky. Soon, the final sliver of the waning crescent moon would rise.

"The Perseids keep coming," she said. "Strange how I'm on the other side of that arc now. Eleanor's five months. She's making sounds on her way to speech."

"It's good you named her for your mother," Marwa said quietly. "Maybe it's time for bed."

Judy stood, momentarily taller than her friend. She offered her hand.

Marwa took it and rose.

They walked in silence until Judy asked, "So what happened in Mecca was what didn't happen. You didn't find God. And now what?"

"That," Marwa said, "is the question."

And as if on cue, the silver horn of the crescent moon pierced the horizon.

"It will be a dark new moon for the next three nights," Judy said. "And then, what."

ABOUT THE AUTHOR

L. Shapley Bassen is a prize-winning author, poet, dramatist, and current fiction editor at *Craft Literary*. Her writing career began in 1984 with *The Kenyon Review* and spans decades of publication across acclaimed journals and presses. Her second novel, *Blue Monkeys*, will be published in print by Shy City House (Chicago) in September 2025. The haunting backstory of a central character in *Blue Monkeys* led to the creation of her newest work, *How She Came to Know*.

She is the author of several books, including *Summer of the Long Knives* (Typhoon Media-Signal 8 Press, 2014), *Lives of Crime & Other Stories* (Texture Press, 2014), *Showfolk & Stories* (Inkception Books, 2017), and the poetry collection *What Suits a Nudist?* (Clare Songbirds Publishing House, 2019). Her play *The Month Before the Moon* was published by Samuel French (now Concord Theatricals) in 1996.

In 2016, Bassen won First Place in *The Austin Chronicle* Short Story Contest for "Portrait of a Giant Squid." She has been widely published in literary venues such as *The Kenyon Review*, *Per Contra*, *Lunch Ticket*, and *The Writing Disorder*.

A native New Yorker now living in Rhode Island, Bassen credits her grandmother—a Wall Street telegrapher from over a century ago—for teaching her to read and tapping secret messages to her in Morse code, a formative experience that ignited her lifelong love of language.

Connect:
Website – <u>lsbassen.com</u>
Fiction Editor – <u>Craft Literary</u>
<u>LinkedIn</u> | <u>Facebook</u> | <u>Poets & Writers Directory</u>

ACKNOWLEDGMENTS

The law may be slow, but publishing might be slower. After my second novel, BLUE MONKEYs, was accepted by a Chicago publisher in late 2023, scheduled for some time in 2025, I thought, great news and actual time for...? Turns out, the people in BLUE MONKEYS continued to occupy my imagination's real estate, especially one whose backstory insisted on attention. I hadn't heard or seen her as a major character before, but she kept reappearing, as if complaining about the plumbing. Originally, she was inspired by a teenager with long wavy hair, a scientific mind, and a real attitude I admired. But I'd written about her as a successful 30-something NYC scientist living amongst others in a West Side building when the pandemic struck. Where did she come from? How did she get there?

Right after Christmas, 2024, the publisher at Page Turner Books, Inc. in Henderson, NV (now in Shelby, NC), Leanne E. Staback, Ph.D. reacted to my Facebook Comment to her *Call for Submissions* post for fiction of at least 80,000 words. I asked if she'd consider something of about 74,000. Her reply, "That could work if the story is good." By January 9th, she sent me a contract, followed by a classy binder and clear directions for its future use. The past few months have been a whirlwind of focus on publication details. What an organized team she leads! *How She Came to Know* could hardly have found a better home.

Since my stories, etc., have been published since 1984, first in *The Kenyon Review*, first thanks should go to *Emeritus* Professor Frederick Turner, [Former] Founders Professor at UTDallas, who has generously remained a longtime friend; he wrote a blurb for my first novel, *Summer of the Long Knives*. I'd like to thank all the many people who have accepted, edited, and advised previous publications and productions of my stories, poems, and plays. I've never been a fan of long biographies & bibliographies at the end of novels.

A great deal of reading and research has always informed my work. In *How She Came to Know*, I was at pains to include the authors or titles of its source _in_ a reference. I also tried to place translations of foreign language [Marwa quotes a lot of Latin!] close to their appearance in the story. If I missed any, I've kept a big box of notes I hope not to search again. It's impossible to credit all inspirations for characters and events in the new novel. I like to believe most of the novel is imagined, but I'm sure some people will recognize aspects of themselves [several high school and college instructors come to mind] and hope they find portraits less distorted than Duchamp's *Nude Descending a Staircase*. Any character flaws a reader finds should be attributed to the author's interior monologues and experiences. Also, the New York metro area and 9/11 are characters who belong to us all.

Once, I dedicated a book to my wry and wise spouse, another time to the characters in their collection. At this time, may I most humbly salute Lady Liberty in the Harbor.

Rhode Island, June, 2025

WORKS CITED

"Annual Rites." *The Writing Disorder*, 20 June
2021, http://writingdisorder.com/l-shapley-bassen-fiction/.

"That Is the Question." *Beneath the Rainbow*, Sept.
2017, http://beneaththerainbow.com/.

"That Is the Question." *Circle Show*, vol. 15, Winter 2016, Seven
CirclePress, http://www.sevencirclepress.com/CircleShow%20
Volume%2015,%20Winter%202016%20Online%20Edition.pdf.

"The Man with Ten Hats." *Have a NYC 2: New York Short Stories*,
Three Rooms Press, http://threeroomspress.com/authors/have-
a-nyc-new-york-short-stories/.

"The Man with Ten Hats." *Per Contra*, issue
30, http://www.percontra.net/issues/30/fiction/the-man-with-
ten/.

"The Night Before the Snow Day." *Lunch Ticket*, Amuse-Bouche,
Antioch University, https://lunchticket.org/the-night-before-
the-snow-day/.

www.ingramcontent.com/pod-product-compliance
Lightning Source LLC
Chambersburg PA
CBHW010740310726

48971CB00010B/2887